a theory of
all things

ANOTHER TITLE BY PEGGY LEON

Mother Country

a theory of
all things

Peggy Leon

THE PERMANENT PRESS
Sag Harbor, NY 11963

For information, address:
  The Permanent Press
  4170 Noyac Road
  Sag Harbor, NY 11963
  www.thepermanentpress.com

Library of Congress Cataloging-in-Publication Data

Leon, Peggy—
  A theory of all things / Peggy Leon.
      p. cm.
  ISBN-13: 978-1-57962-195-7 (alk. paper)
  ISBN-10: 1-57962-195-3 (alk. paper)
    1. Family secrets—Fiction. 2. Domestic fiction.
  3. Psychological fiction. I. Title.

PS3612.E56T47 2010
813'.6—dc22   2009044426

Printed in the United States of America.

*F*or John, Christopher and Kimberly,
whom I love above all things . . .

. . . and for my mom,
who forgot, but still loved.

PART ONE

A BIG BANG

Dear Mary, Ellie and Sarah:

I have not been ignoring your emails. I have been busy. The last few days have presented a number of challenges to my equilibrium, one of which a barely credible social mishap has landed me in hot water with the university, resulting in "sessions" with the department head of Psychology. Quite ludicrous. Ellie, I am sorry to hear that you are feeling ill, but there seems very little any of us can do at such a distance. Get well soon.

 Best wishes all,
 Mark

* * * * *

Mark:

Thanks for the get well, and have at them. Remember, you're the Quark, and always right. Someone else must be wrong. They're infidels! Remember, brilliance is often mistaken for insanity!

 XXXXOOOO, Ellie

* * * * *

Quark:

I knew you would be found out someday!
 XO, Sarah
PS—Coming to SF soon for opening of my show....
 Lunch? (between "sessions" that is)

* * * * *

Mark,

What have you done? Don't worry. I'm sure everything will turn out fine. I'll call this evening.
 Love,
 Mary

MARK

I do not trust memories. To look back is to place an artificial construct on random events. Things happen. Look at existence at the subatomic level. Electrons waver, drop from their path. Must there be a reason? Is it always a sign? Look at the cosmos, a billion, billion stars (my private chuckle—yes, a colleague *did* say something like that), galaxies, black holes, nova and nebulas. How many still exist? How many winked out eons ago? Ah ha, you say, there is memory, the memory of stars! No, I would counter, just unfinished business, light traveling blindly until it runs into something solid. Yet, the ancients looking up from the earth connected the dots, drew pictures in nothingness, charted their courses, prayed. Where are those sages now? It proves my point, really. Do not trust memories.

Perhaps I should explain the genesis of my irritation. I normally wouldn't allow myself such exposure, but being forced to look back, to remember (the university actually made it *contractual*), is unsettling. It pulls me out of myself. So, despite the fact that it was a simple misunderstanding, well actually two misunderstandings, one perhaps a little too public, one private, here I sit, across a glass coffee table from Dr. Ernst Himmel, eminent psychologist, department head.

When I walked into his office, I chose the chair. I wanted *him* on the couch. Himmel, that's heaven in German. Do you know anything of heaven, Doctor? Is your concern more in the realm of private hells?

11

"So, Mark. Tell me about yourself," he says.

Himmel, can you believe it? *Got im Himmel!*

"I am a theoretical physicist," I tell him. "A cosmologist and mathematician."

I deal in the universe, the tiniest subatomic particle, the farthest, most immense curve of existence. I watch. I calculate. One day I will tie it all together. A grand theory. There's one thing I know for sure, Doctor. There is no Himmel. I don't tell him this. Perhaps not the best course, I think, to be combative on the first visit. The Chancellor is keeping an eye . . .

The Chancellor's wife was the subject of the first, public, misunderstanding. Cocktail parties are not my forte. I tried to beg off; however, it was quite an important event, a celebration, really. Compulsory. The physics department had just received a rather large grant. String Theory is a hot topic. I'd written a tidy little paper that was published in *Science* and then received some press, actually quoted on NPR and in *The New York Times*. "Dimensionality, Particular Type and the Journey Across the String," Bennett, Sanders, et al. Five minutes of fame, that leaves me ten more. I need to be careful. They wanted to trot me out, show me off, their little flash. Calling all quasars, all photons and quarks . . .

I had allowed myself an extra glass of wine, though I can't really attribute the trouble to that. A man of my height, 5 feet 11 inches, and weight, 153 pounds, should easily be able to handle two glasses of wine at six percent alcohol. However, I was slightly nervous. That might have been it. I had Clare, one of my post-doctoral students, standing at my elbow. Within the six-inch limit, I might add. Clare was the source of the second misunderstanding. I should have never invited her. I was perfectly aware that she produced an odd physiological effect on me whenever contact seemed imminent: restriction in breathing, slight mental confusion, moisture of the palms. I believe I may be allergic to her perfume, though I enjoy the scent inordinately. I never should have invited her, but I wanted to. It seemed an opportunity. I hoped for an opening.

There was a large group standing around us, among them the Chancellor's wife. She had read a novel recently, science fiction, and asked about a term, entropy. As it happens, entropy is one of my favorite quantities, a pet of mine, really. Quite simply put, entropy measures the disorder in a system, and disorder, of course, increases with time. Entropy is visible everywhere, a metaphor, really, for life. Perhaps it was the wine, perhaps the nervousness, but I have to admit, I waxed poetic about entropy, I was carried away. Then I made the ill-fated analogy. In all honesty, I still don't understand the offense. In fact, as my mouth opened and the words came out, I was rather proud of them, of myself, thought I was being clever.

". . . therefore," I told them using my best professorial tone, "entropy can be found even amongst man and woman, in their relationships of course, but also in their states. There is the argument that woman came from man's rib, a neat piece of entropy in itself, but I put that aside. I'm sure everyone here knows what that story's worth."

Here, I must state in my own defense, that I had no idea that the man to my left was the university chaplain, and, I might add, that he should be used to such arguments. He does, after all, work in a community of higher learning. I can't be the only skeptic around. This was part of the first misunderstanding, the smallest part. I leave it to him to practice forgiveness.

I went on, ignoring the slight murmur. "No, I speak about measurable states. It is quite evident from the way she conducts her life that a woman is more disordered than man. She is an advanced state of man. However, in saying that, the question then implied is: Does this advanced state make woman inferior?"

13

A tautological argument, I admit, but I ask you, how could I have known that the Chancellor's wife had been college friends with Gloria Steinem, was a lifelong devotee—as her husband pointed out, rather heatedly the next day in his office—of women's issues.

Well, what ensued was yet another example of entropy. Things fell apart, flew askew. The Chancellor's wife's face turned an alarmingly unnatural shade. People looked at their drinks, their toes. There was one uncomfortable laugh. Clare moved beyond the six inches. I could feel cool air rush into that space.

My first letter of apology was a further explanation of entropy, its place in the second law of thermodynamics, its importance in the cosmos. The Chancellor returned it, asked for something shorter, more to the point. It took me two and a half hours to revise. It is quite difficult to condense and simplify advanced concepts. The Chancellor provided the third letter himself, my name typed at the bottom, a blue post-it with the instruction—sign here! A dark, accusatory arrow pointed left. Another letter in the same envelope, stated, "An appointment has been made for you with Dr. Ernst Himmel, Psychology Department. Mandatory."

On the ride home from the ill-fated cocktail party, Clare asked, "How could you say that, Mark?"

"Say what?" I wasn't really paying attention. I was thinking of knees, knees in transparent black stockings, knees and the three inches of stocking-darkened skin above that disappeared beneath a black hem, a mystery, a trick of shading. I was thinking how black stockings were evidently invented specifically to enhance the natural curves of a woman's legs. Quite effective. Clare, with her nice legs in her dark stockings, with her dark hair, smooth and long, with her dark eyes, was staring at me.

14

"Mark! How can you say 'what.'" Her voice was sharp, almost a cry. "All that about entropy and women. And the poor chaplain! How could you?"

"It didn't seem to go over," I admitted.

"Mark! You said women were disordered."

I am used to that particular timbre in a woman's voice: exasperation, a tinge of incredulity. I grew up with three sisters.

"I spoke from some experience, Clare. I have three sisters. Believe me, they're very disordered. Try as I might, they continue to grow more disordered. Classic entropy."

"You said women were inferior, Mark."

"In point of fact, I didn't. I put it forth as an intellectual query, a simple hypothesis." We had pulled up in front of her house. The porch light was on; inside, the blue flicker of the television. Her roommate was still up. Now was the time. I opened my mouth to ask.

Clare was groaning, shaking her head. "I don't even know you! Who are you, Mark?"

Oddly enough, my sisters say this same thing to me quite often. Our telephone conversations are punctuated by it. The thought held some comfort, a place that I know, a place to start from.

"Clare, I . . ." I hadn't had much practice at this. "Actually, we've known each other for eight months and—" a slight hesitation here for calculation, "twenty-four days . . . but . . . well . . . I would like you to know me . . . better, that is, because of course you do know me . . . slightly . . . I . . . we . . . maybe . . ." Frankly, no practice at all.

Clare was blinking. I could see the brush of shadow from her eyelashes, intermittent, hesitant, along the line of her cheek. Her profile was caught in porch light, a soft glow against single strands of hair, the curve of skin, the flickering sweep of lashes. Light, encountering her solidity, like the memory of stars, unfinished business. She

15

turned toward me, and her face was suddenly in darkness. She leaned in close, passed the six-inch limit, an arriving warmth, a slight scent, in me that answering dizziness.

"Eight months and twenty-four days," she murmured. "I know that. Say something nice to me, Mark. Say one nice thing. Try."

Alas, the second misunderstanding, not entirely of my making. There exists data to support my position. Scientific studies have shown that mating is not a simple matter of pheromones, that when choosing a mate, the human looks for certain physical characteristics, whether knowingly or unknowingly: a pleasing symmetry of shape, eyes that are large and wide, a regularity of features, without extreme, good hair, teeth. To me, Clare is an excellent example of these attributes, exactly what one would look for in a mate. In addition, she is extremely intelligent, a quick study, quite easy to work with. She seems to defy entropy, really. She is perfect, always will be. However, I didn't say that.

If human communication, just simple conversation, was a mathematical equation, I could do it. No matter how complex, I could arrive at the right answer every time. But, there are complexities here that go beyond calculation, theorems that have not yet been discovered. I don't understand.

I don't want to make excuses; I've made enough already— closeness, nervousness, perfume, confusion, wine. They don't really matter. What it comes down to is this:

"You have admirable symmetry."

Clare slid back into her seat. She was quiet and still for a long time.

"No." She shook her head. Her hand reached for the door handle. "No, Mark. I don't think so. You're lacking. You need . . . I don't know . . . something." She stepped out of the car, turned around in the space created by the opened door, leaned in. "Wake up, Mark. Look at the world, at people, at yourself."

16

"I wasn't speaking in a purely geometric way. I meant regular, actually, very regular."

The door slammed. Clare's long, lovely legs carried her home.

Dr. Himmel sits across from me on his couch. It is brown leather, long, with deep soft cushions, evidently comfortable. Dr. Himmel seems very comfortable. The wing chair I sit in is not particularly comfortable. The black leather, buttoned and stretched taut, is unforgiving.

"So Mark. Tell me about yourself," he says. "Tell me something about your childhood."

"What?"

"Pick something. Something that stands out."

"Why?"

"Memories are important. They give us a way to understand the present, what's happening now. They define us, not just the memories, but what we choose to remember, how we remember it, what we leave out."

I can see that it is an intellectual puzzle, one of those MENSA "mind ticklers" you can buy in a box, the key hidden in what is stated, what is implied, what is missing. The artificial construct.

"How can you trust memory if it is not exact, not precisely true."

Dr. Himmel smiles. "Maybe the truth is found in the imprecision."

I see I will not win this argument. The Himmels of this world coat science in a thick sludge of vagueness. They call it truth, and counter mathematical evidence with faith and feeling. You can't fight that. You have to go along and keep your opinions, your calculated proofs to yourself.

"Where do you want me to begin, Doctor?"

"Well, Doctor," he counters, smiling. "Begin at the beginning."

17

I FIND that now that I have sunk to metaphor, I cannot escape it. Metaphor is everywhere. I call my eldest sister, Mary, after my first session with Dr. Himmel to tell her about it. We talk often, more so now that our father is failing. Mary is his caregiver. She has never left home. She is the part of the universe that remained at the center, intact even after the explosion. Mary is a reader of literary fiction. I am afraid it adds to her sense of confusion; however, it also cultivates in her an open mind, a quick and certain sympathy. Invaluable. I tell her about my misunderstandings, about Clare, about entropy.

"Oh, Mark," is all she says.

I tell her I have found another metaphor, a metaphor for our family's beginning: The Big Bang.

"Peter's suicide, you see," I tell her. "It was our Big Bang."

There is a long silence on the line, and then I hear the soft, short click of the phone being replaced on the cradle. Perhaps Father needs her just at this moment. She has to be very careful of him.

The general theory of relativity predicts that the universe started off infinitely dense at the singularity of the Big Bang. Physics deals in what is observable; space and time are its boundaries. Prior to the Big Bang one could not predict what would happen after it, and similarly, after the Big Bang, our current location, one can not predict what it was like before because the event is the boundary. Before is unobservable and hence has no effect. Void.

I remember every detail of the moment we discovered my older brother Peter. I was three weeks and two days over thirteen, Mary fifteen, six months, ten days, Ellie and Sarah, were eight, four months, five days, and Luke was six, to the day, almost to the hour. He still wore the crown Mary and the twins had made for him. The twins' glitter job was collapsing and his cheeks and forehead were sprinkled with gold and blue and red. I remember the question mark shape that Peter's body made in the spreading blood. I remember Grandpa's shotgun, supposedly hidden from us all those years in the northwest corner of the attic, in the steamer trunk, wrapped in a white cotton bedspread. It lay eighteen inches from Peter's left side. Its muzzle pointed exactly east, at the dining room table. Our large white spatula lay across Peter's feet. That's how he reached the trigger. The spatula's rubber surface would have been flexible and sticky enough to catch and hold the trigger. Peter was clever.

I remember silence, not screams as one would think, just silence, then the hum of the refrigerator kicking on in the kitchen, then the thump of Father's knees hitting the ground next to Peter's body, the sound of Mary's coat brushing against my sleeve as she turned to block Luke's view, the sound of air escaping the twins' bodies as they turned and clung to each other, becoming one. Then there is noise, every noise in the world gathers into the throat of my father, the whimper of the twins, and Mary, kneeling in front of Luke, saying, "Go outside, Luke. Take a little walk. When you come back, it will be okay." The sounds of us flying apart.

If you do not include Peter (who was, in fact, the event), Luke was the first celestial body to break away, to go spinning out, away from the center. We forgot about him. With the blood and the ambulance and the police and the bright yellow tape and the crowds of neighbors, we forgot about him. He walked and came back and it was not okay yet, so he walked again, each time returning, each time straying a little farther, until some of him never came home again.

That is our beginning. That is the story I tell Dr. Himmel. Everything we were, every probability of what we might become ended, was made senseless at the moment of Peter's suicide. We were let loose, new creatures, to travel our ever widening paths with different futures ahead of us. If I must look back along the arc of my life, must provide some artificial construct for the journey, I choose physics, astronomy. The Big Bang is my beginning.

Dr. Himmel is hard to read. He is not particularly forthcoming with opinions, so I don't know what he thinks of my metaphor. At least he doesn't hang up on me like Mary, but since we sit in the same room, he can hardly do that.

"That's a remarkably precise, intense memory," he says. "How does it make you feel?"

Feel about what, the memory? The event? I am a body blown into space, ever accelerating, dark matter screaming past. I have only my science with which to calculate my fate, the fate of the whole universe.

"Ill equipped," I tell him.

CLARE WILL still not talk to me. This is not strictly true, but all the brief conversations we have had seem to hinge on the words symmetrical and regular. She has embellished by adding sphere-like and ordinary. It is amazing how often these words can fit into discussions about the behavior of p-branes in supergravity theory. There is an emphasis in her voice every time she uses one of these words. When she isn't speaking to me, which is most of the time, she sits at her computer by a south-facing window. The sun hits her dark hair and fractures into shades of deep red, slight traces of gold. I watch the light as she dips her head in concentration. Lately, she seems to focus far better than I. I have become fascinated by the prismatic aspects of hair. Quite intriguing. In physics, we can measure a cosmological body's distance, its heat, even its chemical composition by the spectrum of its light. Hubble was the first to discover the red-shifted galaxies and puzzle out the color's importance: these galaxies were moving away at remarkable speeds. Clare, by her window, her hair a red-tipped aurora, is a long way off, and moving further.

20

Mary, too, is angry with me. She has not called since I posed my Big Bang theory to her, though I have to admit my mind has been elsewhere. I did not note the absence of her daily calls. Then I received an email from Ellie, from Patmos, a Greek island where she lives with Stavros, a man (I should say a boy) much younger than she and works as a sculptor. Ellie's email:

WHO R U??!! Call MARY. SHE'S EXTREMELY MAD,
SAD. Y R U BEING IDIOT?
XXXOO E.

Ellie heard about Mary's anger from Sarah, who is doing work in San Francisco. I should visit her while she is there as Palo Alto is only short distance, but it is difficult to leave the lab at this time. Sarah is evidently traveling with her laptop. She must post to her website on a daily basis the new photographs and conversations with her homeless subjects. Homelessness is Sarah's means of expression, her life work, that and being Ellie's twin. Ellie's sculptures of bone and tortured blood-red clay are an abstract, a three-dimensional construct of Sarah's visual and auditory record of misery. They are in accord. My opinion? Entropy as art.

Though they live half a world away from each other, they keep in constant communication. They are a single, running commentary on the rest of us, irreverent and, indeed irrelevant, most of the time. Ellie and Sarah generally email the entire family at once and never delete previous notes, so it is easy to trace an entire conversation. The following is in reverse order, so that it makes a semblance of sense:

Ellie:
Mary called. In tears. Mark the Quark at it again.
Said Peter was the Big Bang. Can U believe it?

21

Mary—much howling. Worried about her. 2 much stress with Dad as is. Quark a JERK. What is he thinking? Would like to string him up with his own Theory! By the way, did U read articles about him, included links below. Also check out new entries on my website. Cool flop house in Philly. Amazing pics. Woman named Ruth especially wonderful—an immediate kinship. Indispensable being. Read interview. Does she look like Mary to you, too.

XXXOO S

* * * * *

Sarah:
Quark DORK. So mad. Cool about the articles, tho. Nice pic. Cute brother! 2 bad a dolt. Also website. Not dolt, cool. Yes Ruth & Mary look alike. Spooky. Similar sadness? Liked man with orange + brown tam-o-shanter and red red gums. 1 gold tooth! What 2 do about M? Dad worse???? Not heard in 5 days. Quark—AARGH! I'm boiling bones for nu sculpt. Perfect baby lamb. Stavi found after last cold snap. Very excited.

XXOOO E

* * * * *

E: Mary says Dad up every 3AM to shave!??!! She says called Sundowner's Syndrome. M exhausted. Won't hire help, misses Q talks. Q FOOL. Could kill! What 2 do? Back NYC 2sday. IM in PM (your AM).

XXXOO S.

* * * * *

S: Need to fix Q-M ASAP. U—Mary. Me—Quark. Quark is Quark—likely oblivious!

XXXXOOOOO E.

At this point, I received Ellie's elliptical, and I might add blunt, communiqué. An interesting aside about this woman, Ruth. I examined the photos. It is true: the lines of her face, the shape of her eyes . . . something of Mary there. Intriguing.

I like reading back through the twins' emails. Language breaks down into essential utterances with them. Though lacking the import, in some way it is reminiscent of quantum physics, its search for the elemental building blocks of matter. In both cases, we take apart so we may put it back together with understanding. This is yet another example of the fact that the principles of physics are in all things. However, Ellie and Sarah's communication goes beyond this. They have always strived for a personal, excusatory language. As with all things, I trace its beginnings to Peter's suicide.

In the weeks after Peter's death, Ellie and Sarah devised a secret language. I am sure it was in response to the scrutiny we were all receiving. Though in size a city, Santa Barbara is a small town in many ways, and our neighborhood was particularly tight knit. Everyone took a keen interest in each other's business. We were without a mother and so already a topic of neighborly concern. Then Peter committed suicide. While we were carted off to the hospital (a useless activity since it was quite obvious that nothing would repair Peter), the street organized. They came into our house, removed the soaked carpeting, scrubbed the floor and walls, replaced the bloodied couch with one of their own, and carried all the mess off and out of sight. To this day, we have no idea which one of them went couchless for our benefit. We returned home in the small hours of the next morning without Father, who was still with the police. Stepping through our front door was like stepping into a parallel universe, one of the seven other dimensions that String Theory now suggests may exist. It was as if what we saw, what we knew, had never happened, had been a mirage.

It was only then, yanked from our stunned state, that we realized we were missing another piece of our history.

Luke, told by Mary to walk away from all the blood and mess, had never returned. I know you are wondering how we could forget him. He was only six. There is no excuse, only fact. It was the moments after the Big Bang, each of us flung into darkness, careening away from a center that no longer existed. What was left of us organized a search. We walked the streets in ever-widening orbits, called out in voices meant to carry but not to wake the houses' occupants. In the end, we found him waiting on our own front steps, his hair sleep-mussed, his upper lip lined with drying hot chocolate, no doubt gathered, cared for and deposited by some neighbor. We were too raw to feel thankful, there was only the pain of being further probed, further found out. When we brought Luke into the house, he looked around at the changed room and asked, "Where's our house?"

All the rest of the week and part of the next we stayed home from school. Every morning, the kids we walked with paused at the edge of our lawn, peered at the windows and wondered what was inside. Food appeared, horrid casseroles in throwaway pans, covered in Saran Wrap, bearing neatly written instructions: HEAT AT 400 TWENTY MINUTES. KEEPS WELL. Mary was the one who collected them from the doorstep, murmured the appropriate words: how kind, how thoughtful . . . The school called. We were excused. Teachers were collecting makeup work, a school psychologist standing by. Looking from our scattered heights, we saw that it would all be waiting for us, the curiosity, the scrutiny, the gentle interference. We each rushed outward, into darkness, further away. Except, perhaps, for Mary. She stood stolidly there and took it, accepted the unbearable press of concern on behalf of us all. I wrapped myself in Einstein, the last Christmas book on my shelf I hadn't read. Luke began his wandering in earnest, drifting away, the front door left open, only to reappear hours later with a cookie, a toy, a baggie of hard candy. Asked where he'd been, he'd point vaguely and tell us in a puzzled, piping voice, "I was looking for our home." For each of us, a genesis of future self.

The twins locked themselves into their bedroom. Strange utterances were heard, low mutterings, snickers. Mary left plates of casserole by their door, carried the plates off later, barely touched. They were creating their new language. They named it Double Talk, a title singularly lacking in sparkle, I thought, but the language itself was ingenious. Until they were eighteen, for the next ten years, they never spoke to each other in any other way. After graduation, they went to far-flung colleges, different lives. But it's still there, that ability to communicate in separateness, to understand as a sole essence. They lapse into Double Talk whenever they need to be not understood, to exhibit their aloneness. For the first six months after Peter's death, the twins uttered nothing but Double Talk, to each other, to the world. It was an instant grievance to friends, a growing annoyance to teachers and a portent to the school psychologist. If he had any grasp of physics, of cosmology, he would have understood. They were spinning off into space, forming a twin galaxy, revolving around each other, perhaps their language was the tinge of red that proclaimed their leaving.

I have told Dr. Himmel about the twins' secret language. He seems to think it very natural behavior, though not usually seen in children quite as old as Ellie and Sarah. Evidently, psychology, as well as physics, has progressed in the last twenty-one years. He asked how I felt about it at the time. As always, looking back.

"Mildly challenged," I told him.

"Ah ha." Dr. Himmel often finds refuge in the noncommittal. A lengthy empty space usually follows these utterances. The clock on his desk will tick, dust will settle. I always know what he's up to, of course—the unnatural disruption in the flow of conversation, the discomfort of the

25

void. He hopes I will fall in, commit myself, reveal something elemental. Dr. Himmel has yet to understand that I work in the void, anti-matter buoys me, so to speak.

"I solved it," I told him; almost immediately, I must admit. Sometimes I am not as successful at mastering conversational discomfort as I intend.

He raised his eyebrows.

"The secret language," I prompted. "I solved it."

Dr. Himmel nodded, smiled as if he knew it would be so, and then waited once again for more. There are times when I find Dr. Himmel exceptionally irritating.

"It was a fairly clever construction. I was quite proud of the twins. A simple structure but very confusing to the listener. Would you like a demonstration?"

Dr. Himmel grinned. "I would enjoy that."

"Yigou wigill giget nigothiging frigom mige. Igi igam thige figortrigess. Yigou igar thige figool." I smiled at Dr. Himmel.

"Impressive. Your sisters were obviously very bright children. How did you figure it out?"

I shook my head. "I promised."

He waited. I listened to the clock tick a full ten seconds before I folded.

"You add a long 'i' to the first consonant of a word, a 'g' to the rest of the syllable. Multi-syllabic words follow the same construction. Words beginning with a vowel will start with an 'i' and then follow as before. Example: 'again' would be 'igagigain,' pronounced 'eye-ga-gye-gain.' As I've said, quite simple, quite clever."

"How did your sisters respond to you decoding their language?"

"They locked me into the bathroom. The doors along the hallway upstairs all opened into the rooms, unfortunately. They waited until I went to use the toilet and then tied their jump ropes together and attached each end to a door knob: the bathroom's and the walk-in closet's across the hall. They told me they wouldn't let me out until I promised never to tell anyone else . . . all in Double Talk, of course. I refused. I lasted five hours, though. I had brought reading material, you see, my Einstein. I ate a tube of toothpaste and a bottle of Tums and drank a great deal of water. Stomach discomfort set in and our toilet paper supply was discovered to be gravely depleted. In the end I agreed to their terms."

"No one saved you?"

"No." I did not mention to Himmel Mary's padded approach, the sound of her soft breath at the door crack, her whispered words, "Promise Mark. It's important to them. Understand." I remember the sound of her bare feet receding down the hall.

There was a soft knock on the doctor's door; our hour was up. Dr. Himmel and I rose from our seats.

"So you see, Dr. Himmel," I told him. "I've broken a promise in giving you the secret of Double Talk. You must be very careful with it."

"Don't worry, Doctor." He smiled at me. "I'll guard it as if it were a key to a fortress." He winked and stuck out his hand. "Igi igam nigot thige figool. See you next week."

I believe my mouth actually dropped open. I couldn't respond. A lesson: Dr. Himmel is not to be underestimated. Indeed, he is not the fool.

I don't remember a time when Ellie and Sarah didn't call me Quark, at first Quigark, of course, then just Quark. I haven't minded. The quark is extremely important, fascinating really. Between 1966 and 1978, Richard Taylor, Henry Kendall and Jerome Friedman conducted experiments to study how high energy electrons behaved when bounced off the protons and neutrons in a selected target. The electrons bounced back with higher energy and at more enlarged angles than could be explained if the protons and neutrons constituted uniform spheres of matter.

The experiments revealed extremely small, dense objects moving around in the protons and neutrons. Enter the quark. In 1968, I might add, my own birth year.

Dr. Himmel has suggested that humans find connection in shared experiences such as memories. I find this problematic. Why should some snippet of lore, insubstantial, likely inaccurate, be the basis of connection? To me, it seems an equation with too many variables and no true answer. But there is Clare, always Clare. She sits in her patch of sunshine and scrolls through notations on the screen in front of her. To me, in the shape of her body, folded into its chair, in the tilt of her head, there is formed some eternal question mark. How?

"I was born the same year that the quark was identified," I inform her.

She looks up from the computer and gazes at me without recognition.

"The twins, my younger sisters, have called me Quark ever since I can remember."

Clare blinks at me.

"See, it rhymes . . ."

"Quark?"

"And of course it's rather funny sounding . . ." I continue, hopeful. She has spoken.

"Small, dense quark?"

"I don't think they really knew . . ."

"Very dense?"

I nod. Oh, Dr. Himmel, where have you led me?

"What color?"

In the identification process, quarks have been further described as having six 'flavors'—up, down, strange, charmed, bottom and top. Each flavor has three possible colors—red, green and blue.

I hesitate, then, "Green?"

Clare nods. "What state?"

I take a wild guess. "Charmed?"

Clare shakes her head and smiles at me. "Strange."

"Really?" I am perfectly happy to be strange. It is a start.

She nods and takes her hand from the computer mouse, offers it to me. "Nice to meet you, Quark."

I take Clare's hand. It is cool and firm. There is force, gravity. Perhaps Clare is not a receding galaxy. Perhaps she is more elemental than that, closer to home. Standing there, holding her hand, I think she must be what has been termed a Strong Force, the strongest of the four fundamental forces. It holds quarks together, helps them form a nucleus.

MARY AND I are talking again. I apologized. I used the epithets provided by the twins in their emails. I called myself an oblivious idiot, a fool, a jerk. I drew the line at dork. It is not in my *Oxford English Dictionary*. I made it short. Keeping in mind the apology process with the Chancellor's wife, I abandoned further explanation of the Big Bang theory as it related to our particular family history. That is not to say I don't continue to think it accurate and, if needed, mathematically provable. I shall wait until Mary is in a less emotional frame of mind to expound. I am sure she can be brought to agree. Mary has always been the one who listens, the one who agrees. Unlike the twins, who have always rolled their eyes and made rude noises when one speaks. Or Luke, who is there one moment, and then simply vanishes beneath one's nose. Mary can sit, can nod and frame intelligent questions, can make one know one's time and words have not been wasted. Mary is invaluable. She is worth an apology. She accepts. I know.

Mary has the numbers for my home phone, my cell, the lines in my office on campus, at the accelerator and in the lab. She may call me at any time. About six months ago, I began graphing the probability for the hour of her daily call. I often engage in these extemporaneous exercises. Quite amusing. When I told Mary I was in the process of doing this, she said I was charting the arc of her desperation. After the month's time I was able to reassure her that the calls did not represent an arc at all, at the very most a slight wave could be extrapolated from the data, but really, even that was reaching.

"Don't worry," I told her. "Your desperation appears to be quite random in nature."

"Well, that's a relief," she responded. Her voice was quite without affect.

Since there was no particular pattern, I asked her, at that time, if she would designate a specific time to call, so that I would know to expect her.

"I can't do that, Mark. That's not how it works."

"How what works?" I asked her.

"My desperation."

"I thought we had proved you didn't have measurable desperation."

"No, Mark. We proved that my desperation was random. I have random desperation, Mark. You'll just have to go with this one as is."

"Actually, Mary, there are theorems which predict outcomes for random events—the movement of herds and flocks, the probable spatter pattern of rain drops, the long term ebb and flow of human—"

"Good!"

"Yes, it's very interesting, very satis—"

"No, I mean you do it, Mark."

"Do what?"

"You keep graphing my random desperation, and when the big picture emerges, Mark, you let me know."

Her voice sounded tired. Of course I could not see her though the phone, but I thought the conversation was wearing.

"I'd be glad to do that for you, Mary," I soothed.

30

"It's for you, Mark. Not me."

"Very well." Obviously time to change the subject. "So, how's Father?"

OUR FATHER is, more accurately, was, a craftsman, an artist really. He began as a cabinetmaker, working for local construction companies. Except for the fact that our family home is filled with beautifully handcrafted cherry cabinets and bookcases, this fact is unimportant since it predates Peter's death. After Peter, Father emerged as an avant-garde furniture maker, famous locally, then nationally and finally internationally. First, he made Peter's coffin. Looking back, it has suddenly occurred to me that that was where he was during those long days after the suicide, while the twins locked themselves in their bedroom and separated themselves from the world by their chain of misplaced vowels and consonants. That's where he was while I was tied into the bathroom with Einstein, while Luke wandered, while Mary stood hollow-eyed and accepting, trying to tether the rest of us together with offerings of casserole and her single presence. Our father was making Peter's coffin. I have no memory of it, of that box of fine-grained wood, no doubt hand-planed and joined with Father's soon-to-be distinctive style, a box with no other purpose than to be the home of entropy. I will not use the word decay.

I remember the funeral, the long line of cars, tailpipe to nose, winding down the cemetery drive like genetic code, the sound of waves on cliffs below, the fog bank two miles out at sea. I remember Luke in a borrowed suit with too-long pant legs bunched at his ankles, sneakers peeking out beneath, restless toes anxious to be on their way. I remember Mary's hands, one on Luke's shoulder, one in my hand. Even then, Mary had long, tapered fingers. She played the oboe. She was quite good at one time, on her way to being a prodigy, I believe. I remember she played it there at the grave site, its low, lovely sound catching in the branches of the cyprus trees overhead and riding the breeze over the cliffs and out toward the fog bank, as if a Bach melody could hold off approaching darkness. After she finished the piece, I held the oboe for her, so she could hold my other hand. We stood there while the coffin was lowered into the grave. I don't remember it, Peter's beautiful casket. I don't remember my father watching his work sliding into earth. For me fog had come, darkness, limitless space, and Mary's hand to stay me.

I wonder what Dr. Himmel will say when I tell him this particular memory, its precise sequencing, its sudden gaps in code. It's like a tune half-remembered. He will have something to say. He always does. Perhaps he will take me back to the edge of that grave, resurrect that box so singularly made, brush it off, trace its grain, have me read there the meaning of my father's effort. Here is the crux of my argument, the reason I have no place for memories. What good will it do?

When Mary and I discuss our father, we seldom refer to the man he was. She has told me that she has packed away the coffee table books that hold glossy photos of his work. They had begun to disturb him. He sent one through the plate glass window into the succulent border beyond the front porch. She retrieved the book and picked glass from the succulents for weeks, their hides bleeding clear drops of fluid with each sliver she pulled out. Glittering filaments of glass hid all through the pages of the offending Museum of Art and Design book, *Modern American Masters: Franklin Bennett.* Mary put the book in the trash. Father retrieved it. Leafing through it, his hands bled over the pages. Another book, *Nexus, Art and Function,* he fenestrated, cutting star shapes from the pages, each star containing some truncated image, the smooth curve of an armrest, the slender spokes of a straight-back chair, the words "beautiful, bold" on glossy white paper. Now, the few tributes left to him are packed away. Mary allows him to dissipate. He is unmolested by the past.

Father has Alzheimer's. Mary keeps him. She has lived with him always, cared for him the past five years. The twins and I each visit when we can. Of course Luke lives nearby, providing, I surmise, small comfort and more worry. He lives in a caretaker's cottage on one of the less inflated Montecito estates, rent free in exchange for light gardening. Mary finds him somewhere on his regular route on Sundays and sometimes Wednesday afternoons and brings him home for dinner. Father sometimes knows him. Father always knows Mary; she is his anchor. I keep up on the latest Alzheimer's research and inform Mary of the new or hopeful; the twins divert with the stories of their lives. Mary listens.

My father is entropy, the inevitable disorder of a physical system, throughout his mind, his body, his spirit, microscopic configurations disseminate. A measurable decline. Parts of him fall away. Mary picks them up and places them in safe keeping. She waits for the next small bit of him to fall. If it is a testament to entropy, then what is Mary? What principle does she embody? I think she is the purest essence of Einstein's theory of general relativity, that measurement of the passage of light through the curve of the infinite. In her resides the classic paradox of space and time. She is the one who stands on earth, shading her eyes and watching our streaking passage into the ether. We travel, taste the cosmos, return unchanged, hardly older, to offer her our tokens. While we've been gone, she has aged beyond us. Trapped by gravity, she has aged for us all.

Mary is the reason for my calculations, for the theory of all things that I will find some day. I will place it in the hand that she still leaves outstretched. It will have the lonely perfection of an oboe piece played in clear, still air. It will explain the universe, how we began, where we are going. It will explain why: why a seventeen-year-old commits suicide; why disease deconstructs lives; why some bodies spin into orbit while others remain at the center, intact, true. It will give meaning to the graph of her random desperation, an end point. It is the big picture she is listening for at the other end of the telephone line.

MARY

When we talk, careful conversations that avoid discomfort, I do not tell him, but Mark is wrong about our past. I can't speak for the stars, but our family has history, a beginning. I was there. I know. Sometimes I think that people like Mark and Ellie and Sarah, people who continually race upward, rush forward, people who achieve, think they have no need for a past. Even Luke, who heedlessly propels himself along roads that go nowhere, doesn't look back. If they slowed, perhaps to see how far they've come, what they've passed by, they might experience that sharp thrust of vertigo that waits at the edges of ascents. They might stumble, fall. I am not as clever as any of them. I am not the achiever. I have always stood in this place: the same small city, the same short street, the same wide tall house, the same narrow bedroom. From the beginning. Knowing this, you wouldn't think I'd need to know where my feet are planted, but I do. If I don't know where I stand, how can I be always looking out, looking up, my arms outstretched and ready to catch them when they fall.

Mark wants to think that we began the moment Peter leaned into that gun barrel and pressed the trigger. Mark's Big Bang Theory. He denies the existence of anything before. He negates me by saying that. He negates all those years I tried so hard to tell them, to show them that we are okay. WE are still here. How does Mark think we got here? Does he think we sprang full grown from our father's head, like Zeus's children, girded in iron, clustered tightly, then exploded apart at Peter's singular act? I changed too many diapers to swallow that whopper.

I remember. Daddy forgets, Luke was too young, Mark reformulates, and the twins . . . fabricate. That leaves me to remember for us all. Once we were a family. We were whole. We even had a mother.

Her name was Jean. She was slender and light-boned and pale compared to Daddy. I'm built just like her, with her skin tone and hair color. Peter was too, with her fine light brown hair and greenish-hazel eyes. It's as if she had just those first few years to express herself before Dad's genes came barreling through, insisting on dominance: height and large lanky bones, dark skin, crisp black hair spongy with curl, brown eyes so dark the irises disappear. That's Mark, Sarah and Ellie, Luke. They look as if they rolled off an all-paternal assembly line. If I hadn't been there to witness it, I might agree that they sprang from Daddy's head, little godlings, legs kicking and ready to run. There's some marker there, some exact point between me and Mark when our mother gave up. She receded. I believe, from that moment on, all she passed on to her children was fragility. Then, she left.

I remember her, though, sun slanting through the pale shield of her long hair and into my eyes, her face in shadow. I remember games of Scrabble one night when the lights went out in a fierce Pacific storm. Her thin fingers fiddled with the ivory tiles, her nails short and chewed. The whole house shook and creaked from the wind; her eyes were shiny in the light from the guttering candles on the table. We didn't have enough candle holders, so she dropped melted wax onto the card table and stuck the candles there to make soft pools of blue and red and green. We still have that table; it's folded in the back of the coat closet. If you move the coats to one side, you can see the stains the wax left, pale hues of memory. So you see, it did happen. Mark is wrong. That night of the storm, the twins were too small to play, so she handed them gobs of warm wax. They sat at her feet and sculpted in the dark. Mark of course, never too young to play, was winning. My father's laughter and cigarette smoke drifted, his hand on Mark's shoulder, proud and territorial. Peter sat intent on his tiles, willing a word that would bring him closer to his younger brother's score. What was I doing? Watching, probably, waiting my turn. Mother was pregnant, big with Luke. Her belly bumped the table and made the tiles rattle. Her cheeks suddenly ruddy in the candle glow. The small hillock of her belly button, pressing through the yellow cotton of her dress, looked as if it wanted to burst out, escape.

It did escape, with the rest of her, six days after she came home from the hospital with Luke. She walked out the door after she fed us breakfast, in nothing but the clothes on her back, leaving everything, everyone. It was the first time she had been dressed since she came home with Luke. Why didn't we suspect? We looked, we searched. There were police and, later, a private detective. The coast guard harbor patrol watched the waves, the beach line, checked the tide pools along the Channel Islands. Nothing but memory. We waited; perhaps, we still do.

There are so many things I don't know. For every inch of Mark's certainty, I tread doubt. I don't know why she left. Were we "too many," like the children in Hardy's *Jude the Obscure*? Was that it, or am I being too literary, as Mark so often admonishes? Did Luke bring us to some sort of critical mass? Critical mass, a term Mark would like. His science finds ways to slip into my speech. Looking back, I can guess at some sort of postpartum depression that probably wasn't even acknowledged almost thirty years ago. Certainly the doctors didn't notice. Daddy didn't notice. I didn't notice. But, since that morning, I've tried to be so much more careful. I've had no success. They still slip away from me, like water in my cupped palms. Witness Luke. Witness Peter. Responsible is a term I know

37

well, it encompasses both action and restraint. I continue to try, to watch. Even now I am scrabbling to gather the pieces, to lay my tiles carefully. I hope for the right words. Together. Family. Stay.

We have a daily routine. I try to get Daddy up by eight. Lately, his internal clock is off and it is harder, a struggle of wills. I feed him his coffee, his juice and hot oat bran cereal with a big tablespoonful of brown sugar. I tell him what I have already read in the paper. He used to pretend interest, now he doesn't. He is silent. We take our morning walk, always the same route, up to the Mission through the back of the Natural History Museum along Mission Creek. In the spring, the ground beneath the oaks and sycamores on either side of the trail is covered in wild vinca. Later in the summer, brilliant nasturtiums will cling to rock piles and roots. The air is sharp with the scent of eucalyptus. This is the longest part of the journey. Daddy stops often to gaze around and comment, his voice tight with wonder.

"It's just beautiful here."

"Yes. I love it." I have to watch, to keep him from walking from the path to gather flowers. I don't begrudge him a handful of wild flowers, even though he'll throw them away before we reach home, wondering how he came to have them, but poison oak lurks in the undergrowth. By now I know that trying to keep a man with Alzheimer's from scratching himself raw and spreading the itch is not worth the fistful of temporary color.

"It's beautiful here," for him, a refrain.

"I know. I love it, too, Daddy."

"We've never been here before. We should come here again."

"That's a good idea. We'll do it. Maybe tomorrow."

"Tomorrow would be good. I don't think I'm working."

There's a point where we cross the stream before heading up an aged staircase on the other side of the ravine. Crossing, I choose the wobbly rocks carefully. Daddy goes straight through the ankle-deep water, the first grin of the day on his face. It buoys me. I return the grin. We are equipped. We sit on the bottom step and I pull out a hand towel, an extra pair of sox and loafers from my backpack. I strip his feet and wipe them, redress him.

"You always treat me like I'm . . . like I'm . . . like I can't do anything," he'll say as I work on his feet, an edge of anger in his voice. "I can do it." But he won't. Instead, he gazes through the green of the trees at the museum.

"That's a very interesting building. I wonder what's in there."

"It's the Natural History Museum, Daddy. You used to take us there when we were kids. Remember the rattlesnake in the glass box. You would push the button and its tail would rattle and we would all scream."

"Oh yes. I'd like to see that sometime." But his gaze is vacant, troubled. Sometimes, he becomes momentarily upset by this lack of willing recall, and if not distracted, he will falter into fear or lash out. It is time to be moving.

"Should we go on?"

"Absolutely!" he'll say with a smile. "I'm not feeble. I take a longer walk than this every day, you know."

"Do you?"

"Yes. Some days I go way up into the hills."

"You'll have to take me sometime, Daddy."

"Tomorrow."

Up the steps and through the old seminary to the Mission, solid, beautiful and pink as sunrise. We sit on the steps and watch the people in the park. Daddy takes a childish delight in dogs and children now. Sometimes a park worker knees his way through the rows of roses. If it is too hot or cool or rainy, we go into the chapel and sit in its quiet sanctuary. We can never stay long; Daddy is liable to say something inappropriate and loud: "Why did they paint it these ugly colors?" "These chairs are poorly made. You'd think they could afford better," or my personal favorite, "Why are those people kneeling? Get up you over there! Can't you see you're in some sort of church? Show some respect!" We have to scurry out before my fit of giggles will seal our certain damnation. As a family, we have never been churchgoers (Ellie's flirtations with the village priest aside). We have viewed those who are with skepticism, perhaps even cynicism. In years past, we, just Daddy and I, were even guilty of certain, small vandalisms of some of the local churches, rearranging letters or adding words to smug aphorisms: JESUS RESIGNS! or GORY BE TO GOO! However, watching the faithful at their rituals, I suspect we have been wrong. Daily I listen to their whispered prayers. They enjoy the luxury of hope. I envy them. Daddy and I perform a different ritual, the ritual of disintegrating minutes, of time that slides like tide through the channel, past the islands and out to sea, carrying with it small bits of a man, of a life.

From the Mission, we head home along streets. It is here, where the sidewalks are straight and narrow, that I always notice Daddy's gait. He has developed a funky walk. It is rolling, slightly silly, Popeye on land after a long ocean voyage. Someone else out with their dog might stop to watch, wondering. We are not back to our own neighborhood yet. There, they know not to notice. I am long past concern and embarrassment. I have moved on. I embrace. We are in this together. I galumph along with Daddy, who is happy, scenting home, feeling accomplishment. I feel a loosening of tension, of disasters avoided. Safety is ahead.

SARAH HAS emailed us pictures and interviews from her latest work. Across the bottom of one photo, she has

40

typed: "Mary, don't you think she looks like you?" I am trying to decide whether to be offended or intrigued. The woman is old, lined with living outdoors. Her hair is short, spiky, a mousy gray. I suspect creatures burrow and crawl there. She wears a filthy flower-print dress of which Sarah has painstakingly colorized each faded red rose, each twining green vine. Her name is Ruth, no last name. What has Sarah seen in this face that reminds her of me? The line of the cheekbones? The level, pale brows? The slight widow's peak? I hope it is not the eyes.

I take it to Daddy, laughing. He is kneeling in the flower bed next to the barn, pulling weeds, flowers, too. I hand him the photo.

"What do you think, Daddy? Sarah says she looks like me . . . why are you pulling up flowers?"

Daddy ignores me. His dirty fingers trace the face. "Jean," he says. "Darling Jeanie . . ."

I open my mouth, close it, will the words not to come, then say them anyway. "Oh no, Daddy. That's not Mom (the word so foreign in my mouth). That's some woman Sarah's found, a stranger." It is useless, even hurtful. He is already hooked.

He is instantly angry. He gets to his feet, clutching the picture. "Jean," he tells me. "She called. She's coming." He stomps to the house.

I cannot help it. "When did she call, Daddy?" I ask his retreating back.

He waves the photo vaguely as he opens the screen door. "A day or so ago. You just don't believe!" The screen door slams.

I try to imagine the face, but it is a blank. As always with Daddy's sudden, grand illusions, I cannot resist the tug. Could he be right? Did she call? Was I away at the store, or in the yard and not hearing the ring of the phone? Has she surfaced from that watery spot in my dreams?

41

Standing at the edge of the flowerbed, a sprinkling of weeds and bedding plants dying around my feet, I surprise myself. I want to believe it. I want it to be her. I want to believe that all that is lost can be reclaimed.

Twenty-five minutes later, Daddy emerges from his bedroom, white shirt, blue suit jacket, green school tie tied in a sailor's hitch. He clutches his suit pants at his waist.

"I can't find my zipper." His voice is belligerent, unyielding.

I have regained my equilibrium. I have just finished emailing Sarah, detailing Daddy's quaint response. I know she will laugh. I turn to Daddy and smile. "Dad, you have your pants on backwards."

He looks down. "Damn." He drops his pants to his ankles, not a stitch on underneath, and goes through a complicated maneuver to correct the errant slacks. He pulls them up, does the top button, tucks his shirt in, one white tail poking out from his unzipped fly.

I come over to help. "Here, Daddy. Since you found that zipper, why don't we use it?"

He goes out the front door, down the walk. I trail behind.

"Whatcha doing Daddy?"

He stands still and straight at the edge of the lawn. He is a handsome elderly man, formal in his suit, regal.

"I'm waiting for my Jeanie." There is in his voice that edge, that sharpness that expects contradiction, but I am ready for him this time.

"Can I get you a cold drink?" I ask.

"No, I want to be ready."

"Okay, I'll wait with you."

Illusions, delusions are stronger, more constant, than truth. I am prepared to be here all day and into the cool, lovely evening. I will come up with some story to get him inside and to bed. There is a strong chance that we will do it again tomorrow. We will wait until she comes or he forgets.

Oh, Sarah, what have you done?

THE MOMENT before our mother walked out the front door, she handed me Luke, swaddled in a thin gray blanket, six-day-old head peeking out, spiky black hair, blue-black eyes, pink cat yawns. I was nine and I wanted that baby. I don't remember what my mother was wearing, whether she had on sensible shoes for running away. I remember us: the weight of Luke in my arms, his thin ruddy not-quite-human skin and crinkled black eyebrows like little smudges of worry; the twins, somewhere in their mid-twos, making a nest of blankets under the coffee table, meowing like kittens; Peter, eleven, at one end of the couch with Mark seven-going-on-forty-five at the other, the pads of their bare feet pressed against each other, defending turf. Peter read a comic book, Mark something weightier. Dickens comes to mind, but I think that is what I hope he was reading, something thick with the messy juices of life in it, rather than what is in character for him or true. No doubt he was reading science.

Sunlight in the living room, children noise, a normal morning.

"Can I give him his bottle?" I called to her.

No answer, an open doorway, a rectangle of empty California summer. So, I assumed. I went to the kitchen, heated the bottle, returned and settled into the wide, ancient leather armchair. Luke chirped like a cricket as he ate; the twins mewed under the coffee table, "We want milk too!" I set Luke into the crook of the chair and returned with a bowl of milk apiece, placed them at my feet on the wide pine planking and returned to feeding Luke. The twins crawled over and lapped; their noses dripped, pink tongues extended to catch the drops. Peter chuckled at his

Archie comic; Mark, furrowed his brows in concentration, his fingers creating the soft swish of turning pages. The smell of milk, of children, of sun, of wood. I remember that exact moment. We were still whole.

The private investigator Daddy hired to find my mother showed up after the local police and the coast guard gave up the search. But I knew where she'd gone. I dreamed of her breathing salt water, her hair drifting like seaweed, trapping small bubbles like stars; her mouth opened, she spoke. Her words were currents of blue, unreadable.

"He won't be able to find her," I told my dad.

The private investigator asked for a photograph. Peter chose the one on the mantle, handing it to Daddy so he could remove the backing and photo. The investigator slipped it into a square white envelope, the size that usually contains greeting cards or condolences. Did he keep them, I wondered, all those unused cards, or throw them out? Did his wastebasket contain a stack of discarded wishes? After he left, Daddy stood for a long time in the middle of the living room, holding the empty frame. I was the one who took it from his fingers and placed it back on the mantle. His hands remained in his lap, empty fingers crooked, molded to the shape of the frame. It stayed there, blank, for four years, until a poorly aimed beanbag frog knocked it from its place, shattering the glass and chipping the green enamel frame. It was the end of an era, a point of acceptance. That night I slept without dreaming of water, of her. I never blamed her. I always thought that she would come back, if she could, that she had left the door open for just that reason. She handed me Luke in his gray blanket, left the twins, kittens in a nest, at my feet and stepped away. Left Peter and Mark, and I took care of them all. I took care of them for her at first, then as the weeks, the months, the years passed, for myself and for us. We waited together. I never realized until Peter's suicide that one of us might want to leave on purpose. I had assumed too much.

In the interim years between the two departures we were not unhappy. We went on with ourselves much as we had. We were young, resilient, with the attention span of puppies. At that period of our lives, Daddy was making custom cabinets, and though much of his work went on in the carriage barn next to the house, we could not be trusted alone. There were a series of short-lived Mexican housekeepers, each in turn terrorized into leaving. Picture Luke, age two, a huge butcher's knife in his hand, scuttling toward Carlita, fifth in the long line of horrified help, and from the kitchen behind him, whispered instructions from Peter and Mark: "Tell her we require ice cream immediately." (Mark of course) "Tell her or else!" (Peter) I could have stopped them. They behaved for me when they knew they needed to. Instead, I crouched with the twins, hidden behind the sofa, hands wrapped across our mouths and noses to stifle our giggles. Waiting for Carlita's reaction, I was so excited I almost peed.

Luke mimicked Mark as best he could. "Smire ice cream meadly. Else!"

A pause. Carlita took a moment to look away from her soap opera and knitting; then, pay dirt. A shriek and the vision of Carlita hoofing it past us and out the door. Perfection.

"Else!" Luke brandished the knife at the slammed door.

"I'll get that ice cream," I announced as I crawled from behind the sofa and took the knife from Luke's grip.

There were other instances of torture: Maria Number Five scrabbling on shaky limbs across the slate roof, three stories up, to retrieve the five-year-old twins who had climbed through the attic window in Peter's bedroom and sat at the peak of the house, feet dangling, singing "Itsy Bitsy Spider," complete with precariously exuberant arm motions; and Maria Number Eight praying for the ump-teenth time in the middle of the living room floor, rosary clicking, knees already pink from overuse. Luke, of course, was gone again. We never told her or any of them that he always came back. Where was the fun in telling? No, we encouraged her worry with stories of children stolen, of small body parts found in empty lots, of bloody little Oshkosh overalls torn and rolling in the surf. It was much better to enjoy the show.

We were too much for them, Luke with his wandering, the indistinguishable twins with their tricks and single will, Mark with his ponderous, argumentative logic, Peter with his inventive schemes, Daddy oblivious, and I, watching, enjoying, undermining. I kept score. We were a handful, a team. We always won.

They still amuse me, divert me, draw me in, but here is a confession: Sometimes, these siblings of mine are too much even for me. Sometimes, when Daddy decides to take a midday nap, I turn off the computer, the cell phone, unplug the wall phone and go into the back garden. I replant the annuals that Daddy has once again weeded and then I sit. Silence. No confusion of voices, no mes-sages, no need for interpretation—such a risky occupa-tion. A flock of sparrows have built a condo complex in the long back hedge. They trill and complain, blissfully unintelligible to anyone but themselves. Occasional traffic ticks by out front. A dappled quiet, like the shade where I sit in the twins' old swing. If I move, the branch over-head will creak, memories will stir, voices will come. Duty will sift down like a fine dust and coat my shoulders and head. So I remain still, just for a few moments, the length of an afternoon nap, just until I hear Daddy's footsteps. Then it's time to bundle him into the car and go in search of my brother.

They call Luke "Can Man." Locals leave bottles and cans in clear bags for him at the roadside. He collects them, lives and creates off the returns. He covers thirty miles or more in a day, Montecito to Carpenteria and back one day, the next day to way past Goleta and back. That dogged, foot-sore walk, those faded yellow coveralls, a list of roads, a bag of booty. Highway 152, Foothill Drive, Mountain Drive, Mission Ridge, Stanwood, Sycamore Canyon Road, East Valley Road, Toro Canyon Road. A familiar sight on the landscape. He insists on shaving his own head. He shouldn't, it's a mottled, patchy job. He's easy to find if you know the route. I collect him on Sundays, Wednesdays too, if he'll let me, to make sure he gets a good meal. Locals wave when he passes.

He's been in the Sunday section of the *Santa Barbara News Press*. We sat together over Sunday dinner here at the house that day, ham, green beans and scalloped potatoes as always, and pored over the article. "Eccentric Artist," they called him, "A Tin Can Alexander Calder." There was a picture of him standing in the doorway of his tiny cottage, the eves dripping with the weightless, origami mobiles he makes from the best of the cans. It is hard to see his face in the picture. It is slightly blurred with movement. Coca-Cola cranes, Pepsi flying fish, fantastic sea creatures, constellations of stars and planets, a Pythagorean dream of angles and shapes. He could sell them. Modern Americana. Pop Folk Art. They clamor for it. Everyone here wants one. Santa Barbarans tolerate, even encourage a certain amount of eccentricity. He doesn't sell them, though, he can't. It would mean standing in one place too long. I had two, matching strings of cranes that hovered lightly above the sink and swayed delicately, their graceful necks and wings working in the faintest breeze. I woke one morning five months ago to find them in the garbage under the sink, stomped to an unbearable flatness, like road kill, hideous, untouchable dead things. I don't know why Daddy did it. He couldn't remember.

Before the end of each day, Ellie will email, occasionally call. She will regale me with her sexual adventures with that Greek boy. She explains her latest projects. Currently she is fascinated with bones, they puncture the red clay of her sculptures, or lie barely exposed beneath the smooth, faultless exteriors. The photos are stunning, the work alarming. She has always lived for extreme exposure, of herself, of others with an uncanny knack for seeing the inside of life, its mess. She flirts with the village priest, who is a friend, and the abbey monks, who, I suspect, are not. She fights with the matrons of her little village. They represent rules, sobriety, everything she hates, except their sons. I counsel patience, tolerance. She is the weed, the invading species in their garden. Secretly, I encourage. Conquer, Ellie. Show them who we are. I can hardly wait to hear the next installment. I miss her.

Following Ellie's lead, Sarah, too, contacts me almost daily, but while Ellie exposes, Sarah conceals. Her black and white photos are smooth and hard, the exterior life of her homeless ones is shown sharp and clear and heartlessly bleak. She has recently taken to colorizing small bits of her pictures: a gold-hued tooth in an otherwise dark and empty mouth; a bright red hat set at a rakish angle over long, stringy gray hair and black eyes that sparkle like shattered glass. She is the twin who follows, who wants. I suspect Ellie's conquests, her boy lover, her life on Patmos, leave Sarah feeling bereft. She records desertion, aloneness. I worry about her. When will she find someone for herself? Is that what this latest obsession is about, this grubby old derelict that looks like me? How can I help her? Look through the windows of houses, I want to encourage her, photograph family, find a way home . . .

And Mark? He looks down from the stratosphere, offers advice on Daddy, his newly concocted life metaphors, and anecdotal evidence of his science and his days from the safe reaches of an outer galaxy. He's been snagged. He doesn't know it yet, but he's locked in orbit (to use his terminology) around another heavenly body. Clare. Mark in love—I can hardly wait! And what about this Dr. Himmel? Mark thinks his sessions are an amusing saber fight of brains and tongues. His weapons are prodigious. I know. He spent two months with me in seventh grade before the teachers happily handed him up to the next grade. He will triumph. He does. I hope for more for him with this doctor. I want Mark to look back, to sway with vertigo, to see us, to see himself, to feel.

We are different voices clamoring to be heard, separate lives woven together by the glue of my memory, of my worry. We are almost like a novel I could be reading, bit by bit in stolen moments. The meaning is eked out in emails and phone conversations, in careful words and daily protocols, but I can't quite get the sense of it. I don't know where we are headed, how our book will end.

Frankly, I envy Mark his Dr. Himmel. I have so many questions. I would begin with why. Mother, Peter. Why Luke's wandering, why Ellie's hectic sex, why Sarah's loneliness and Mark's self-deceiving luminosity? Even more pressing, though, are questions about Daddy. Where is this illness taking him? What will he become? He is my last child, my latest, most chronic worry. Dr. Himmel, I would ask you this: Are my father's nightly dreams, the dreams that change his nights to fretful day, are his daily delusions, stories offered to me as truth, are they desires? Are they needs, wishes, hopes disguised as sickness? How do I answer them? I need a face to look into mine and to tell me these things, not the pamphlet, not Mark's gleaned facts offered from a safe distance. I need the touch of a hand, the low, warm murmurings of human understanding. I am slipping past diversion. I want someone to whisper me the ending. I need help.

MARK

*T*he uncertainty principle, as formulated by Heisenberg, states that one can never know exactly both the position and the velocity of a particle at the same time. The more we know of one, the less we know of the other. I try to use this principle with the esteemed Dr. Himmel to point out a major failing in his psychological study of me. He may seek to know who I am and how I became who I am, but he will never be able to know both accurately at the same time. To contemplate one is to lose the other. He must choose. He disagrees.

"A human being is not a particle, Mark," he tells me. "We are vastly more complex, more capable."

I disagree with his first point. "The laws of physics apply to all things, Doctor, the macroscopic as well as the microscopic. Human beings are macromolecular, subject to mechanical laws. We cannot pick which laws to follow. They *are*."

"All right," Dr. Himmel counters. "What about that part of life that is not physical, that is immeasurable? What about conduct, emotion? Human connection? Love? How does love behave, Mark? Is it a particle? Is it a wave?"

I see Dr. Himmel has been brushing up on his physics. He is clever, and obviously interested in our little intel-lectual repartee. This is what our hourly sessions have become, a sparring match of ideas. I must admit, I've come to enjoy the contest, to look forward to each Wednesday at 4:00 PM when I settle into Dr. Himmel's chair and he into his corner of the couch. Though we are sparring partners, we are connecting. He seeks me through my ideas as well as my past. Past is position, ideas velocity. Am I wave or particle, Dr. Himmel?

"Love is a string, Doctor," I answer his question. I might have him here. Is he familiar with String Theory yet? Does he know that what were previously thought of as particles are now, in String Theory, considered to be waves traveling down a string, much like the vibrations along a piano wire? Have his studies taken him this far? "Emotion, human connection—strings."

"How so, Mark?"

I ask him for a sheet of his paper and a pen, and sketch an "X" the lines of which are made of tiny loops.

"In String Theory, energy vibrates like the wires of a violin; particles and their corresponding antiparticles are described as waves along an oscillating string." I pointed out a tiny circle on the X. "When a particle and its antiparticle collide along the string, they annihilate each other, emitting energy which creates another pair, another string, a different pattern." I glance up. Dr. Himmel is not looking at the sheet, but at me. I shade in the circles of the X, then the empty space between. A thick rod is created. The tiny circles are barely visible beneath the light blue shading of the pen. "Look here. If you look at the strings not as single moments, but as history, they become something we call a 'world sheet.' Infinite connection. Infinite possibility. Do you see it, Doctor? Doesn't it sound like love?"

Dr. Himmel takes the piece of paper from my hands. "May I keep this?"

"Please do. I'd be more than happy to explain any aspects of quantum mechanics to you at any time."

Dr. Himmel shakes his head. "You surprise me, Mark. You're speaking metaphorically, not mechanically."

"I've recently embraced metaphor, Doctor. You've heard me speak of my Big Bang theory as it relates to my family history, and of course, the ever-presence of entropy, the

51

uncertainty principle we currently argue . . . As metaphors for the human condition, they are very apt."

Dr. Himmel grins across the table at me. He holds my sketch lightly in his fingers. "And yet there is this, Mark." He flaps the sheet. "A String Theory of love. History. Infinite connection, you called it. Infinite possibility." He tucks the sheet away in his notebook and snaps it shut. "I suspect you harbor a romantic inside you, Mark." Dr. Himmel leans back against the couch, displaying a full set of teeth, with what I must describe as a very self-satisfied smile.

I'm tempted to ask for the return of the sheet. I no longer want him to have it. He thinks he has caught me out, determined my position. I smile. I believe it was Heisenberg himself who said, "What we observe is not nature itself, but nature exposed to our method of questioning." While Dr. Himmel has been pinning me down, my momentum has carried me forward beyond his view. I am miles ahead.

"On the contrary, Doctor. Applying the laws of physics to the human experience is releasing it from the romantic and making it practicable."

Dr. Himmel's face has sobered. "Practicable? Oh, Mark, I think you will surprise yourself. I hope you will."

To this there can be no response. I am saved by the soft knock of the receptionist. Time for me is up.

I LIVE a reasoned, regimented life. I rise at six, run in the neighborhood for thirty minutes, then walk back home for ten, shower for ten minutes, eat three-quarters of a cup of All Bran cereal with a sliced banana and a cup of one percent milk, and drink eight ounces of low acid, vitamin A & D-enhanced orange juice while listening to NPR and waiting for my coffee to brew. I drink one cup of coffee, black, no sugar while doing the *New York Times* crossword online (no more than fifteen minutes, usually less, except

Sundays when I like to linger). I am in the office or at the lab at 8:30. My workdays are executed with precision. Possible consequences are monitored, eventualities planned for. I am home by 6:30, with time to check my messages and emails, heat some dinner and then eat it in front of *The NewsHour with Jim Lehrer* on PBS at 7:00.

I admit it: I take comfort in routine. Is Dr. Himmel accurate? Perhaps I am a fraud. Entropy is enemy, uncertainty fear. I can't embrace my metaphors. I fight them, try to stand apart, keep to regimen. I believe it is working. Each morning I begin again.

Then Clare walks into the lab, 8:43, carelessly shakes the water from her umbrella, droplets flying everywhere. Without my knowing it, it's started to rain. She walks up to my desk, plants her hands on two piles of computer printouts (calculations of mathematical dualities in plus dimensions), leans close to me.

"I did it in twelve and a half minutes this morning." She is talking about this morning's crossword.

"Nine."

She narrows her eyes at me, stares. "Nine?"

I nod.

The moisture has made her hair curl. A few strands form loose ringlets that cling to her temples and tremble slightly. She wears her perfume. I hold my breath.

"You had better come over tonight, Mark. I'll make dinner for you. Seven o'clock, not six, not eight. Seven."

She has moved on before I gather in breath to answer. I stare at the piles of paper. She has left two wet palm prints on my calculations.

"Yes," I say to them.

Copernicus and Galileo discovered that the planets circle the Sun, not the Earth. Newton, in turn, determined the laws that governed the planets' motion. By doing so, he made possible a later theory called scientific determinism, which states that, knowing the laws that govern

53

the motion of a body, we should be able to predict where it will be at any time. In effect we should be able to know the future of the entire universe. Alas, later still, enter the subatomic. Uncertainty is all. Particles run riot. Chaos is king. In this era, however, quantum mechanics works to alleviate some of the confusion. Using the Schrodinger equation it is possible to calculate the evolution in time of the wave function of a particle. Some scientific determinism has been salvaged. We may never know the exact future of the universe, but we can chart its probability.

P-branes in the tenth dimension have little appeal for me today. It's hard to concentrate. I catch myself running my fingers over the dried, bumpy imprints Clare has left on my printouts. Every time I look over at Clare in her workspace, I hear particles collide with their antiparticles, a slight popping noise. I think I see sparks. Perhaps I'm unwell. New strings are forming at unpredictable angles. What is the probability of their future? Perhaps I should go home early. Perhaps I should have my hair cut, just a trim. I'll need time to shower. Speaking empirically, the freshness of a ten-minute shower does not always last an entire day.

When I arrive home after my haircut, my message machine is blinking red, and next to it, my laptop indicates I have emails waiting. I push the play button and click on the email icon with my other hand. Over the whir of the laptop's modem engaging, I hear Mary's voice, thin and high with anxiety.

"Mark. Mark, please call. Daddy doesn't know who I am! Twice today. Twice he didn't recognize me. I had to convince him! And there's something else, something worrying about Luke. Please call, Mark."

A second message. "Mark. It's me again. Please, please call."

Another. "Mark. Please call."

As I listen, in front of my eyes, six emails scroll onto the screen. Three ads, then this from Sarah:

M & M:
Have you heard from Ellie?!? Big news!! Here too.
Think homeless woman in Philly that I emailed
about—Ruth—may be our MOTHER! Just think!
XXXXXXXXOOOOOOOOOO S.

Our mother? What mother? A fourth ad announces tickets available for a new traveling Broadway show. Then Ellie's one word message, all the way from Greece:

PREGNANT!!!!!!!!!!!!!!!!!!!!!!!!!!!!!

No X's and O's from Ellie. It seems too many kisses and hugs have landed her in trouble.

I need that shower more than I ever imagined. I stand with my head directly underneath the spray, feel the hot stream of water wash away the tiny specks of clipped hair that always adhere to my neck and shoulders, even after the stylist has brushed at my neck with her rough towel. The flecks of black swirl between my feet carving the serpentine shapes of question marks before escaping down the drain. Einstein would have called them Fragezeichen. I know what I call them. Entropy.

It seems the historical imperative of my family is to create chaos. I leave myself out of this equation. I observe, compute. An errant, fading father . . . a worrisome brother, a sister at her wit's end (pick any of the three!) . . . a long-lost mother . . . a baby, each stands like an irrational number, irreducible, truculent. Then factor in this: I have a date!! Well, Schrodinger, where's your probability now? Perhaps you should take your theories up with Himmel.

In my work, both on the cosmic and subatomic level, I have always found it easiest to address glitches in calculation as they arise rather than put them aside. A wait and see attitude usually ends in a great deal of waiting and very little seeing. Hence, straight from the shower, this email to Sarah and Ellie:

GREETINGS

SARAH, UNLIKELY—STATISTICALLY A 1 IN 295,734,134 CHANCE.

ELLIE, ARE YOU CERTAIN? BEWARE OF FALSE POSITIVES. DON'T PANIC.
    YOURS, MARK

With Mary, this phone call:
"Hello?"
"Mary. It's Mark. How are things now?"
"We're better. Everything's back to normal, seemingly. He just said, 'Mary, I'm going to take a nap.'"
"Excellent. Perhaps it was just a small, anomalous spike, then. Not significant to his overall status."
"Oh, but Mark, it was so awful! You can't imag—"
"Mary, I can't talk for long right now. I have a date."
"Oh! Well. (a long silence) A date?"
Silence from me this time. Women seem to require unwarranted repetition.
"With that Clare?"
"Yes. I am going over to her house for dinner at seven. You mentioned something about Luke?"
"There's a girl, Mark! I saw them together two days ago on the road, and then again yesterday. I think she's attached herself."
"Mary, there's nothing wrong with Luke having a . . . a girlfriend." (Admittedly, I hesitate on the word, such a suggestion of intimacy, of connection. My hand is wet and slick on the receiver. Perhaps I haven't toweled off enough.)

"Of course, there's nothing wrong. It just seems so . . . What are you wearing?"

"Currently, an undershirt, briefs and socks. Seems so what?"

"Unlikely. Are you planning on wearing more than that to dinner? Jeans and a nice polo. Do you own a polo?"

"It depends on what a polo is."

"God, Mark! What planet are you from?"

"In actuality, Mary, I could be from almost any planet. Speaking on the subatomic level, the celestial makeup of the universe consists of the same few basic elements. The Big Bang—"

"No Big Bang, Mark! A casual, button-down shirt with jeans, then. Got that?"

"No Big Bang, button-down shirt. Mary, about Dad—"

"Don't worry, Mark. We'll be okay. I'll handle it. It was probably just a spiking anomaly, like you said."

"An anomalous spike."

"Yes, that. Roll up your sleeves."

"What sleeves?"

"The sleeves of the casual, button-down shirt you are wearing to your date at that Clare's house at seven, Mark."

"Roll them?"

"Yes. Roll them to just below the elbows. Trust me, it's a nice look, a little less . . ."

"A little less what?"

"You, Mark."

"Oh."

"Call me later and let me know how it went. Have a good time."

"We can have a long talk about Father then."

"That would be fine. Remember, roll the sleeves. Relax."

"I will. Mary, thank you."

"Any time, Mark."

"I'll call later."

"Bye."

It is a longer conversation than I had anticipated, though informative. I have just enough time to iron a shirt and pair of jeans. This question arises in the cloud of steam from the iron: Does one roll the sleeves while on the ironing board and then press them into place? I should have asked Mary.

As I am walking out the door, the phone rings.

"Hello?"

"Mark, it's Sarah."

"Sarah, I can't talk. I'm sorry about the mom issue, but—"

"What mom issue? There is no mom issue. I'm calling about wine."

"What wine? Sarah, you're not making sense. I have a—"

"A date. I know. Bring a bottle of wine."

"How did you . . . ?"

"Mary just called. Red is best."

"Red?"

"Red. Spend about twenty dollars. Medium body."

"No, in fact she's quite slender. She's—"

"The wine, Quark."

"Oh. Twenty and red?"

"Right. Medium body."

"Okay."

"So go already."

"Okay."

From the other end of the line, a decided click . . . pause, then dial tone. Medium red twenty dollars in jeans and rolled-up cuffs. Deep breath.

Wine . . . again. I shall have to be vigilant. I shall have to titrate the amount carefully. Don't panic.

On the way over, I make a mental list of possible topics of conversation: a recent article on the Higgs field; my thoughts on the new Large Hadron Collider in Geneva and whether it will help to prove multi-dimensionality; the relative importance of gluons; the new work coming out of Oxford on non-mass particles; the rich hopes for NASA and the European Space Agency's Laser Interferometer Space Antenna finding gravity waves. Any one of these topics could provide a roomful of scholars ample discussion for many evenings, except perhaps the gluons, and so I arrive at Clare's house, $19.95 bottle of Bordeaux in hand, feeling quite adequately prepared for the evening.

Clare at the door. Her hair is pulled back from her perfectly symmetrical face, her lean legs are clad in faded jeans, her curving torso draped in a long, soft, shimmering top reminiscent of the charged ion curtains of the aurora borealis, her bare toes tipped in a deep, satisfying red. My list of topics disintegrates into wayward neurons in my brain.

"Mark." She smiles.

"Gluons," I mutter.

She laughs, "Well, absolutely," takes my hand, takes the bottle and pulls me into her house. "We're having vegetarian lasagna. This will go perfectly." She waves the bottle before me. We have reached the couch.

"Sit," she orders and walks toward the kitchen with the bottle. "Say something, Mark," she calls from the kitchen. I hear the pop of the cork from the bottle.

I open my mouth, but frankly I am afraid of what might come out and close it again. I close my eyes, too. More sparking like this morning. Zipping neurons collide, inappropriate combinations of impulses that fade into darkness. There is an explanation for everything, and I am beginning to believe that interpersonal communication creates an interesting physiological stress reaction in my body. It seems to go beyond the ordinary sweaty palms, pounding heart and dizziness into a realm of confusion that affects my motor functions (witness my evident lethargy and inability to facilitate vocal muscles), language usage and speech patterns. I will have to speak with Dr. Himmel about this. I am sure he will find it fascinating.

"Mark?" Clare is standing in the doorway of the kitchen, eyebrows raised in perfect arches. She wiggles the bottle and two empty wine glasses.

I open my mouth. "Interferometer," I wheeze. This evidently goes beyond a mere stress reaction. Perhaps I am contracting a neurological condition.

"You need a drink." Clare is at my side in two seconds, dropping into the thick cushions of her couch, sinking toward my greater mass. Gravity. Our hips touch. Collision.

"Don't say another word until you've had some of this." She fills my glass to the rim, places it into my hand. She pours herself a glass and leans back sighing. "That's better."

The knob of her shoulder, the length of her upper arm and thigh press into me. She suddenly leans forward. The air is filled with her scent. My vision swims. She holds her half-filled wine glass to her wriggling toes, red to red. "They match! Well done, Mark." She leans back and looks me over, reaches out with long, tapered fingers and examines my shirt cuffs. "Ironed?"

I nod. I should have called Mary.

"Interesting. Drink up, Mark. Then let's talk Interferometer." She smiles.

There is an interesting feeling in me, perhaps the wine on an empty stomach, perhaps the perfume, the smile, but whichever it is, I think I now know what a free-traveling stellar object, an asteroid or satellite for example, must feel like when it is suddenly pulled into the gravitational field of a planet or star. Compelled is the only word I can think of, physically, mentally compelled. Of course an asteroid or satellite wouldn't be able to feel anything let alone conceptualize it, but I stray from my point. My point is that the sensation is akin to a sudden sense of purpose, a movement toward completion, wholeness. It isn't unpleasant, not in the least. It is true that something is lost when orbit has been joined, a certain, aimless freedom is gone, but then, so much may be gained.

ONCE AGAIN, Dr. Himmel sits across from me. In this hour we have discussed Sarah and her illusory mother; we have discussed Ellie, her unwed pregnancy, her teenage lover; we have even discussed Mary and her struggles with my father's disease. He has asked me how I am responding to these crises.

"With logic," I tell him. "There is a function called a Lagrangian, which represents how particles interact. Using it, one can calculate the behavior of elementary particles, including how they combine. It's somewhat the same with my sisters. It was predictable that Ellie would become pregnant, that once she did, Sarah would need something in her life, too, and that Mary's panic would escalate with my father's disease. That leaves Luke, and of course, he walked out of the equation long ago. Straightforward math, really. Mary can be encouraged, Sarah can be discouraged, and Ellie, well . . . Ellie will always be Ellie. All that's required there is a mop-up."

Himmel nods. "You seem to create a comfortable distance from the world with your logic, a cushion that keeps you untouched, secure."

"I am not untouched." I open my mouth, but I cannot say Clare's name. She is inside me, and I cannot get her out and display her. She is a hard kernel of heat, a tiny nuclear reaction somewhere in the region of my intestines (though that could also be the vegetarian lasagna), and I suddenly want to hold her there, feel the buildup of secret energy.

"I respond to my family in a logical manner. I try to with everyone."

"What happens then, Mark, when your logic, when your math and theories don't pan out." Dr. Himmel reaches for a pile of magazines on the coffee table. From half way down the stack he draws one out, *Discover*, in a provocative bold yellow on its cover, the question: "Is String Theory About to Snap?" "I think you may be right, Mark. I think science and human relationships may be alike. They are both tentative, liable to failure. Isn't that a cause for insecurity, Mark?"

As usual, I am way ahead of him. "Have you read the article, Dr. Himmel?"

"Yes."

"So have I. You'll know then that it is written by one of the leading proponents of String Theory and talks about the many ways in which String Theory may be provable in the future. The math is there, the proof will follow."

"And what if it doesn't? Won't that affect your perception of everything? Won't that affect all your other theories, your Lagrangians and your Big Bangs? What will you do then?"

"Doctor, science is process. The universe is everywhere, around us, in us. Something holds it together, makes it work. The equation is there, somewhere. Science inquires."

"Then what's the answer?"

"Wait, and perhaps I will be able to tell you."

I would call today's session a draw. Himmel has thrust with uncertainty, I have parried with the unassailable: process, math, science, time. I hope I have given him something to think about. Indeed, I must admit he has provided me with a slight jab that festers. He said that human relationships are liable to failure. I had not thought of it. Failure. There is, however, historical precedence in our own family: suicide, and before that cataclysmic event, the other failure (I choose to think it less germane), a mother leaving. They are quantities, calculable, subject to rules. Mass, force, acceleration. It is a matter of function.

But, Clare. Only you defy my mathematics. What is your value? Where is the outcome? Science is inquiry, love is a string. Entropy threatens, makes me tentative. The math is there somewhere. I shall go back to the drawing board, redo my calculations. How do two people meet, touch, become one? Whatever this equation between two humans, it will be my work to solve it.

LUKE

I am doing the math, recounting cans in my head and walking. She just appears, pulling up next to me on the highway and asking if I need a ride.

"No. I walk."

She rolls alongside me. "Where you heading?"

I point. Her dog leans out the passenger side window, the VW bus so close that I can feel the dog's wet breath on my face.

"Mutt."

I don't usually do humans, except for Mary and Dad, who doesn't really do humans either. Not sure what I am supposed to say to this girl, I keep moving. She inches forward with me as I walk.

"Mutt. The dog's Mutt. I call him that. It came to me in a dream one night. I found him going through a line of trashcans in an alley in L.A.. For a while I called him Trashcan Dog, but that was a lot of work. So I slept on it, and it just came to me. Mutt. A lot of things come to me in dreams. I bet I dream you tonight. Why do you wear those coveralls? It looks like you just got out of jail or something."

I shrug.

"Did you just get out of jail? 'Cause I dated a guy who was in jail once. I met him on the internet, and then visited at the jail a few times. It was pretty cool, but he was going to be in there for a long time, so I kind of said hasta la vista to that whole thing. Hey, I can't be hanging with no payoff, right? Plus he was pretty spooky when you got right down to it. Know what I mean?"

I shrug. A long line of cars is forming behind her. There are a few light honks.

"So what's your name? What do you do? What's in the bag, man? Sounds like trash."

"Walk," I tell her. "I walk." Then I stop and turn and look at the line of cars, hoping she'll get the idea. There is a can back there, Pepsi Lime. She made me miss a can. The wheels of the bus crunch to a stop next to me. She rolls down her window and waves people by. I can feel her eyes on me as I head back for the can.

"Hey! What you doing? What are you, like an environmentalist or something?"

I bring the can back and stand by her bus, the dog panting and grinning in my face. I might as well get this conversation over with. I show her the can.

"I make things."

"What kind of things?"

"Things that move."

Her face just lights up. She has a beautiful smile, bright and white with perfect teeth.

"That is so very awesome, man!" Down the road behind us, a police car taps its siren and slows. She looks over her shoulder. "Oh boy. I better be moseying, Dude. Don't want to end up in jail with my ex. That would be uncool!" She pulls out onto the highway and rolls about thirty feet down the road, then pulls over again. Her park lights go on, and her head appears above Mutt's. "Hey! You never told me your name!" The cop pulls up behind her and taps his siren again. "Never mind! I'll call you Motion Man!" She throws her arms around Mutt and buries her face behind one of his ears. He accepts it with a nose raised in salute. She lifts her head and lays it on the dog's head.

"What do you think, Mutt?" she says so we both can hear. "You and me and Motion Man."

The cop taps his siren again, but I can see a grin on his face. She waves at him. "Better go, Motion Man. I just

65

know I'll dream about you tonight! We'll walk!" She goes another fifty feet maybe, then pulls over again. "Hey! I'm Willow!"

"What?!"

"Willow! My name! Willow!" And she is gone in a sudden rush, the cop following and checking her speed.

I pull the trash bag off my shoulder and put the can in it. Pepsi Lime, a good find, pretty rare. I swing the bag back up onto my shoulder. The cans rattle like conversation. When she talks, her fingers race back and forth along the steering wheel, the muscles in her face move in a hundred ways and the tattoos on her arms seem alive. The tips of her hair quiver and sway. She is Willow . . . Willow who carries her own breeze. I have another twelve miles to cover. Cans wait. My feet itch to feel the hum of the pavement below them. I am Motion Man.

MARY

Who is this woman-child who pursues our Luke? I see her VW bus parked along the verge in front of his cottage. A number of times I've seen them walking together, he, as usual, silent, head down, hands in the pockets of his coveralls; she, matching his long stride with an occasional skip, skinny arms flying, talking four times as fast as they're walking. There is a motley dog, large and overfed with a loping gait that reminds me of Daddy's. I am inclined to like the dog. I'm spying, of course. I can't help it. I bundle Daddy into the car and make excuses about groceries or dry cleaning, as if he ever questions me or even cares.

The girl's hair is spiky and dyed an impossible magenta. There are tattoos at her wrists and biceps and more crawling up her scrawny calves. I suspect piercings. She is young, much younger than Luke, somewhere between seventeen and twenty-two, I'd say. Where are the parents of this bright-hued illustrated waif? Why don't they rein in their child, scrub her and send her off to school to make goo-goo eyes at boys her own age, boys that stay in place? But no. It seems she has chosen my brother. Even from behind the windshield of my creeping car, from the distance of my hiding places, I can see she is in love.

I can't quite understand myself. I have enough to occupy me, days filled with activities, duties, Daddy, but still it rankles. Luke has found someone, or rather, someone has found him. Will she feed him, clean him up, make sure he arrives home safely? I suspect yes. That is a good thing. It seems there really is someone for everyone, someone for Luke, for Mark, someday there will be someone for Sarah, and of course, many someones for Ellie. Once there was even someone for me, someone who was nothing more than a shadow that slid though our night-dark yard, but still *someone.* I remember his eyes lit by moonlight; I remember the promise of his vigil. I remember, too, he pulled my eyes away just when I should have been watching the closest. No one knows this but me and Peter. Peter, I'm sorry. I should have stayed to listen. Perhaps he stands out there still, my midnight Lothario, my personal Peeping Tom. But, I learned my lesson; I stopped looking. It's been years. Years that have been filled, filled with brothers, sisters, a father, a family that has chirped and quarreled for my attention, has clamored just like chicks before they leave the nest. So why am I worrying about Luke?

My days are filled.

Mark,
She has tattoos. I've been worrying for days now.
What should we do?
    Love,
    Mary

* * * * *

Mary:
Please be precise in your language. Who has
tattoos?
    Mark

* * * * *

Good Lord, Mark! Are you paying any attention at
all? Luke's girl! This family is falling apart, Mark,
and you are going out on dates! How was it? I
hope you had a nice time.
    Love,
    Mary

* * * * *

Mary:
A very enjoyable evening, though I must admit
to some slight shyness at the onset. Re family, if
you will remember, it fell apart long ago. Don't
worry about Luke. Frankly, I find it encouraging,
tattoos aside, that he has found someone—or as
you say, someone has found him. I find Sarah's
"discovery" far more problematic. There is no
mother, Mary. She is evidently delusional. You
must speak to her.
    Mark

* * * * *

Mark,
Re date: glad you had a good time. Re shy: don't
worry. Re Sarah: talk to her yourself!
    Love,
    Mary

SARAH

$\mathcal{M}$ark annoys me. He always has. I have heard his Big Bang theory, of course. Mary told me, called me right after she had hung up on him. Over the line, her voice had a jagged edge of hysteria, at its core, deep, blunt hurt. Mark and his theories, I'd like to stuff one up his nose. He doesn't have the right to do that to Mary. None of us do. She deserves more of us. She deserves everything. Of course, Ellie and I have always thought Mark is from a different planet. He might look like us, but he's an alien. "I come in peace, Earthling," he seems to say, but in reality, he nudges the status quo into chaos. He can't help himself; he has no understanding of the precarious balance of human existence. Mark the Quark. He may think our family is blown apart and drifting, but he couldn't exist without us. Mary, Ellie and I make him acceptably human. He wouldn't have a chance with this Clare creature without us helping every step of the way. We lead him by the nose to some state near lovable. Without us he really would be speeding along into deep space; he would be all alone with his concocted theories.

It's not that I don't believe in his Big Bang theory when it comes to our family. I actually do. Undeniably, it fits. But theories can cause enormous harm. Look at our Mary. Or better yet, look at Mark's little idol, Einstein, and the atom bomb. "Look vat I figured out," he said (of course, I paraphrase here—I haven't the slightest idea what Einstein actually said). "Heer ist dee potential for a fery big boom." Nice one, Einstein. Welcome to the modern world's

Big Bad Bang. Harm on a global scale. Theories. Once the words are out, you can't take them back.

Ellie and I have always hated to admit when Mark is right. It's one of our codes. Nigeviger igagigree wigith thige Quigark. We really do try never to agree with him. In this one case, however, I fear he may be right. The thing is, there actually is very little Ellie and I remember before Peter's suicide. We were eight and we should remember more. For me, that time is like an ancient sepia tintype, the images faded beyond ghosts and shadows to a simple rusted haze. All that is left of the vibrancy of that previous life is Ellie. Snapshots in my head of Ellie in full color caught at different stages of young childhood: Ellie sitting on a blue paisley-print lap (our mother?); Ellie running ahead of me through dappled green shade toward the rope swing in the backyard; Ellie grinning in a yellow dress that stuck out like a circus tent over the upward press of petticoats; Ellie holding a Popsicle on the front step, clear red melt running down her fingers; Ellie giggling, open pink mouth, at the thump of Peter above our heads in his bedroom in the attic.

He was our favorite, so much larger than us, gentle and patient, not ordering us about or buttoning us up like Mary, not Mark in any way. Our favorite. My favorite. He showed me how to use his new camera. An Instamatic. Just me. Where was Ellie? He showed me how to fit the viewing hole to my eye, guided my index finger to the black button, gently pressed it.

"Smoothly," he whispered in my ear. "Look. See what you want. Hold your breath. And click. Smooth, perfect, real. Now you try on your own."

I remember his fingers sliding off my own, the lightness of the camera in my hands, an intense need, a longing for ownership. Well, I guess I lied. There are a few pre-event recollections. There are some things that can't be forgotten, must be carried, like the obligatory oh-so-ugly school photo in the wallet. The next day I stole the camera out of his book bag and hid it between the mattress and box springs of my bed. Mine. That night he killed himself.

Here is another memory: Black blood on our pale gray carpeting, white walls spattered in clots of darkness, an articulation of dusky, angled limbs. The moment when the world became something to be looked at, recorded, a news item, a human interest photo. Hold your breath and click. Put it out there and let the public react. I wanted to put the camera back, place it on Peter's shelf as if it had never been taken away. I never had the chance. That night and many nights afterwards, I waited for Ellie to fall asleep, for her body, in bed with me, to loosen with sleep, but she never did. We stared into each other's eyes. I could feel the lump of the camera beneath my knees. I never told her. I've never asked her. Did she know? She never said, but how could she not know? I slept with it for years, couldn't take it out, couldn't touch it, an uncomfortable lump of guilt and desire, until it was lost to one or another cleaning lady's avarice or zeal.

Between me and the world is the camera. The camera and Ellie's eyes have always been my focal point, where I turn, the camera for truth, Ellie for belief, ever since that day, that night, eyes that I have been studying ever since.

A FACT about Ellie and me: We are mirror twins. When you compare us, we are identical opposites. She is left-handed, I right. She has a mole on her right kneecap, I, a twin one on my left. Our hair parts naturally at cowlicks that whorl in opposite directions in the exact spot on opposite sides of our heads. Growing up, we lost mirrored teeth at the same time. The black flecks in the irises of our eyes match. Exactly. We are two halves of a whole, yin and yang, light and dark, though which is which, I'm never sure. We are linked, inextricable. It has always been this way with us, a natural order: I think something up, she jumps ahead to do it. I follow. The rest is mutual action, entertainment.

Damn the consequences.

THE IDEA snuck up on me. Even after the first session of shots, it never occurred to me that the homeless woman, Ruth, could be our mom. We never think about her, our missing mom; we never talk about her. She left before it could matter. That's what I always thought. It mattered to Mary, though, and Mary is always in my thoughts— Mary's life, all that Mary does, all that she can't do—we owe Mary, we love her. Mary has always been our audience, our acceptance, our applause. The point is, I see her face sometimes, in crowds on the street or in the subway, maybe in the tilt of the head or the dreamy, waiting look of some lone diner in a restaurant window. I never see Ellie's likeness until I look in the mirror, but Mary I carry with me, always. Even so, it snuck up on me. Need and Ellie made me believe.

The woman was sitting against the cement wall of Wicker Place, a flophouse in Philadelphia I had come to shoot. It was hot, and she sat at the edge of deep shade created by the burnt-out factory across the street. She sat with her knees drawn up to her chest, but her bare feet were in full sun, the toenails painted a deep, pristine red on filthy toes. It's what drew me, that urgent red. Recently, I have been awakening to spots of color, noticing sharp points of color in gray life. I don't know what has triggered this turn in my vision. The colors stick out like necessity, and I can't ignore them. I've taken to tinting some single item in a photo, a gold tooth, a child's pink drinking cup, a brilliant yellow black-eyed Susan glowing in a field of featureless trash. I've talked with Ellie about it. You'd think I had just invented white bread. "I knew it would come. Go for it, Sarah!" she whooped over the phone line from five thousand miles away. Ellie's standard response from the time we were five, whenever she rushed forward and I held back. As with most things, she's right about this though; it feels right.

I never ask my people to pose, to even change position. The way life presents itself is the way it should be seen. I wanted to catch Ruth (I didn't know her name yet) just as she sat, deep in shadow, those toes gleaming. I squatted down and asked if I could take her picture.

"Why?"

"It's what I do. I love your toenail polish in the sun."

She wiggled her toes. Points of white light danced. I was afraid she might move her feet. The toes settled in the dust again.

"Go ahead. You can take a picture of me doing what I do."

She looked out at me. In the deep shadow I could just discern the whites of her eyes, the angles of her thin cheeks through my lens. It wasn't until I developed the photos from the shoot that I saw it, the resemblance. That's what I love about the camera, the truths it finds and leads me to. A trick of shadows really, the features transferred from the negative as I exposed it to the lamp, blackness turned light—a straight thin nose, wide lips, long eyes, widow's peak, heart-shaped face with wide, sharp cheeks and pointy chin. Then, the face slowly darkened, withdrew back into shadows, threatened to be lost as the picture exposed. With each subsequent print I used a little less lamp, dodging my hand between the light and paper then swished each page in developer, stop bath and fixer. I pulled them out one by one, dripping and underexposed, and hung them on the drying line. Photography is a game of patience, fiddling with possibility, waiting to see what will be revealed. All ten shots of the woman presented the same face. They hung in a row by their corners on the drying line and stared back at me from different

74

angles, each of them Mary's face, twice her age, dirtier than Mary would ever be, but still Mary, all of them Mary. Almost a twin. Later, when they were dry and spread out across my work table, I was so engrossed I forgot to tint the toes.

I emailed Mary and the others, knowing it would amuse them.

"Please don't tell me I look like that!" Mary emailed back and added Dad's reaction. And there it was, The Idea, the Great What If, triggered by Dad's sweet, stubborn hopes. I know he has Alzheimer's, is sometimes confused, sometimes deluded. I know that, but there was that face looking up from my work table, clear pale eyes that had something to show me. Photography has taught me this about life: you have to be ready to snap the picture, to capture the moment.

I took the train to Philly four more times over the next two weeks. She was always there. The Queen of Wicker Park, she called herself. Her name was Ruth.

"That means mercy," she told me, slurping up the lo mein noodles I had brought her. "Did you know that?"

I shook my head.

"Very few people do, but everybody needs mercy." She grinned and held out a hand, palm up for change.

She said she came from "out west." She told me she had had a family there somewhere, six kids. We were six once. She said they left her, grew up, moved away, no word. She couldn't do it on her own and ended up on the street.

"What about your husband?" I asked.

"I didn't say I had one."

I wonder how much of a husband Dad was.

Back in my apartment, I listened to the tapes of our conversations over and over, tried to tease out the lies, the fantasy. I knew that, like Dad, she couldn't be trusted, but that face stared up at me through the pauses, the mumbled answers, the occasional sharp retorts and frequent evasions. I remembered the pale eyes, so like Mary's eyes, sliding away from my questions. Through the chirping of the rewind, I waited and wondered and listened again. A waiting game. Who would be revealed?

My voice: Do I seem familiar to you?

Hers: Sure. You were here a few days ago. The lo mein lady.

Mine: Sarah.

Hers: Sure.

I finally called Ellie to see what she thought of my big "what if." She didn't give me a chance to say a word.

"Sarah! My God! I knew you'd call any second! I'm pregnant! Pregnant! I just found out! Me! Pregnant!" Ellie is screeching. The connection was tinny and odd, as if she was screaming from the bottom of a deep well. Panic bubbled up from down there, panic, excitement, accomplishment. Joy. "I wasn't sure! We had to go all the way to Kos to get a kit to check it out! Can you believe it?! They are so backward here! I swear, this island! Just last week—"

"Ellie!" I hollered. "I think I might have found Mom!" She might have gone on forever. I had news too. I dropped my voice, "I think I might have found Mom."

"Mom? What mom?" An utterly blank quality in her voice.

"Ours."

"Our mom?" Confusion, perhaps awakening.

"Yes! It's remarkable, Ellie. I sent pictures. She's in there. She could be Mary, only so much older and worn. Ellie, she had six kids. Six! She says she came from the west! Haven't you been checking your email?"

"I told you, we went to Kos. My God! We had the most fabulous weekend! This incredible taverna! Dancing! They make their own wine. Oh my God, Sarah! I was polluted! Absolutely shit-faced! I woke up naked on the balcony of our room!" Ellie's voice faltered. "But, Sarah. Mom? Sarah, are you sure?"

"Ellie, I think so. Can you believe it?"

A tribal scream reached up to me. "Yes! Of course! Sarah! Mom! And me! I'm pregnant! I can hardly wait to tell Mary! Sarah, just think! It's perfect! Two new family members at one blow! We're so amazing! Oh my God, I have to go! I have to tell—" From five thousand miles away, the phone clattered into its cradle.

I sat holding the phone, her news sinking into me. Ellie's pregnant. Ellie was going to have a baby, a thought, an action entirely her own. Someone else inside her, a part of her. Her own little being. My fingers cramped on the handset. I don't know how long I had been clutching it, how long the connection had been lost. A baby. Sarah and Ellie . . . and Ellie's baby. What had always seemed inextricable loosened, unraveled just a little. I felt dizzy. A precarious balance had been tipped, a natural order lost. I knew what she'd do. I always know. She'd rush ahead. She'd offer it up, this little artwork, her own creation, a gift, and Mary, our Mary, our special audience, would be amazed. Mary would be so happy. What did I have to give? *Something of my own.* I looked down at Ruth's face, at Mary's face, at so much more. A discarded, forgotten being found, resurrected, offered up. I saw mercy.

I think so. That was what I told Ellie, and she jumped at it. That is how the two of us are—idea, agreement. The rest is action. Instamatic. As Ellie says, we are amazing. We *are* inextricable. We must be. I traced the lines of each image with my fingertips. Peter once told me, "Look, see what you want, and click."

"It's you, isn't it?" I whispered, then answered, "Yes." Once the words are out, you can't take them back.

I emailed Mark and Mary. Luke would just have to find out through the grapevine. Mary's response was a muted, "Oh Sarah, how can you be so sure?" Mark's, of course, was anything but muted. He thinks he's so clever. Only the Quark would know the exact population of the United

States on any given day. Yes, I checked his figures online. Since his email, that little phone call, his reasoning voice, his reassertion of statistical impossibilities. God, he's annoying.

But Mary, how can I answer you? Here are Ruth's faces in various stages of shadow. A vision, a creation, a gift. For you. Mary, here's something to complement Ellie's squalling bundle. Something for all of us. I'm righting the balance. Can't you see I must.

A FACT about our family: we're all artists; Dad with his single, perfect pieces of elegant furniture, Ellie and me, Luke with his airy menageries, achingly precise and delicate. Who knows what Peter might have become; perhaps a photographer like me, though Ellie thinks an actor. Mark, being from another planet, doesn't count.

I think Mary is an artist, too, or could have been. All over our big old house, in out of the way corners and crannies are painted murals. In the upstairs tiled bathroom, a blue ocean washes along the upper edges of the walls, fish swirl in schools, an octopus peaks out from a sand-bound rock and reaches one long arm towards a crab, a gray whale dives into the space behind the claw foot tub, delicate strands of seaweed reach toward the ceiling, sheltering a family of sea otters that float on their backs. Above the back porch door, sunflowers sprout brilliant yellow, lightening that spot of perpetual gloom and spiders. Ivy grows from corners all over the house, and a beehive throbs with activity in the library, its bees scattered all over the ceiling. If you pull out a book from the white-painted shelves, you will find them there, too, tiny yellow and black secrets. A climbing rose creeps out of the front hall coat closet; one red rose, huge and blown, drips petals that drift and collect at the baseboard. There are touches like that all over the house. Bits of whimsy done with moderate skill, they predate my truncated memories. The murals, their quiet spark, remind me of Mary. I'm sure she painted them, though she denies it. That, too, is so like Mary, self-effacing, modest, and then . . . surprising. Ellie agrees with me. Mary did it. Who else?

Ellie is the true genius (I don't count Mark's mental talents) though, despite Dad's world-famous armchairs. She creates the most amazing art. It's visceral. She sculpts now, but she started out with paint. It's how she was accepted into Cooper Union here in New York, her paintings that seemed to scrape the surface off ordinary life. Her paintings and *I* got her into school.

Ever since the first day of junior high school we exchanged classes, each of us going to the classes that were easier for one or the other. It was something we had worked out the summer before. My idea. I have always been the one who comes up with the idea, she the one who sets it in motion. We knew they'd never put us into the same classes, too much potential for trouble. The way we spoke in Double Talk (another of my ideas) rankled. Warning notes preceded us with every matriculation. We worked out how to change clothes between classes, practiced the first few days of school. We were careful to appear as different as possible from each other, then, as soon as class bells rang, T-shirts, jeans and skirts sailed over toilet stall dividers in our appointed bathroom. Seventh grade through senior year, Ellie did every single English and P.E. class for both of us. I did math and science. History we switched by subject. I hated American history, but liked world history. Ellie was ambivalent about both and willing to be led. Art was a different matter. The first year we flipped for it. She won. I took two semesters of home economics: Miss Thurber, burnt cakes, and two skirts on the bias. The second year, Ellie begged. I conceded—two semesters of music theory with Mr. Marvel. I'm not kidding about that name, either. "Listen to this Marvelous melody," he'd say with a grin at least once a day, only I'd hear it twice. By sophomore year, it was a settled thing. Seeing her progress, I couldn't say no. What she was producing was startling, a movement from mimicking others' styles to her own clear vision. The only one who ever knew our secret—even including the family—was the art teacher; and she, a true believer in divine talent, went along with it. For high school teachers, an Ellie comes along so seldom. What about me? I knocked together two birdhouses that still hang under the big sycamore in our backyard, typed twice as fast as anyone else in my class(es), shot off two rockets of my own design; shared sticky teen angst (with some slight imaginative changes) in double Life Skills, became extremely intimate with the health, care and functions of the human body, and learned to drive twice. Ellie still doesn't drive. She'll never learn. There will always be someone to drive her. Me.

The series of four paintings that landed her at Cooper Union were titled *Beneath*. Four ordinary houses and yards, one with a white picket fence out front, but in each, every surface is missing. The fronts of houses are missing and we see the complicated life inside: a couple's drunken dance, a woman weeping on a bed, children arguing over a toy as their parents make love above their heads. An old woman stirs poison into a heating can of Campbell's tomato soup. Inside faceless refrigerators, lettuce rots surrounded by beer cans, moldy cheese, a dead rat, a slice of fresh wedding cake. Worms hide in porch and fence posts, termites in foundations, bats roost with pendant menace in dark attics. The earth itself is sectioned and its secrets lay open: dinosaur bones, a mole's nest, rocks and shells, a musket and potsherds, the skeleton of a man. Lower still, at the very edge of the paintings, a ruddy, hungry glow is barely glimpsed, the hot heart of the earth. In one, my favorite, a young boy swings, pumping for the sky, slicing the interiored picture in two, a sneaker soars, a pink grubby toe thrusts through a holey sock. Seedy, voracious life displays itself behind him, but on his face is an openmouthed shout of purest joy. I asked Ellie for that painting, but she had already sold it. It paid her way to Europe and kept her there until she no longer needed to come back. But I have the photograph of it pasted onto my computer as my screensaver. It slides across my vision when I sit down to email or work on my web site. Sometimes the face of the boy reminds me of Luke, the black weightless hair, the pink toes that socks and shoes can't hinder. Sometimes the face of the boy is Mark laughing at me. Mostly, the face is Ellie. Ellie knows secrets, she knows without seeing the darkness inside people. She gives it light. She knows how to walk away. She is escaping with a laugh.

I couldn't go to art school with Ellie. No art. I went to Berkeley as a chemistry major, then transferred into the journalism school my junior year. I worked in the photo lab to help pay tuition, and then one day picked up a camera, the first time since I was eight. It was heavier, bulkier, more complicated than that first, never-used Instamatic. Yet holding it, it felt light and simple with lack of history. It felt right. I looked through the lens and focused on the world, one small square, smooth, perfect, real. I moved to New York, but Ellie had just graduated Cooper Union and flown to London. I have stayed, sitting at the edge of this continent, waiting, ever since.

It's hard to explain how my art came on me. I started out in one of those kiddy picture studios, photographing rich little darlings in oh-so tasteful clothes. On my own, I wandered the streets, noticing the people, absorbing the shadows. It was so dark and dirty compared to California. My eyes were drawn to trash, the left behind, the discarded. I photographed trash. Dogs and birds and butterflies love trash. They value what everyone else has dropped or passed over. The first photo I sold was of a dog gleefully rolling in the lurid contents of a ripped garbage bag, the dog's owner looking on with comically pronounced repulsion etched on his face. Later, as I sat on a nearby park bench praying I caught the shot, an old man came by and patiently dug through the garbage bag, finally carrying off two items, a heel of bread and something dark, unpalatable and mysterious. The homeless find a use for refuse as well.

I have settled into my surroundings here, into myself, into a routine. My apartment is in Tribeca. It sounds far more glamorous than it is: fourth floor walk-up, one room with a slight little nub of a wall toward one corner to suggest an alcove for a bed, a tiny sink and stove beneath one of the two windows, a toilet and shower where a closet once was. I have painted the walls a pale gray, the ceiling a bright white and all the trim a flat black. I've just paid off a black leather couch and armchair. Little black cockroach traps hide in each of my four corners. The two windows are fitted with blackout curtains that turn the apartment into a darkroom when I'm working. It's much cheaper than renting lab time at the university. The entire building is set up for wireless internet, which is perfect for me. I can sit at my desk, or lay on my bed, or sit on my just-paid-for couch or chair and put my feet up on my not-quite-paid-for black iron coffee table, and instant message Ellie, email Mark (against my better judgment) or Mary, connect with curators, galleries, work on my web page and check the number of hits it has received that day. In this building, in this room, there is everything I need. I am in touch. I have lived in this city long enough to know that this is the only connection available. I look through my window, through my camera. I see.

My first award-winning photo was taken five years ago. You see, like Ellie, I am good at what I do, too. It is shot almost at pavement level, no more than eight inches off the ground. A homeless man is wrapped in a plaid blanket, on either side of him pale low mounds of city snow. With grubby fingers he holds out a plastic cup. In front of him, around him is the gray blur of passing legs. Bars of movement, they scissor the image of the man into triangles of stillness. It took five rolls of film to catch that shot, the face and hand and cup, the plaid of the blanket, the white of the upturned eyes echoed in the piled snow, little clippings of crisp, clear need between oblivious legs. I crouched in the gutter for an hour, felt the slushy runoff seep into my Doc Martins, felt the cold rise from the pavement until I thought I would never be warm or dry again. Here is my theory of things (something to rival Mark's): if you wait, let things develop, if you watch you will see the darkness rise. Unlike Ellie, I do not want to know the inside of life. There is enough shadow on the surface. All the damage people do can be seen there.

Some days I stand at the window of my apartment and look down, watching the people, crowds that walk tightly packed but with careful, almost dancer-like avoidance. Proximity without touch, that's New York. In late spring, the café across the street sets a few tables outside on the sidewalk. People sit in twos and threes and talk on their cell phones to people other than those they are sitting with. Their eyes wander, offering their tablemates occasional, absentminded contact. Once in a while, one looks up, notices but doesn't see me. Between us is the glass, grainy with dirt, four stories of city air, the width of the street and everything we don't want to know. I am reduced to a picture, an Edward Hopper painting, all stark lines and alienating distances. I am in danger of becoming my own subject. Then I wonder why I haven't heard the musical chime of my computer telling me Ellie's online with an instant message, why I haven't heard the soft "boop" telling me an email has arrived. Distance invades, behind me a continent, before me an ocean and half another continent. I am alone in this gray space. The absence of a ring on the phone is like hunger, and suddenly it is as if I am huddled in plain view, holding out a plastic cup. Ellie? Mark? Where are they all? Mary? I need you.

MARY

I step out of the shower and I know something is wrong. I have become attuned, have grown a mother's antennae.

"Daddy!?!"

No answer except the low bleat of distant television.

Lately Daddy has become addicted to soap operas, any soap opera will do. He wanders over to the set and punches buttons until I come and turn it on for him. I give him the remote and show him the channel up button. He nods and clicks through channels until his own internal tuner finds a soap opera. Perhaps it is the garish, plastic sets or the large hair of the women, but he is never wrong. He always finds his show. He can't follow the long-term stories, but each fresh indiscretion of the moment, each emotional outburst delights him. "Oh she's a nasty one," he'll point and tell me, having no idea who "she" is or why she's behaving so badly. I admit I've encouraged it. To see emotion carve the wooden planes of his face, astonishment, anger, amusement, is wonderful. My own addiction. We watch together.

But this one day, I don't. Sweating from digging out a mass of daisies in the back garden, I decide to settle him in and take a shower.

"Daddy!?!"

I wrap a towel around me and hurry downstairs. Living room—no Daddy. Kitchen, dining room, library, toilet—no Daddy. Up the back stairs, through each of the bedrooms, bathrooms, closet doors are yanked open, down the front stairs hollering at the top of my lungs, rising panic making my voice higher and higher. No Daddy. I run outside and into the street, pushing wet hair from my eyes, looking, searching both ways.

"Daddy!?!"

The pavement sears my feet and my wet towel feels heavy and tight against my pounding heart. The man across the street waters his arborvitae and stares.

"Did you see him?"

He shakes his head, looks disgusted. We are a house of crazies, towel-clad women and wandering old men. A history of insanity resides behind our wall. Water your garden and beware!

"Daddy!?!" I turn and run up the driveway. In front of me the carriage barn door gapes wide.

He hadn't been in there in years, not since the thoughts, the plans in his head no longer translated through his hands. Or perhaps the wood has stopped listening. Somewhere, nature is at fault. At first, he was merely annoyed, then angry. His burst of temper ended with thrown tools, sliced fingers and twice a broken window. Bewilderment set in, then finally bereavement, a slow, frightened turning away from the very center of his existence. One would think we would be there, at the core of him, a knot of troublesome children, his offspring; but we were never there, or perhaps we had been carved out. It was his art, that unique convergence of vision and hands and cool wood. Wood is capable of being shaped, incapable of hurt. It was almost an enactment of the stages of dying. What was missing? Bargaining, but then, with what did he have to bargain? Acceptance? By that point, it was too late. He had become his medium: a man of wood, all expression sealed inside. I watched it happen. Then I closed and locked the door behind him.

Now it stands open.

"Daddy?"

Dusty sunlight filters through the high windows. He stands with his back to me, looking down at his work table.

"Daddy? What are you doing, honey?"

He turns. "Look, Jean. Look at all these things I found." Sunlight falls across his face, his outstretched hands and flashes along the blade of the German drawknife he holds between them.

In the stuffy, heat-baked barn, the air is suddenly chill. Goosebumps rise along my arms. At the nape of my neck, tiny hairs spring to alert. My towel isn't enough protection. There will never be enough protection.

"Aren't they interesting? I think . . . I think I remember someone using them when I was little." He blinks and smiles. "Someone in my family. How was your shower?"

"Just fine, Daddy. Come inside. The soaps are on."

He has called me Jean.

LUKE

*D*oes a name mean something? Mother Mary? Our family genius, Mark? Peter? Wasn't he the one the Romans crucified upside-down, so he could not rise to heaven? Did our Peter rise? What about the name Willow? Willows are flexible, tenacious, graceful. It's not a wood my dad would have approved of, would have ever worked with. Too common. It's a soft name, Willow, gentle and quiet, a name that won't set the soles of the feet itching to run. In my mind I see the wind through a willow, how the leaves, the supple branches flow. Willows are along for the ride.

She takes me on a hike up the Montecito Peak trail. She throws a packing blanket around my neck and carries a stuffed backpack herself. We drive high up into the maze of streets along the hillside, pull over in deep shade, then hike following a creek that drops in pools and cascades beneath huge old trees. We have started late and the trail is dark underfoot. Her dog trots in front of us as if it is heading home. When we come out in the scrub it is dusk. The ocean is aluminum with the sunset dying orange and red beyond the reach and way up the coast. All the lights of Santa Barbara, Goleta, Montecito and even as far south as Carpenteria are winking on beneath our feet. All the paths I walk, the roads that know my feet are spread out before me, shrunken, packaged like glittering gifts. We come out on a fire road, and Willow takes the blanket from me, lays it out and flops down on it. I am already tired. I have walked past Goleta this morning, gathering cans.

"It's going to be too dark to make it back down if we don't keep going," I tell her, still standing there.

"Then we'll spend the night." She grins and pats the blanket next to me.

"We might get into trouble." The rules of things are a confusion to me, how to talk to people, when to stay or walk away. You can't stand in one spot too long or you are a vagrant; you can't wander too much or you are homeless. I don't like trouble. Trouble makes me walk. But I have to be careful, because sometimes walking can get me in trouble, too.

"You worry too much. I've done this a million times." She pats the blanket again. "We'll have a little fire . . ." She fishes in her backpack, pulls out a Bic lighter and waves it. "A little wine . . ." A bottle of red appears. "A little weed . . ." She sets both items down and rummages in the front pocket of her jeans, carefully extracting a battered joint. "A few munchies . . ." She has returned to the backpack again. A bag of Fritos emerges. "And then we'll just see what happens. Now sit, please."

I sit. She has been dogging me for weeks, following me in her car, walking with me, waiting for me at the cottage when I get back. She loves my mobiles. She has taken thirty-two of them to hang from the ceiling of her VW Bus. She says they hang about her head like stars at night. She says that when she drives, they sway against each other and tinkle and chime. My mobiles are meant to be silent, but if she wants them to chime, that's okay. When I think of it in my head, the mobiles swaying and chiming with the movement of the bus, it is her voice I hear the mobiles making. She talks a lot, too much. But her voice is light and windswept. She has a take-it-or-leave-it kind of voice, and the more I hear it, the more it's okay. The more I hear it, the more I listen.

"I used to come up here all the time with guys and have sex. It was a kind of rite of passage. If they could make it up the trail, I'd do it with them. I had about a fifty-fifty average. Then, I started liking the place better than the guys, so I just lived up here on my own for a while, going down for food and getting water out of the creek; but then I got giardia from the creek, which reminds me—don't drink the water in that creek on our way down tomorrow because giardia is one nasty bug. So then I just came up when I wanted to, not drinking the water, of course." She stills, which is unusual, and watches the last of the light draining out of the sky, her long fingers picking at a run in the fabric of the blanket. "I brought you." Then she focuses on my face and suddenly grins, her teeth white in the darkness. "And you made it! So let's get that fire started and smoke that joint, man! Great things are going to happen here tonight!"

Later on, I feel it, that itching in my feet, that slight, longing ache in my calves. She is trouble and my legs want to carry me away. The fire is just embers. Her dog presses to one side of me, and she is curled into the other side. I can feel their heat inside my body, warming my ribs and even deeper, reaching into my lungs and warming the air I breathe. I am wedged between these two creatures and, above me, the stars sharp and bright. They sway like mobiles. The itch, the ache eases. I am twenty-nine, and she is maybe twenty, maybe eighteen, but she has lived her life in movement just like me. We are always leaving.

Laying there pinned down by stars and hemmed in by Willow and the dog, I remember Mary, kneeling in front of me, her hands holding my shoulders, her body blocking my view of what had happened to Peter. "Take a walk," she said. "When you come back, it will be okay." I am still walking.

Willow is noise. She is complication and trouble, but her name whispers to me. The voice it uses is soft, the quiet sound of mobiles touching, of slender branches and leaves molding to the wind. When I walk, I can hear her name, her voice between the beats of my feet. It is becoming a part of my journey. I whisper into the space between her sleeping breaths, "Stay now. Stay, or let me come along."

ELLIE

Some nights I lay on my roof, spread-eagled on a blanket, the stars pressing down on me with the weight of a lover, and the earth of this land sighing out its heat all around me. The priests are wrong; heaven is here. I love this island; it's addictive like art, like sex. It makes me want to shout, to sing out loud as if no one was listening. Quite often, I do. Every morning here the light erupts, a brilliant molten platinum, and coats all reality, each rock and blade of brittle grass, each solid, squat house, each solid, squat Greek inhabitant. With evening light ebbs, slows, softens to tarnished silver and slips from thought. Between the morning and the evening there is russet earth and azure water, store, house and church the surprising white of long exposed bone. If Sarah were here (and, oh, how I need someone), she would notice the shadows, their smoothness, their uncompromising depth. The play of light and shadow reminds me of Sarah, of her photos. It keeps her near. Her art is like this place, stark contrasts, unforgiving surfaces. The people she presents are like the earth, the stones, the buildings and people here: weathered, enduring, fortresses with bleak faces, all life locked inside. I look at her photos and I think, *Yes! Yes!* Then I want to crack them open and see all the mess, see the red truth that's hidden.

There is abundant, tantalizing subject on this tiny island, laid out like a feast just for me, and I, avoiding its shadow, molding its clay, collecting its heat, squinting into its light . . . I open myself to it, drink it in, lick it up, and grin like the she-devil the people around here think

I am. Patmos reminds me of Santa Barbara, not just the scrutiny of the people, but the landscape itself, the color of the earth, the scrub and dusty olive-covered hills that rise from the sea. It is less ordered here, less planned and tamed. Nature here is primal, orgasmic, a wildness of spring wildflowers, the tickle of dust between the toes, the searing of sun, and of men's eyes, erotic like the press and slide of warm fingers along arms and across shoulders. At least forty ladies of my acquaintance from the village below would drop where they stood if I said any of this aloud. Such naughtiness, such blatant sexuality calls for more than the ritual crossing of oneself, calls for more than prayers on knees in dim, stony churches. Such wickedness, such black sorcery calls for a dead faint or, better yet, death itself. Faint away, ladies! As one might guess, the people are not quite as embracing as the surroundings. They are prudes, their mores as archaic as the land. As always it brings out the worst in me. It always has.

We are at war, a Homeric conflict that has recently turned grim. It began immediately upon my arrival three years ago. I landed a job waitressing in a tourist café down by the harbor. I slept on the beach four miles away, hid my gear in the rocks and biked into work every morning. I was great for business. The tourists loved me because I could speak their language: "You're American!" the relief in their voices and on their faces, comical. The local fishermen began hanging out at the café, ordering Greek coffee, thick as sludge and sweetened with honey, or later in the day, bottle after bottle of Fanta. I flirted, pretended I didn't understand a word they said. The girls followed the fishermen. They tried to copy the way I dressed, walked, moved. A pair of tattered, paint-splashed jeans, a peasant skirt, five T-shirts, a mini-skirt and a pair of cutoff cords that showed way too much cheek was the extent of my belongings, not counting, of course, paintbrushes. I blame the escalation of hostilities on the cords, but I swear I didn't start wearing them until I heard the hissing.

In Greece it seems, where virginal, blushing girls go, mamas follow, prowling like packs of Rottweilers forever on guard duty. One thing was quite obvious: they didn't want their tender young anywhere near me. Seeing their little dears in moral danger, the mamas would lock onto their daughters with muscled, black-clad arms, and with wrestlers' strangleholds they would haul them away. Erect heads and stiff black-clad backs shed sunlight like dandruff and left the echo of a soft, sibilant hiss in their wake. It was a warning shot across my prow. Formidable, they wanted me gone. What does one do when faced with black condemnation, with the hiss of enmity? *I* put on my shortest shorts and slept with the first man whose offer interested me. Stavros, sixteen, a miniature Greek god, brown skin sleek and slippery as watered silk, eyes the color of bittersweet chocolate. Yum. I was twenty-eight, but he didn't know that, still doesn't. All he knew of me was no tan lines, no inhibitions, no rules. By fall, I had enough tip money combined with the last of my art commissions from my wanderings through London, Amsterdam and Prague, to buy a wreck of a house in the upper village, on the winding main road that leads to the monastery. Stavros moved in and we began mucking it out together, mucking and . . . well, living in glorious sin.

Whore, sorceress, baby thief, the Greek words clattered off the mamas' tongues like bullets from a Gatling gun. I grinned from behind a layer of thousand-year-old dirt. I sang out loud. We had discovered a fresco on the back wall of what would become our bedroom, a lean, bloody Jesus levitating above a ring of praying saints. We put our mattress right beneath the gathering. Our lovemaking was blessed. I was happy. Then, the real war began. The mamas brought out the big guns: the village priests, first the young one then the old, a delegation of monks from the monastery, the mayor. Here's a tip from me to all the mamas everywhere: never send a man to deal with a woman. Stavi was staying. I didn't realize then that only I could scare him away, only my body with its hidden secrets, its dark, viscous potentials. Stavi, if you could only see into me as I can see into everything, you would know that creation is art and art is truth and truth is always beautiful. Ha! Even I can have a grand theory.

I mined local clay. My first sculpture was of the monks from the monastery that perched on the cliffs above us. Only vaguely humanoid, the monks I fashioned were a line of narrow black eruptions from a terracotta base, a drape of glazed clay for sleeve and cowl and abundant beard. The tall formal headdresses were like sharp black chimney pots aimed at heaven. The first in line held a crude approximation of the Orthodox cross before him like a shield. That first year, an Athens gallery owner saw it in my window on her way up the street to midnight mass. She said the figures seemed to march, too, in the flickering candle light of the Easter procession. She had to have it, she said, and anything else. Mugs and small takeaway pieces for the tourist trade kept us in food, the larger pieces—what I feel, what erupts from me—for the galleries. We were getting by, doing well.

History intrudes; it carves this ancient rock and soil; it molds these people and dictates their sacraments. History binds. It has led me to see that my art has been an expression of my own particular past: my family. I have moved forward, through years, through cities and through the sweet, forgetful touch of so many men, but still they bind to me. My family. Our sacraments, our sins. They are inside me like an extra set of bones, a beating heart, a growling stomach. Everything is inside me; it explodes out of my fingertips in wild splashes of color or in the sharp edge or smooth round rise of bone from clay. I can't cover it; it wants light. I expose in metaphor, in clay and paint. It isn't the truth, just my version. I am not the mirror.

Growing up, Sarah and I looked out at our world, at our family, and I thought we saw the same things, thought

94

the same way; but my art, and now hers, have lead me to see the differences between us, glorious opposites. She is the one who reflects the surface, and I have always been the twin who noticed what was beneath and behind. I knew about Dad and Mary's hidden cache of letters, their midnight word games played with church notice boards when we were still little and Peter was alive. I knew that Mary had a personal Peeping Tom that she didn't mind at all. His eyes reflected the moon, and her eyes reflected his. I knew that Luke sucked his thumb long after Mary worked so hard to stop him, and probably still does. I knew that Mark kept a diary once and in it were all his pre-teen dreams of becoming an astronaut written hastily in his scrawly, loopy hand, such ordinary little boy dreams for the genius, the Quark. I knew that Sarah stole Peter's camera and then slept on it for years, a private scourge for the penitent. I heard what Mark said to Peter the day before he committed suicide and the long hollow silence of Peter's response. I knew that Dad carved beautiful lean women from leftover scraps of wood in his carriage barn workshop. I know he burned them, one by one. When I was four or five, I took one and used it for a doll, until he found me playing with it and made me throw it into the workroom fire. Later, after Peter died, Dad's furniture always reminded me of those women, lean and graceful, sometimes sprawled and erotic. I knew that Peter was a fake. I told him so. It was the first, the last time I ever revealed a secret. So I learned to let my clay, my paint, speak for me.

I immerse myself in their lives from a distance. I email everyday, offering little trimmings of my life for them to hold onto and make of it what they will. I call Mary just to hear her voice, thinned by distance, but always there telling me about Dad, about Luke, never herself. And Mark, my sweet, strange Quark? Sarah thinks I share her constant irritation with him, but she's wrong. I love his clipped emails, his sureties that hide so much. If I were to paint him, it would be with the top of his head exploding upwards into a constellation of sparks, bits of mathematical equations, atoms and molecules, question marks and tiny broken hearts. I'd call it Mark's Big Bang. What a glorious idea! I will paint it . . . when I feel a bit better. He has a girl! His first I think. Woohoo! Mary says he talks about her endlessly. I bet he's still a virgin. He'll need some advice. Mine.

I was the first to lose my virginity in the family, Sarah about ten minutes later. I am pretty sure Peter died before he had the chance, and Mary lived at home, raised us, went to UC Santa Barbara, but was always home by three to ask us about our day. Her nights were spent at home, too, in games of Scrabble and overseeing homework. Someone waited for her beneath the window, but she never went out. There was mooning at the window, but not that plunge into velvety darkness. That would be my job. Quark left for college days after his fourteenth birthday, hopelessly out of sync, mind ahead, body behind.

It was Sarah's idea, as always. She said we shouldn't spend too much time in high school burdened with our virginity. Burdened, her word, I swear. Sarah's brilliant, an unerring sense of what's needed at any exact moment, so many lovely schemes to carry us through our childhood. A great deal of effort went into that particular escapade, months of research and reconnaissance before fruition. But, ahhh, what a fruition! I don't know how it was for Sarah (her comment, "Okay, that's taken care of," leads me to suspect not well), but as for me—I was hooked! Cowabunga!! Look out Santa Barbara High, I had arrived! Oh, Sarah, how can we look so much alike, and experience everything so differently? I am sorry.

Sarah is my mirror in shadow, my pinprick of guilt. I have not been fair to Sarah. Here is another secret I hold inside: I betray her, my sister, my twin, with everything

I do, with who I am, I betray her. I will never be enough like her. And in answer to that, some pirate part of me screams, "Thank God!" She thinks we share everything, memory, thought, feeling. She guided me to myself, to my work, to this glowing island. I have paid her in silent disagreement. It is only in art that our minds meet. Like mine, hers is so perfectly who she is: black and white, uncompromising, complicated. Vulnerability bleeds from the razor edges and deep shadows of her images, as if she is saying, "This is what I see. Please take it away." She is unaware in her art, in herself.

I have hope for this woman she speaks of. She *must* be our mother. How perfectly it fits, such symmetry! A mother, a baby. This woman is the first image since me that Sarah has taken into her heart. This woman gives Sarah someplace else to look. She will save Sarah, and, thereby, save me. I cherish Sarah, cherish them all, but oh, I have cherished the distance. Until now.

On this borrowed island, my war escalates around me. There is no one on my side. I can laugh in the old bitches' vengeful faces. I can ignore the giggles of the lean, jealous girls. I can even wink and joke at the sneers of the old men. But not alone.

ALL I can manage is eggs. Not to eat, even the thought makes my stomach roil. From the moment when I wake up until well after one in the afternoon, I can't hold down a thing except fresh mint tea and those tasteless Greek cookies that suck the saliva from my mouth. This morning I opened the front door to find that some concerned neighbor had emptied a bucket of piss and shit on my front steps. I threw up on the spot, adding the contents of last night's meal to all the other crap, then I closed the door and went back to bed. I want to sculpt these women, a thick, fat ring of black crows with hunched backs and grasping claws. I have been collecting rusted metal from all over the island. With Stavi gone, I do it myself. I want it poking out from all over them—old bed springs and crowbars, pick heads and ruined blades—I'll call it *The Mamas*. But all I can manage is eggs. My fingers work the clay, prod it, mold it, smooth it, and there it is before me—an egg. The studio is filling up with eggs, egg-shaped mugs and vases, tiny whole eggs glazed in delicate hues of sunrise, partial eggs with peeled away layers exposing tender lumps or sharp little bones, cracked eggs glazed black with throbbing red centers. Frankly, they don't sell. I make them, hold them in my hands, feel their weight, their portent. I sit in stillness, alone with my eggs, wondering if it is the baby that I almost feel move inside me, that strange fluttering, that settling. Is it my new tenant taking stock of his surrounding, moving in? My own little egg, no longer hidden, no longer safe.

I've counted backwards. I think I conceived the night of this year's Good Friday procession. If memory serves me, it was an Extremely Good Friday. Every Good Friday, the holy icons are placed on a conveyance, a kind of canopy bed, covered with fresh flowers and candles. Four strong village men carry it through the town, following the priests and altar boys who swing incense or carry candles. There are candles everywhere, flickering in the narrow streets, in the hands of the devoted and of the gawking tourists, in the dark windows of the shops and homes. And because this is Greece, there is wine, retsina, ouzo and plum brandy. And because this is Greece, there is dancing. The penitent, the hopeful, the brave, or simply drunk join hands and weave through the streets, following the icon. They say that if you pass between the men, beneath the holy icon, Jesus will hear your prayers and answer them.

"What a hoot!" I laughed and moved to join the line.

"Don't do that," I remember Stavi warned. "Newlyweds and barren women do that to conceive. My Aunt Sophia had a baby at forty-eight from passing under." He looked stern and worried, a teen caricature of the old man he would become. I was filled with wine and incense, with flickering light and the almost carnal intonations of the chant. I slid my fingers over his face, smoothed his severity to youth and kissed his wet, sweet mouth.

"Superstition is for the weak, Stavi," I whispered into his ear and kissed the hollow of his neck. I broke into the line, grabbing hands and yelling back over my shoulder at him, "Watch me!"

There were fireworks later, out over the beach. Young boys threw firecrackers at the feet of unsuspecting revelers and passing cars. All that chaos and joy coalesced in our bed, in our bodies. No protection that night, I wanted to prove something, my strength, my lack of faith against all the mutterings, curses and unanswered prayers of mamas everywhere for all time. I didn't know that the clay of this land, this island, gets into you, it covers you and molds you with its ancient, golden imperatives. All the time I thought I was in charge.

Two months later we went to the island of Kos, more cosmopolitan than our own virginal rock. It took me that long to notice. Kos was sure to have one of those home pregnancy tests, hidden on the back self of some alleyway pharmacy, and Kos had other amenities, springy hotel beds, tavernas filled with the bland cheerful stares and laughter of strangers. We were riotous! On the morning we left, I took the test. Such a simple thing, so far-reaching. Savros left two days after we returned from Kos. The blue line on the test strip hung between us in that time, a wire that tripped us, that tied us together and made the last two times we had sex seem needy to me, dirty to him. He showered after. He slipped out while I was walking in the hills, singing at the top of my lungs, of course, unaware that someone was finally listening, jealous island gods, listening and working their mischief. I came home to his few clothes pulled from the hangers, his box of teenage music gone from its spot by the stereo. He turned nineteen three weeks ago, not too young to be a father in this country. He took the bike we shared and left no note. They never do. They never tell you why, not my little Stavi (though I suppose it's obvious), not the ones before him in different places but the same life, not my brother, Peter. I loved them all, still do, but they disappoint. I have been thinking of Peter. Is it Stavi's leaving, the bloody Jesus that hangs over my half-empty bed, or Mark's latest silly theory that has set me off? Perhaps it is the time-honored rumination that comes from sitting on an egg. I am brooding.

We always thought Peter levitated, Sarah and I. He was going through a swami stage, that's what Mary called it. He meditated, announced it to the house, climbed the attic stairs to his room and shut and locked the door. A late afternoon, during one of his sessions and while Sarah and I played in our room beneath his, we heard an enormous thump above our heads, the sound of a heavy body falling from a high distance, hitting the floor. We took the stairs by twos and pounded on his door.

"What?" his muffled reply.

"Are you okay?"

He opened the door, smiled down on us glassy-eyed, "I was coming down."

"From where?"

He pointed up. "I can't help it. When I meditate, I rise. Don't tell."

We shook our heads. It was simply the coolest thing we had ever heard. Our brother levitated. He couldn't help himself. Of course, we told everyone. Daddy nodded absently, Mark intoned, "physically impossible," and Mary rolled her eyes. School friends didn't believe us either. It didn't matter; we had proof. We heard it almost daily;

we made a point of being in our room when Peter went upstairs after school. We listened, we grinned in bliss each time the thump shook the ceiling. It went on a good eight months before I decided to sneak upstairs to see for myself. I told Sarah I was going for a bike ride, then rode around the block, hid my bike, snuck back into the house and up the back stairs. I hid under his bed and waited for the sound of his steps across the floor boards, the soft, rubbery tread of black Converse high tops. He sat on the bed with a squeak and a downward bulge of springs, and pulled his legs up onto the covers. I could hear him shrugging off his book bag and letting it drop next to him, the bed's muffled response, then more squeaking and rocking of the springs above me. "Lotus position," I silently mouthed to the underside of the mattress, imagining him winding his legs into a pretzel position. It would happen soon, now, the releasing of the springs, the easing up of the mattress, the rising of Peter. I waited. I felt the tick of excitement in my chest. I heard the click of a lighter, the sharp sweet smell of burning lawn trash. I waited through the sound of slow inhales, one, two, three, then slower sighs. I waited, fighting the need to squirm. When would he do it? I waited, but he never did. It was only smoke. Then, the sounds of him gathering his book bag and edging to the brink of the bed, the springs protesting his passage. A final groan from the bed and he lifted himself off and landed, cross-legged and clutching his book bag, on the floor next to me. He unwound his legs, lay back on the floor boards, turned his head and unseeing, looked right into my eyes. Surprise, Big Brother.

"You're a fake," I said to him, crawled out from under the bed, stepped over him and walked to the door. "You're a fake." I thought I would never love him again. I was so sure. I was eight. In a week and a half, Peter would be dead, leaving us all bereaved and guessing. I have seen the inside of things, the inside of Peter. Standing just inside the front door, Sarah next to me, our shoulders and the length of our arms touching, almost becoming one, I learned early. Open up the human body, the human heart or soul, and it is red, red and messy, slick like wet clay with bits of bone exposed. It is frightening and beautiful. It is the basis of creation.

I have not told Sarah, Mark or Mary about Stavros' leaving. I have kept my phone calls and email elliptic. They would be unfailingly supportive, but between their words, the "I told you so's" would leak out. I don't want that. I have always been the one who rushed ahead, the one to taste, to try, to plunge. I have been splashes of color and gritty texture, I have been life in brilliant color and in 3-D for them. They have lived vicariously through me. This has been my chosen role. Now, I shall have to swallow the "I told you so's" whole, take the advice, ask for help. My role is changing. I am two, and we are in a mess.

Since Stavros has gone, the mamas and even some of the men (oh, my old flames, how you have turned on me!) spit at my feet when I pass. I hold my head up and gird myself in my short, short cord cutoffs with my painter's smock to hide that I can't button them. *Look at me! This is what I am!* I want to scream at them and laugh, but I am afraid that my voice will sound hollow in the tunneled streets between these ancient buildings. They are winning the war. Even the young priest, my sometimes friend, hurries by, eyes down. He used to wander through the shop, fingering the pieces, talking with me about classic Greek sculptures and the aesthetics behind Byzantine iconography. He seemed, himself, an icon, lean and hollow cheeked with a dark and thoughtful gaze. He has let me down, too.

I don't think men are to be trusted. They require too much of us. They want body and heart and belief, and in return they offer the glazed surfaces of their selves. Then they leave. Mark is the exception, I think. He is something less than a man, something more. Perhaps he is an alien being, as Sarah and I have always joked, zipped into the handsome casing of my older brother. He is incapable of deception; it is not standard operating procedure. To the woman who finds him (perhaps this Clare!), he will be an equation, tough to crack, simple and undeniable once solved. I am pulling for him. With all his faults and oddities, he is a precious commodity. He is sensible, of clear thought and steady course. There is no vividness in him, no splash of wild recklessness or smooth, hard danger to draw the eye or cause the tips of the fingers to tingle. I should look for someone just like him, but I don't, and, let's face it, I won't. I'll run.

I love this island, its light, its earth, its one young man, but I have to leave. It is not *I* anymore—such a strange, unexpected thing. *We* have to leave. We won't call it defeat, never that! We'll call it a strategic retreat. We may be back, and when we are, believe me, they'll know it. But for now, we need someone to come claim us, one of my own. Who should I call? Mark, sure, economical of action and emotion, would bring me home with nothing more than an explanation of the workings of jet engines; or Sarah, my avenging angel other-self, would stand like a smooth, hard protecting wall and reflect back on these people their terrible rancor. Mary would gather me up, hold me close, allow me to return to the heedless, hopeful child I was, I want to be again. I shall call to them each, put the word out on the wind. Come get me. Me and my baby.

I'll make a child like this land, filled with light and heat, with skin the color of its fine golden clay, with hair and eyes as dark as the deepest shadows. I'll carry her far away, my little egg. When she cracks open and rushes out, red, messy and screaming, I'll teach her to laugh. I'll teach her to sing. We'll lay beneath distant stars with the heat of this island rising from our souls. She'll be my spoils of war, my triumph. We'll begin again . . . again.

MARK

*D*istance is relative. Some facts: one astronomical unit is equal to ninety-three million miles. The cosmic horizon is the distance from which light must travel for the entire age of the universe to reach our location here on Earth, a distance represented by the number ten to the twenty-sixth power. Light travels at a speed of six hundred and seventy million miles per hour. This is "c" in Einstein's famous equation. C is for celeritas, which means swiftness in Latin. However, ten to the twenty-sixth power is a very large number. The cosmic horizon is a very long way away. On the other hand, when any two substances, any two objects touch, their electron clouds become intertwined and distance between them no longer exists. In a sense, they are one. Clare leaves tomorrow at 7:45 PM from San Jose International Airport for Geneva, Switzerland, where she will attend a symposium on "Substructures of Atomic Decay." A Boeing 757 travels at an average celeritas of five hundred seventy-two miles per hour. Airport to airport, it will take her 10.174825 hours. She will be gone for one month, not an overly lengthy time. However, Geneva, Switzerland, is five thousand eight hundred and forty-two miles from this exact spot on Earth. Five thousand eight hundred and forty-two miles is a very long way.

More facts: Clare and I have had ten dates, twenty-three shared lunches and one tour of Alcatraz Island together. Seven and a half of the ten dates were extremely successful in my opinion. One of the remaining two and a half ended in a quarrel about the foreign language film we had gone to see. The other one and a half were early on in our relationship with all the attendant problems of beginning communication and negotiation. Clare and I have a relationship. I have held her hand seventeen times, and on our last date I successfully put my arm around her waist. Clare kissed me on the cheek. We have shared electrons, obliterated distance.

Clare is going to Geneva and taking her electrons with her. She will be 5,842 miles from me, but I already know it will feel like five thousand eight hundred and forty-two astronomical units, like she has slipped over the cosmic horizon. Einstein pursued light. He found that it could not be caught. It seems I pursue light as well. Clare's light will not reach me for an entire month. I have been contemplating my situation and possible reactions. How does one grapple with distance? She has asked me to take her to the airport. I will. Once there, I think it very likely I will kiss her, a collision of molecules and atoms, a last exchange of electrons.

Distance is relative, but it matters.

PART TWO

A CALCULABLE CHAOS

Dear Mary, Mark and Sarah:
Morning Sickness & Horrible People!!! Puking
my guts out and a dead cat nailed to my door
this morning! Donkey dung thrown at me in the
outdoor Saturday market and a town of silence
and staring eyes that waits to see my reaction.
I picked the shit up and sniffed it and said as
loudly as I could, "This isn't fresh enough," then
dropped it in the gutter. I giggled all the way
home—insane, unstoppable giggling that left
me scared. I've bought the little glass disc, their
symbol to ward off the evil eye, to place on the
front door and wear around my neck like a great
blue and white albatross, but still they come at
me. These fucking people don't even believe in
their own myths! I didn't say before—Stavros is
gone. Gone for weeks now. Please, please, can
someone come get me?
    Ellie

A note left on Luke's front door:

Luke,
Came to collect you for Wednesday dinner.
Where are you?
    Love,
    Mary

Ellie:
I did a quick search for you. It appears that
in most cases, the phenomenon of "morning
sickness" lasts no longer than three months.

From my calculations, you are at the end of that period now and should be feeling physically better quite soon. As to the other matter, perhaps you are overreacting. Subsequent reading from the above mentioned search suggests that pregnant women have a hypersensitivity to their surroundings and periods of emotional instability. It appears that this, too, subsides with the advancement of the pregnancy. I've attached pertinent websites and article citations below for your perusal. Should these not answer your questions or reassure you, perhaps a visit to the local police would help. I assume that this island of yours has a police force?

 Best,

 Mark

cc: Mary, Sarah

* * * * *

Ell:

Don't listen to Quark. He is an idiot! Mark, you are an idiot! How can you talk to Ellie as if she's one of your amoeba! Ellie, if I were there I would tear those nasty little Greek people limb from limb—and I would start with Stavros—another jerk! Don't let them see they're getting to you. A pack of dogs—don't turn your back on them. You don't know what they're capable of. Ell, you should have never gone there at all. I can't help you when I'm here, and I can't come. I've just moved Mom into my apartment, and we're having quite an adjustment. I can't leave her here, and I can't bring her there. Just buy a ticket, Ell, and get on a plane. JFK is a cab ride away.

 XXOOOO, S

cc: Mark, Mary

* * * * *

Sarah:
1. I do not study amoeba.
2. If Ellie were an amoeba, she would be unable to talk, email, or, in fact, become pregnant since amoeba reproduce by division rather than sexual means, in which case this entire conversation would be moot.
3. You assume that I am unsympathetic to Ellie's situation, when I am merely attempting to inject some objectivity and logic-based thinking into this situation.
4. There is no mom. Who is this woman?

       Best,
       Mark

cc: Mary, Ellie

* * * * *

Mark:
The real question is: WHO ARE YOU????
   S
cc: Mary, Ellie

Note written on a cardboard box and leaned against Mary's front door:

Mary,
Willow and I stopped by to get a mattress. I am too tall for her VW and she doesn't like the floor. Be back soon.
   Luke

Sarah, Mark, Mary:

Let me field that question—Mark is Mark, Sarah. Or should I say Quark? He's our brother—we love him...remember???? He is not an idiot, however, sitting here typing these words, it occurs to me that the real question is: Is Mark a virgin? I've been wondering about this for quite some time—well, actually only since he acquired himself a GIRLFRIEND!!! Mark, are you a virgin? I can offer advice as necessary—no web search or article citations will be needed this time. I know all the ins and outs.

As you can probably tell, I am feeling better. It is midnight here, cool and still and black. I am sitting on my bed emailing all of you (via an extremely long phone and power cord) as my personal Jesus floats just above and behind me on the wall. He is watching over me for the time being... When I open my eyes in the morning I'll be sick again, so I linger awake as long as I can. I've just finished consuming my 21st Greek cookie and my 9th cup of mint tea. A singularly unsatisfying repast. I dream of fat hotdogs with ketchup and mustard and relish, of submarine sandwiches at least 3 inches thick with meats and cheeses and every known condiment. Not likely on this rock in the middle of the ocean. Are these pregnant cravings? I've heard of pickles and ice cream, but preservatives and fat??? Mark, perhaps you can help me out here, O Ye Font of Pregnant Knowledge. My belly, my baby, my mind urge me toward the land of processed meat. So, in fact, the real question remains: Who will come get me?
 XXXOOO,
 Ellie
P.S. Where has Mary gone? Is her computer down?

A note left for Mary on the kitchen counter:

GON FOR WAK

E:

Mary fine, computer fine (presumably). Had a call
a day or two ago. Something about carving tools.
I wasn't really listening, though. At the time, Mom
was trying on all my clothes. A trip to Macy's will
be needed very soon. She's much shorter than I—
closer to Mary's size. Come home, Ell. Just jump
on a plane! I'll (we'll) be waiting at the gate with
the biggest sub sand you ever saw! We are off to
dinner—taking Mom to my favorite Ethiopian...

    XXXXXOO S

cc: Mark, Mary

* * * * *

Ellie,

I concur with Sarah's initial email (though little
else). Buy an airplane ticket and fly back to the
US; however, once here I urge moderation with
regards to the consumption of processed meats. I
am sure the high chemical and sodium levels are
not conducive to fetal health.

In response to your question: Mary is fine, though
busy with our father. She called to tell me that she
had found Father in the carriage barn (after having
pried the lock from the door). He was sorting
through his woodworking tools. She had left him
alone in front of the television while she took
a shower. She was understandably agitated, as
many of the tools are quite sharp and dangerous.
I suggested a more substantial lock and perhaps
nighttime showers after Father is safely asleep.
The computer, I believe, is working adequately. I
am sure she would have informed me otherwise.

    Best,
    Mark

cc: Sarah

* * * * *

Quark:
You have only answered one of my questions. Are
you a virgin?
    XXXXOOOOOO E
cc: Sarah, Mary

* * * * *

Ellie:
There is no need to focus your frustration in
regards to your personal situation by baiting me.
Work to solve your own problems, not mine.
    Mark

* * * * *

Are YOU having a problem, brother?
    E

* * * * *

Dear Mark:
Geneva is chilly, even now in late June. The
conference has been interesting. I have some data
to go over with you when I return. I went out with
Rory to an amazing French restaurant last night
in the old part of the city. Tomorrow we are off
to the Hadron Accelerator. I'll email you as soon
as I'm back to the hotel. It is beautiful here, and I
think you would appreciate the precision of these
people. In truth, they remind me of you. How
are you? I find I am missing you and my *Times*
crossword—though not equally. Please say hello
to everyone at the lab.
    Love,
    Clare

* * * * *

Dear Clare:

I am pleased to hear that your time in Geneva
has been fruitful. I will pass on your regards
to those still in attendance at the lab. We are

113

winding down for summer break. Though nothing catastrophic, there have been a number of small emergencies here and with my immediate family: one deleted Senior Project, one lost Doctoral Thesis, one wandering father, one ravenous, homesick sister and seemingly numerous mobs of angry Greek villagers. A fairly typical day in the life of a fairly typical physicist...

If you have a moment, I should like to know two things:
1. Which do you miss more, the crossword or me?
2. Who is Rory? A man? Was it a date?
In point of fact, that was four questions. You will have to excuse me, sudden attack of imprecision. I find that I miss you, too.
Mark

* * * * *

E:
Of course he's a virgin. Can you imagine anything else?
S

* * * * *

Dear Mark:

Quite the drama going on there—admit you need me, my cool intellect and keen interpersonal skills. I think perhaps you are lost without me.

Rory is a man, Rory Steen from Manchester, England. Was it a date? Maybe. Answer me this: If I find that I miss you slightly more than the *Times* crossword, how much do you find that you miss me?
Love,
Clare

* * * * *

Dear Clare:
Enough to become imprecise.
   Love,
   Mark

* * * * *

Dear Mark:
I am flattered, and quite satisfied.
   Love,
   Clare

* * * * *

Mary, Sarah, Mark,

It is night again, but hot. I am sticky and queasy and naked (no longer a pretty sight, I assure you) in the middle of my bed—a little more information than you need, I know. Just be thankful you're not my floating Jesus or his circle of saints—they are getting a Byzantine eyeful. No wonder the long, sour faces.

Today, Stavi's mother ran up to me in the street, she called me a witch and a whore and spit in my face. I saw Stavi sitting at the taverna across the square, looking my way, his beautiful face smooth and cold as porcelain. He didn't need to spit. Whatever spell was there is broken. I walked home with his mother's spit drying on my face and on my handful of apples (the first healthy food I've bought in weeks). I chopped them to pieces with one of my clay-working tools and threw them out. Let the crows choke on them. Please. I am sick and miserable. I can't do it alone. I want to come home.
   Ellie

* * * * *

115

Mark, Sarah and Ellie,

Stop the electronic bickering NOW. Mark, I know it is almost end of term; make arrangements. I need you here to watch Daddy.

Ellie, hold on, Sweetie; I am coming.

Love to all,
Mary

MARY

*D*addy sits across from me, his scrambled eggs cooling on his plate. His eyes are bright and happy. He is full of news this morning.

"I didn't tell you about my walk yesterday, did I?"

There was no solitary walk yesterday, or any day. I've arranged for a neighborhood guard. Life provides such ironies. I've turned to the very people whose scrutiny used to drive us kids crazy. Peter used to call them The Watchers, to whisper it in a deep, dread-filled voice, as if any moment our neighborhood would spiral into the dark setting of a horror film. It was a term he coined not long after our mother's departure. He hated them, and on his cue, we all did. Now I find The Watchers' interest helpful, almost comforting. Our little guard unit has been running for more than a month. We are lucky to live in a part of the country where people spend time outdoors. The children are forever playing in their tiny front yards or expanding the games into the street; the adults are in their gardens watering and weeding, in their open garages tinkering. The elderly sit in lawn chairs on porches or inside at glass windows facing the street, keeping a relentless eye. From the youngest to the oldest, everyone is keeping an eye, alert, ready for the breakout. The Watchers have interdicted five attempts so far.

"It was way past . . ." He cannot think of a street or area and so waves his hands toward the hills behind town.

"Above Mission Canyon?"

"Oh yes, way up . . . there. I was walking along, and here was this little house. Just a shack really. There was

117

a big garden out in front. Lots of vegetables. And here were these two little people, a little old man and a little old woman working in the garden. You'll never guess who they were! My parents!" Daddy grins and shakes his head. "Isn't that amazing! I was so surprised. I didn't even know I had a mom and dad!"

"Oh my gosh, Daddy." I have been hearing this story every morning for six days, every morning at breakfast, then during the day every time he has more than fifteen minutes of quiet sitting. It started the morning after I told him I would be gone a few days to collect Ellie from Greece. "That is pretty amazing. What were they doing way up there?"

"Living. Mining. There was a big hole out behind the house. They showed me. It went way back in. They don't ever come down. They eat out of their garden."

"Wow, Daddy. They must be in their nineties by now." I try to change the trajectory of this discussion, "Mark will be coming in a few days. You'll have to tell him. Maybe he can go up there with you."

Daddy nods vaguely and nudges his eggs with a fork. "I don't think I like eggs." His face clears and he smiles at me. "I told them they should come down and live with me. I have all this room. But they said no. They like it up there. They want me to come up there. But I said no, I liked it here in my own house." He nods again, satisfied, then adds, "But I thought I'd maybe take them some things they could use. Who knows, once I get up there, maybe I'll just decide to stay!"

"I'd miss you too much, Daddy. Besides, Ellie's coming home, and I know she wants you to be here. But we could make a pile of stuff for your parents, though." So every morning he spends about an hour and a half gathering stuff, always the same stuff, and dropping it by the front door: a quilt, a bucket, two silver knives and forks, a gallon of milk, eight ballpoint pens, a wash cloth, a potted plant,

"Just for some color," he says, two pairs of his own pants, "They can share," and a hairbrush. His hunt becomes frenzied, disturbed. At this point, I convince him it's time for our own walk to the Mission. He goes reluctantly at first, then easily once we join the creek, and the activities of ten minutes ago escape him. Once home, he will nudge the pile that makes the front door resistant to opening and say irritably, "What's all this junk doing here?"

"It's for your parents," I'll remind him.

"Humph!" He'll kick at the stuff. A couple of times he has picked up the hairbrush and glared at me, "This is mine." He growls that he is exhausted and stomps upstairs to his room to take a nap. Once I can hear his lengthened breathing, I put everything away for the next day. Soon he will awake, and it will be time to watch our daily soaps.

Here is the scary thing: the first time he told me, I believed him, almost. I always do, an ingrained filial piety that runs deeper than the knowledge of madness, of disease. A walk? People? My mind raced backwards. When did he take a walk and I didn't notice? Aren't his parents, my grandparents, dead? Could there have been a mistake? Who are these old people? What do they want? His parents died in those hills, a fiery car wreck in a deep ravine after a day of horseback riding in the Santa Ynez Valley. I imagine their Cadillac fishtailing through a guardrail and arcing through blue air, over brown hills and silver scrub, graceful, relentless motion, something out of a Hollywood movie. It was a Tuesday. Daddy was ten. He, this house, the lucrative properties all over town and along State Street, the 35-foot sailboat and the slip in the harbor, everything left under the keen, and legendarily cold, managerial eye of a dowager aunt. He told me once she never called him by his name, never addressed him directly. He was The Boy. "The Boy must be in bed by eight." "The Boy will not put his feet on the couch." No wonder the boy wants a refund on his past. What if they are hiding in those hills?

What if it was not the first of a string of leave-takings for my father, his parents, his wife, his son, his mind? What if people come back? What if they want us back? What if? He draws me in.

I need distance. That is the guilty truth behind my trip to Greece. Let them think I am the savior. I am saving myself. A few days, an exchange of complications and worries, just a little distance. I have my passport, my ticket, my bag is almost packed. Mark can do this. Of all of us he is the most capable, the most task oriented, trained in procedure and outcome. I have listened, agreed, consoled, encouraged since our mother walked out the door. I am calling in a favor. The refrigerator is stuffed. The channel changer explained in detail, clothing, sheets and towels cleaned and ready. I'm compiling a list of our day, of names, numbers and contingencies, of habits and delusions. Mark can do this. He must.

MARK

*T*he truth must be stated: My sisters are becoming an imposition. There is entirely too much communicating going on currently in our family, too much sharing of the intimate minutiae of our very separate lives, too much freedom of opinion, too much overt curiosity. Too much ordering about. We are, after all, no longer teenagers. In point of fact, I don't think I ever was, except in a purely chronological manner. On the other hand, I am finding an exciting freedom of speech with Clare via our emails. I find I can engage in flirtation long distance, and I have signed the last thirty-two emails with "love." Dr. Himmel has assured me that my inability to speak in Clare's presence, or rather to speak with any sense, is simply an aspect of "juvenile, tongue-tied longing." It seems, at last, I am to experience my teen years. As alarming as that is, it is better than the alternative. After using an internet-based diagnosis program and inputting my symptoms, I feared Tourette's Syndrome.

I hadn't planned on telling Himmel about Clare, but frankly he pinned me down one session in which I was particularly out of sorts, right after Clare left for Geneva. He watched me for three full minutes, then stated, quite astutely I must admit, "Mark, you seem to be mooning."

"Physicists do not moon, Dr. Himmel. Cosmologists do not even moon. It is not in our nature."

"Nevertheless," he said and raised his eyebrows. Another long silence ensued. Sitting there, I felt the knowledge, my secret inner kernel of energy, being drawn to the surface of me. His was the stronger element that day, tugging electrons from my field. Then it was out, clear of me, the secret, the name, even the hopes. They were all his to hold, to use. I was exceedingly uncomfortable waiting for his response. As I could have predicted, he challenged me. Really, Himmel, when will you learn?

"From my understanding of your science, Mark, most physicists are deconstructionists. They break things down, take them apart. Theories aside, Mark, how will you treat this new thing in your life? How will you treat love?

"Like an unstable substance."

ELLIE IS right, of course. I am a virgin. I am a thirty-six year old virgin, but I offer these extenuating circumstances in my own behalf:

1. I left for college when I was barely fourteen.
2. I was five-one and my voice hadn't changed.
3. Women I associated with on campus were always considerably older than me.
4. Any other female was considerably younger— mentally.
5. I have been very busy, occupied with the universe, if you will.
6. I suspect I am a late, a very late, bloomer.

However, the past twenty-two years of companion-less study and training have taught me how to approach a problem and how to solve it. I am addressing Ellie's concerns. I have a plan. I am faced with a lack of personal empirical data; however, the acquisition of practical, scientific knowledge is a process: research, followed by controlled experimentation, then synthesis and analysis. Outcome: expertise.

First, one must clearly state the problem: sex with Clare with a semblance of ability. Possible limiting factors: time, access to information, entropy. Time: Clare has emailed that she has decided to travel in France before she returns home. This gives me approximately two extra weeks to acquire data; however, the next week will be spent putting things in order here at the lab and standing on two dissertation boards. Mary has emailed telling me that she expects me in Santa Barbara no later than next week, Wednesday, as her plane leaves Saturday. She seems to believe that she needs some time to "explain the routine," her words, though I feel a simple typed list would suffice. However, once in Santa Barbara, I should have ample time for study and analysis. I have supervised dozens of postdoctoral students and overseen the workings of a nuclear accelerator. How time consuming can one empty house and one elderly man be? I believe Mary is prone to miscalculation, to poetic hyperbole. Objectivity has been sacrificed to drama. As a side note to my personal quest, I hope to address this issue and correct it for her.

Access to information: Using the internet, though quick, would unfortunately tag my email address with an unspeakable wash of smut, so I shall be pursuing traditional methods of research, and of course, I am thoroughly versed in the use of libraries and book stores. Controlled experimentation presents its own set of moral dilemmas. Acquiring any short-term practical sexual experience would be anathema to my ultimate goal, a long-term relationship with Clare. Hence, we return to books.

Entropy: I am unable to calculate the part entropy may play in limiting my process. The universe is ruled by probability. Let it suffice to say that the probability of something going wrong is high. The question is what will be its measure. I shall keep alert.

SARAH

*H*er nighttime travails instill alertness in me. I watch as she snores. She thrashes her legs, and her arms flail as if she is fighting off a terrible evil that hangs over her. There are gaps in her, huge holes where bits of her have broken away and flown off into the universe. Missing are restfulness, security, trust. Into those spots, demons have rushed in. My queen-sized bed is suddenly narrow and dangerous. I sleep on the couch. In the black shadows and gray light of night I watch her. She murmurs, calls out with a noise like a bark. I go over to her. The light from the window lattices her face, her outstretched hands. I take one.

"Mom . . . Mom. Wake up."

She opens her eyes, stares up without recognition.

"Ruth, you were having a bad dream." I do not call her Mom when she can hear me, though she told me I could call her anything as long as I was feeding her. "Can I get you some water."

She struggles up in the bed. "Maybe some milk. And some crackers, too. Or a little cookie or two."

She is always ravenous. Here is another hole that cannot be filled. She eats at every opportunity, is never full. She hoards food. I find caches in the cracks of the couch, under her pillow, stuffed into the pockets of my out-of-season coats. I leave them be. They will not be forgotten. They will be consumed. When we sit down to eat, she shoves food into her mouth until her cheeks bulge and her lips cannot close. Only then will she begin to chew. The food travels down her throat in visible clots.

When the cheeks are half full, she begins shoveling again. It is hard to watch, but what the hell, she has just cause. I am trying to train my saliva, my jaws, my throat to not respond with sympathetic mimicry. She will eat anything, though Korean pickled dishes and Argentinean steaks are her favorite. We are making our way through every ethnic offering in Manhattan, chewing our way through, the termite and the guide. We have had people in restaurants ask to be moved away from us, to different tables. Even here in New York, where nobody notices, her eating is the stuff of spectacle. Fear and loathing in Dim Sum Palace! Honestly, it's a hoot! I am offering my fellow diners a lesson: What you don't focus on may turn and bite you, literally may gobble you up. I am beginning to believe if all the homeless opened their mouths, they could swallow the world. Hungry eyes, empty hands, hearts and souls hollowed by the wind in the streets, my camera has recorded this for years, but now I see it. This is the ashy, bitter dish she offers me in return for all I have done and not done.

The woman who is my mother prepares for Armageddon or perhaps for dismissal, and I watch. She cannot be deterred, consoled. I have given her clothes, my only bed, feed her her fill and enough also to squirrel away, but she is still not safe. There is too much ground between the front door that she stepped away from so many years ago and this small apartment we share now. I have so much to make up for. Watching her eat, watching her sleep, her face etched in night shadow and eerie street glow, I see her as an image, a negative, the opposite of reality. Her darkness evident and harshly bright, her light steeped in blackness, hidden beyond retrieval. If she were a photograph that I had taken, I would know what to do. I would go back, check my meters, my angle, the aperture settings. I would start over, retake the shot.

MARK

*A*las entropy. Things fall apart.

A number of years ago, there was a game dispersing across America called Six Degrees of Separation. I know that my sisters would be surprised that I am even aware that such a game exists, but I am far hipper (perhaps it should be more hip) than they suspect. I am current on a number of popular trends—electronic pets, Starbucks, eBay . . . I digress. *Six Degrees of Separation.* I believe there was a play or movie or something, but I must admit I don't know whether it came before or after the game. Here, we are interested in the game. The idea behind the game was that you could connect any two human beings by only six degrees of separation. The popular connection was, I believe, to Kevin Bacon, unknown to me, but evidently a man of some import. Perhaps a descendant of Sir Francis. Baconian concepts are now of more historical interest than actual scientific use, yet it seems the great man has kept a finger in the scientific pie with this descendant son or nephew who focuses us on a fundamental principle of physics. I speak of connectedness, indeed, the very essence of physics. As I've said, we search for the unifying theory that connects all things—strings that vibrate a universal truth, a computation that explains all existence. Connectedness is everything. I believe Six Degrees of Separation to be literally quite possible. Should one draw the connections of one human being to another on the other side of the earth, and that second person to yet another in another distant, unrelated location, and so on, I believe that what might emerge would be a form of fractal, an immensely beautiful and complex design made from seemingly disordered systems, that, despite its enormous intricacy is still mathematically sound.

Connectedness and entropy. One would think that these two would avoid each other, would be measurements working at odds, phenomena eternally at war. However, as I have unfortunately found, they can work in concert. The effect is quite . . . annoying. I feel as if I have been the brunt of not one but two theories of physics this last week. Entropy, my pet theory that all things, all endeavors, tend toward disorder, and the very connectedness that ties all things, all people together, joined hand in hand to thwart me. I did, however, emerge triumphant, though at some cost to my dignity. Clare, you will never know what I go through for you. Of course, Clare is the core of it all, the unifying concept. However, unifying is presenting some problems. Of course, I speak again of sex, or rather, how to . . .

Having established a plan of research, I began my studies in the university library. I went late, twenty-five minutes before the stacks would close, in the hopes of meeting no one. Enter entropy. I was perusing the catalog file trying to locate a likely section when I felt a soft tap at my shoulder.

"Can I help you find something?"

I turned around.

"Oh, Professor! Hello!" A very large smile leered up at me. "String Theory and Multi-Dimensionality lecture last fall. Too cool! What can I help you find?" She was squat, round and strong enough to push me from the computer keyboard. "Sometimes these things are touchy!" She said in a distinctly chirpy voice, then, "Oh!" She was looking at the selection of titles I was scrolling through. "Oh!"

"I was looking for models of the Serxalian galaxy G7 (an utterly fraudulent, yet rather quick-witted response), and it misinterpreted my entry." I tried to smile back down at her, but it felt more like a painful stretching of the lips. I don't know whether it worked on her or not.

"Well! You must have been surprised!" She gave a laugh like breaking glass. Let's see what I can do." Another clerk was approaching, drawn by our conversation and late evening boredom. I panicked.

"That won't be necessary." Perhaps I spoke too quickly, pushed past her blocking body too boldly and hit the escape key with too much force. "I have a general idea where they can be found in the stacks. I should go before the library closes." I fled. The two girls' laughter pursued me.

It was not unreasonable that a library clerk could have attended one of my lecture series, nor that the very stack I made my way to was inhabited by two young grad students doing some sexual research of their own. However, that the grad students in question should be two of my own, Matthew Schneider and Emma Pope, sprawled out on the floor with a very rare text of the *Kama Sutra* open to some extremely explicit pages, I find hard to accept. I wanted that book.

"Professor!" There was a great untangling of limbs and adjusting of clothing. "Hi!" Hi, indeed. A rather inadequate response, I thought. "We were . . ." Poor Schneider's voice trailed off. "I guess it's pretty obvious what we were . . ." Schneider grinned while Miss Pope continued to grow pinker by the second.

"Yes. Well. I was passing through," I told them. I pointed to the book. "You should handle books with a little more care, Schneider, Pope. I think you know better." I moved off down the isle. "Carry on."

More laughter followed me.

Evidently the university library was not the location to carry on research of a private nature. A more anonymous location was called for. I thought perhaps one of those large chain book stores with a little bit of everything, but nothing very stunning. I was under the impression, from various conversations, that no one I knew frequented such places. Once again I must state: Alas entropy, alas connectedness. I met two people, separately, in the parking lot on my way into the San Jose Borders, whom I hadn't seen in a number of years—one from my own grad school days and the other an ex-neighbor from Santa Barbara. Once in the Borders, I was called to from the location of the café. A group of three fellow professors, one from biochemical engineering, and two from applied sciences, with, I might add, offices just down the hall at Stanford University, insisted I sit with them for a cappuccino and a muffin. I see no reason for a book store to have a café. What is the point? However, spotted as I was, I had to join them.

"Mark. It's good to see you. Sit."

"I thought none of you supported these places. 'Soul-sucking conglomerates that stifle individualism and true free enterprise' I believe were the precise words I heard at last year's department Christmas party."

There was a certain amount of sheepish grinning and shrugging until Murphy, always the brightest of the three, shot back, "And what brings you here, Mark?"

"The cappuccino." I grinned. Laughter all around, and in fact, the cappuccino was delicious.

So far, I had racked up eight acquaintances in a matter of two days without ever coming closer than twenty feet to the research material I wanted to acquire. I was running out of time. Mary expected me south in two days. I wanted to take with me materials to peruse. Where was I to look now, I asked? Obviously distance was the key to thwarting the combination of connectedness and entropy that seemed set to disappoint my efforts. San Francisco is an easy distance from Palo Alto, and yet a world away. I would go there.

Shopping unmolested at a Barnes & Noble in downtown San Francisco was a very satisfying, indeed, leisurely experience. Dozens of complete strangers jostled me, not a hint of familiarity in the lot. There was even success in my pursued topic. In the social science, family and relationship aisles, I was able to pick up my own copy of the *Kama Sutra*, the original Kinsey Report—as well as a DVD of that movie, the books *The Feminine Mystique, The Art of Masturdating: A Guidebook for Single Heterosexuals* (unappetizing pun, but useful information I hope), the DVD of *What Women Want* with that Gibson actor (I liked his work in *Gallipoli,* but feel it has suffered since), the books *What Women Want Men to Know, A Very Lonely Planet: Love, Sex and the Single Guy,* and *The Girls' Guide to Hunting and Fishing* (for a light touch from the female perspective). Additionally, I found the indispensable *The New Quotable Einstein,* not, of course, in the same section. I admit, I wandered, but I feel that Einstein would agree, everything is relative. I decided to pass on a manual obviously written in the early seventies, replete with photos of two naked and doughy looking, longhaired individuals on a futon on the floor. No thank you. Armed with this stack of materials, I headed for the checkout counter. I stood behind a nattily dressed, middle-aged woman with a broad back and hair that could not have been genuine either in color or in attitude. I was contemplating its structure—an approximation of turbulent waves frozen in mid-crash, something akin to excited molecules trapped in an extremely strong ion net—when the hair in question suddenly turned and I was presented with the face, an unfortunately familiar face. Yes, of course, it was the university president's wife, she of the cocktail party mishap, she of the Gloria Steinem fan club, she, the recipient of the non-explanatory apology, she, the initiator of the Himmel Era.

"What are you staring at—Good Lord! You!!"

I opened my mouth to respond. Nothing came out. She glanced down at the pile of books in my arms. She stared; her lips moved silently. The hair quivered to activity.

"I doubt, Professor, it will do you any good." Then she stepped from the line and moved to a far checkout counter. I saw her raise her hand to the back of her head, as if to calm the advancing tide.

For the very first time in my remembered life, I did not check the clerk's addition skills. I could think of nothing except escaping. It seemed that six degrees of separation is far too many. Everyone I knew or have ever met appeared to be attached to my very elbows. Driving home, I passed along Mission, with its row of adult book stores and peep shows. This, too, could be considered research. I admit I was tempted, but then the thought of running into someone else of my acquaintance stopped me. Mary and the twins tell me I have no imagination, but they are wrong. It was fully functioning that day. I imagined my third-grade teacher, the ancient and ever-terrifying Miss Holypot, lurking somewhere behind one of those grimy, mirrored shop fronts, or perhaps even meeting Himmel himself in the rubber accoutrements section (if in fact there is such a section). This once I must agree with the eminent wife of the university president: Good Lord, indeed. I call it entropy.

LUKE

Willow's body is a path I am following in this strange landscape. She is a neighborhood I remember, a familiar street, a home that is open and waiting for me. I am walking toward her. It has been a long way. If I ever get there, I think I'll be able to stay.

MARY

$\mathcal{A}$s I go in the morning, I check on them: Mark, in his room, flat on his back, snoring, and Daddy, in his room, a gray-haired version of the previous, flat on his back, snoring. Harmony. I don't know if I ever noticed how very much alike they are, so much more than simple bone structure. It makes me sad for Mark somehow, as if walking from one doorway to the next is moving through the dimension of time, seeing one man and then what might be before him, waiting. Their duet follows me down the hall and stairs and out the front door. I have left a note for Mark on the kitchen counter, propped against his precious French press coffee pot. Who even knew he'd be aware of the existence of coffee, let alone be able to make it? I count it as a positive sign. He will need his wits about him. Physics will not help him now. I have done what I can, especially since he has chosen to show up late, last night at midnight in fact, and now will be utterly on his own. Every appliance in the house has a sticky note attached to it with instructions. I have left him with daily lists and hourly activities that Daddy will recognize, will tolerate. I have left him with a roster of subjects that Daddy can talk about. I've even drawn a map of our daily hike with notes on how long Dad spends with his feet in the stream, how long he can usually manage the Mission church before he'll need to move on. Doing all this, I've realized something: Mark will have to be the big brother he has never been. He will have to be Peter, the Peter that should be. I guess that makes Daddy one of us, the younger ones, left behind and in need of a hand. My, we

133

have a complicated family dynamic, changing roles and surrogates, neediness grappling with independence. Mark has always tried to be beside it, above it. Peter's suicide was the last straw, he stepped back forever, or perhaps he had been inching away in embarrassment all along. Each year another step closer to science, farther from home. Now he looks at us as if we are failed experiments, bugs gone bad, interesting, instructive in a negative sense, and generally unappetizing. So I have left him a note.

GUESS WHAT, PROFESSOR MARK, YOU'RE ABOUT TO STEP INTO THE PETRI DISH. FOLLOW ALL INSTRUCTIONS. DO NOT DEVIATE. TAKE CARE OF DADDY. I'LL CALL FROM THE ATHENS AIRPORT TO CHECK ON YOU.
MARY

From our house by the Mission, LAX is two hours with light traffic, first through empty early morning streets in Santa Barbara, then onto South 101, the ocean a dull morning pewter on the right, and the coastal hill, brown as burnt toast on the left. Often the wide, arcing bay before Ventura will offer a display of porpoises in its surf, sunlit backs and shining dorsal fins curving through the rough foam. It is a calming ride, lovely and solitary. I am waiting for an easing in my nervousness; I am waiting for liberation. But that is not what I feel. Each mile from home stretches the string that connects Daddy and me, our secret umbilical cord. It tautens, and each slight movement of the car sets it humming with memory.

Even when Daddy and I traveled 101 to the airport, so many times, seemingly so long ago, we hardly spoke. We took the time to enjoy a certain feeling the ride engendered, a skimming of the bright margin between two worlds, land and water, home and away. To see us now settled in our little routines one would never think that we have been world travelers, Daddy and I, attending international competitions, shows, seminars. I was the mousy little secretary, the gofer, the tag-a-long. Dad was the star, a gregarious and erudite stranger that replaced the intense, tortured man of wood that I lived with. If he introduced me at all, it would be by first name, never adding that I was his daughter. I don't think he meant it to be hurtful; it was just that his craft was sacred space, created from the remnants of Peter's coffin, a place in which he could shut himself. At home he clung to it as if it were a lifeboat, all that kept him afloat in the wash of mess and pain that his other life, our part of his life, had become. Away, that sacred space was opened, offered for viewing, and suddenly he was a brilliant success, a master craftsman. It only worked if we weren't there. Even I, who cooked and cleaned, oohed and ahhed, did the books and the laundry, fielded calls, encouraged, read to the quiet scraping sounds of carving tools and swept the leavings, small curls of pale wood, all that was left of something living and real, even I needed to disappear. It would come over him slowly, this weaning away, during the plane flight or during the drive to whatever venue. So the moments before were always special, filled with closeness that was offered like an apology. I have never been particular. I accepted what was offered and was thankful.

Daddy and I used to play a game while we sat in the airport waiting for our flight to be called. We would survey the crowd, scan for drama, pick out potential for catastrophe. The game was based on the disaster films of the seventies and early eighties. Planes crashed, earthquakes devastated cityscapes, buildings turned into raging infernos and cruise ships sank into dark ocean depths all hands on board, but not before the requisite number of human dramas was established. Little Timmy was traveling alone with his black and white cat, Bobo, in a carrier under the seat. Two nuns in full habit were returning from a missionary stint in the Congo. An elderly lady with knitting and an oxygen tank chatted in a gaspy, thin voice to anyone who would listen. A man in a messy suit was already drunk by eleven AM; his wife sat near him, pleading, nervous fingers moving ceaselessly. It usually took four personal dramas to reach critical mass. Then look out . . . the city would crumble, the boat sink, the tower burn to the ground, the plane was bound to go down.

This trip the game begins before I am even through the security line. A plump woman in a purple velour track suit rifles her purse, declares she has left her passport behind. Hysterics ensue. The line inches past her. Then, a returning Greek national refuses to put out his cigarette. He blows smoke into the check-in attendant's face. Security is called. That's two, Daddy would say if he were standing next to me. The line inches forward. In the waiting area, no nuns with guitars waited, but in their stead, two backpack-encumbered teenagers, shining pimply faces attempting insouciance, displaying instead freedom and joy. Identical long blond hair and deep tans, they hold hands, share an iPod, each with one earphone.

"I wish we could sit together," the girl says.

"That's three, Daddy," I whisper under my breath.

"We're lucky we got on the plane at all." The boy squeezes her hand. "We'll be sleeping the whole time anyway."

The Greek shows up, looking disgruntled, patting the pocket of his jacket for the confiscated cigarettes. He checks all his remaining pockets and finds a single cigarette. He sticks it behind his ear and grins. I am perplexed. I have already counted his as an incipient drama, yet here he is again with a contraband cigarette. I envision smoke wafting down the aisle, raised voices, a tussle.

136

Should the Greek remain a single drama, or should I count him as two?

Two elderly women sit down next to me and begin to compare every item they are carrying. They seem to be similarly prepared for every emergency, including biblical plagues, judging by the amount of bug repellant, SPF clothing and flashlight batteries. When they finish the list, they begin again at the beginning, this time comparing name brands. They cannot be counted as a potential drama, but they might be a couple of handy gals to have around should a crisis arise. I leave them to their discussion and head for a quiet corner to call home.

I know I have said that I would call from Athens, but the urge is beyond my control. Mark might have some last-minute questions. Maybe we both need reassuring. The phone rings six time and cuts to the answering machine. I check my watch. It is too early for the walk and too late for Daddy to still be in bed.

"Where are you?" I call into the phone. "It's me. You should be at home. Where are you? Mark, you're not following the schedule. I can't believe you! Where are you?"

We have forty-five minutes until boarding. I stand by the phone for the next half hour, calling every three minutes, feeling that umbilical cord that ties me to Daddy draw tighter with each ring. The last attempt ends with me slamming down the phone after saying, a little too loudly, "You are so fucking untrustworthy, Mark. You are not even my brother. I don't know you!!" A few people glance up and quickly down again. They are the unwise travelers, the "uninitiated" as Daddy once would have pointed out. What would he have to say of me now? I'm in danger of becoming one of my own statistics. I call back and whisper.

"I'm sorry I swore at you. I'm sure there's a perfectly good explanation why you aren't at home, even though the schedule clearly states that you should be home,

137

at the kitchen table having breakfast, either oatmeal or scrambled eggs, buttered toast, orange juice and one cup of coffee. For Daddy. You can have anything you want . . . I'm sure there's a perfectly good, non-disaster oriented reason for you not answering the phone, but I won't know until I arrive in Athens, will I?" My voice is rising. I clear my throat, lower my voice to a furious whisper. "It makes it a little hard to fly out of the country when my father and my brother have suddenly gone missing! (once again, people looking up) I'm going, though. Don't think I'm not. So you damn well better follow that schedule, Mark . . . and Mark, if you don't have a very good excuse for not answering the phone, I will reach through the wires and strangle you. And when I get back . . ." The message machine clicks off while I am calculating the damage I will do. I return to my seat, umbilical cord twanging. What a stupid idea this all was. Whatever made me think I could just traipse away to a Greek island? Family is luggage you carry with you. I am definitely over the weight limit.

A new traveler has settled in across from my seat, a thin, shaky woman dressed in an extremely beautiful, probably expensive, suit of violet. At her feet sits a huge white dog that stares up at her with eyes that exactly match her clothing. His head is large and oddly shaped and his ears are small and clipped-looking. He looks powerful and possibly mean, and he is completely absorbed in his mistress.

"He's a service dog," she tells me. Her voice is as shaky as the hands that travel restlessly over each other, to the dog's head, back to the lap, up to her hair, a constant circuit. In contrast, the dog is utterly still.

"Oh, uh-huh." I am afraid I have been staring.

"I'm a diabetic. Lance has been trained to tell if my sugar is low."

"Wow." I have broken two of Daddy's cardinal rules of flying: never look, never speak. I slip my hand into my purse and finger my book. I have followed all the other rules: pick a book that will keep you interested, but will not interest anyone around you, nothing sensational, no best-sellers, no self-help or political books that might elicit an unwelcome commentary. I've picked Kazantzakis' *Report to Greco*. It is well worth a second read, appropriate for the trip, and the dull blue 1970's cover will instantly bore anyone sitting near me who takes an interested peek. Too late now, though. Once you have responded to a fellow passenger, they own you.

"I also have seizures, and Lance can tell if one's coming on. He nudges with his nose and I take my medicine. I was attacked as a child and now I have seizures. They don't know if they're connected, but I think they are. I was attacked, then I had seizures. Then I had juvenile diabetes. I also have an anxiety disorder . . . because of the attack, but I don't like to talk about that. Lance calms me and protects me if he needs to."

I notice the intrepid, every-emergency ladies are nodding, bursting with questions, possible solutions. I look down, thinking I will find Lance nodding, too, but he is still, rapt.

"Some people don't like the idea of a dog on a plane, but he's my Lance and I need him every minute. I sit in first class, and he sits right next to me. That way I don't have to sit too close to any strange man."

More nodding. Sweet Jesus, I think, we don't need the smoking Greek and the separated young lovers. This woman singlehandedly fills the quota for disaster dramas. Add my own worries to the balance, and this plane is going down. I hope I'm sitting with the intrepid, emergency ladies. They're my only hope.

Mary:

Where are you? I thought you would be here by now. I think I must have been confused about the

dates, and I can't find the envelope I wrote them on. I think this little creature in me is sucking the brains out of my skull. I don't seem to be able to keep two thoughts at once. Is that normal? What if it's a monster? I'm worried I'm dying. If I do, no one here would know or care. If you don't come soon, you may find my stinking, bloated body lying on the cold stone floor.

In the afternoons, the baby flutters inside me, as if it were running restless fingers along the walls of my stomach, kneading and pinching. Perhaps she will not be a monster, but a sculptress. Perhaps she is already trying to mold me. No sculpting for me though, I've run out of clay, and I haven't the energy or the mind to mine it. I don't much fancy climbing into the hills with the island filled with hostile natives, either. I've taken up my paints again, but oh, Mary, where are you?

XO

Ellie

* * * * *

Dear Mark:

I am back, but where are you? No emails, calls or notes at the lab in the last week. Have I lost my fascination for you? We were four days in transit from London. The plane experienced engine trouble midway across the Atlantic, and we had to make an emergency landing at some military base in Greenland, complete with screaming women, assuming the crash position, wailing sirens and sliding down that slide apparatus. What a drama! It was like something out of an old disaster movie! I slept on a cot, or didn't sleep, as it was too cold to do much other than lay in the dark and shiver. Greenland is not in my future vacation plans. While we waited for a replacement plane or spare parts or something, I did crossword puzzles in my head and thought of you. I thought of you a lot, Mark, and now I want to see you. Where are you?

Love,
Clare

* * * * *

Mary, Mark and Ellie:
What am I, Limburger cheese? No one writes. No one calls. Never mind. Big News! I'm bringing Mom home. The city is hot and stinking and crowded with tourists. There is a restlessness in Mom that worries me. My questions annoy her, and I don't think I'll ever get the story of these intervening years. The important thing is, she is found. So we will begin again where it all began. We will all be together. I am so excited to see you all, and for you to meet (I should say, "remeet") our mother! Tell Dad and Luke my news. I'll keep in touch along the way.

XXXXXXXOOOOOOOOO
Sarah

A message (along with her own) left on Mary's answering machine:

Hey! Mary? Oh yah, uh, Mark? Are you there? Pick up please . . . Where is everybody? It's Luke. I only have one call . . . so . . . so . . . we're in the county lockup, and we need to be bailed. Nothing serious. Sleeping naked on the beach, well, not exactly sleeping, and a little bit of pot in the VW. The cop was extremely uncool, and Willow said a few things back at him. And the dog . . . well, anyway, can you come? Please? I don't like being stuck in here . . . well, bye. Hurry. Bye.

MARY

*T*he umbilical cord snaps somewhere over the Atlantic. I can almost hear the pop. My book forgotten in my lap, I have been talking almost since takeoff. The intrepid traveling ladies have been sandwiched between the window and me. Poor things, they have acquired a glazed, beaten look. They have stopped talking; their nods and clucks have become automatic. There is nothing in their well-equipped bags that will ward off me. I am a force of nature that no cream or spray or SPF fabric will deter. I am a woman with a captive audience and a story to tell.

I have brought them up to date on our entire family history, our current situation, Ellie's pregnancy, Sarah's dubious old woman, Mark's foibles and the emergence of that Clare woman in his life, and am building up some steam in my recitation of the complete and unexpurgated list of Daddy's daily delusions and antics when the intrepid lady next to me interrupts.

"I'm sorry, but I really have to use the restroom." She smiles at me, a weak, painful attempt. Her companion bounces in her seat.

"I should, too, as long as you're getting up."

They are up and scraping by my knees before I can move out of their way. I have kept them trapped for nearly six hours. They scuttle down the aisle as if they are fleeing a volcano. In fact, they are. Mount Mary is spewing! I begin to giggle, high-pitched hysterical whinnies that gain glances. I wrap my fingers over my mouth and nose and snort. More looks.

"I haven't been drinking." I inform all those listening. "I'm hysterical."

That does it. Everyone looks away. They are learning Daddy's rules. Two or three more frantic giggles wobble up from the pit of my stomach, and then, at last, I can sit still. I sit, staring straight ahead, without moving a muscle for thirty-two minutes. They aren't coming back. The intrepid ladies are hiding in the galley or have squeezed into any open seat they could find. They have left their neat little daypacks nestled below the seats in front of me. They won't be back to collect them until the plane has landed, but that's okay, because they have taken something with them. They have carried my story away. I am empty. I am so still, so serene that I actually hear it, the slight pop, the umbilical cord, my personal tether to home disengaging, snapping back and away. I am free. For a space of five blissful minutes I don't even care how the jar and sudden slack must be affecting those at the other end of the line.

MARK

Upon awaking this first morning back home in my old bed, I find I have overslept. The bedside clock reads 9:30. The last time I have slept so late was in this very bed, more than thirty years ago. A bright pink sticky note clings to the alarm clock and reads, *"Be sure to set your alarm for no later than 7:00 am. You'll want to be ready to wake Daddy by eight. PS Sweet dreams!"*

I find an elderly man, physically recognizable as my father, standing over my bed stark naked, in complete disarray and smelling of a bowel accident. Staring up into the blinking, curious face with its cap of wild corkscrew curls and patchy grizzled beard, I do a quick calculation and realize I haven't been home in two years and a little more than five months. This is not the forgetful, doddering father I had left that Christmas. This was an entirely different creature. This stranger with my father's features is frightening.

He asks, "Where's that girl?"

"Mary," I tell him. "Your daughter. She's—"

"I know that!" he says. His features draw in on themselves, tight and angry. "And I know you, too. Don't think I don't!" He leans in closer and glares.

I have to move away, space, air being essential. I smile and try not to breathe. "I think you might have had an accident, Father. You had better—"

"I have not!"

He becomes a portrait of injured dignity. He turns to the door and stomps out, his skinny white buttocks splattered and crusted. I hop from bed to follow. Evidently,

144

one of my myriad duties will be toilet tutor. I catch up and guide him towards his room and bathroom. I will not go into what I found there, first in the sheets, then the floor, then the tiles of the bathroom, the toilet seat and the bowl. Nor will I attempt to find a metaphor to suit my discovery. There is nothing in physics, neither on the cosmic nor subatomic level which correlates. Science fails me. There was, however, a large blue box of baby wipes with a green sticky note attached: *"Your best friend. If you get him up and to the toilet by eight, you may only need one or two to finish the job. If not, there are extra boxes in the cupboard below. Remember, be gentle."* I am gentle, but still Father whimpers and winces, then stands and watches, still naked, as I use the rest of the box of baby wipes to clean the bathroom. I discover another sticky note on the toothpaste, *"Put the toothpaste on the brush and stay to watch. Help him rinse and give him a capful of dental rinse. Don't let him swallow it. It gives him diarrhea—see baby wipes note."* The note on the electric razor states simply, *"You do it!!"* The note on the shampoo bottle is more elaborate: *"It's your job to wash him head to toe, Mark. Try to do it every two or three days. He'll complain. Don't listen. Use your massive charm to coax him. Don't get soap in his eyes! Don't leave him. Have a towel ready—he'll be freezing!"*

Behind me, Father's voice is high and whining, "I'm cold. Why is it so cold in here?"

In fact, upon delivering a shaved, showered and dressed father to the lower atmospheres of our house, I find the place is pasted with fluorescent sticky pad notes covered in Mary's neat handwriting, containing obscure instructions and mild threats. A longer, more pointed note on the kitchen counter, exhorts me to take care of Father and warns me of petri dishes, which proves, in writing I might add, that no one in this entire family has any idea what I actually do. This is a point I plan on taking up with each of them at a future time. However, what I must do, currently, is breakfast. Father has already asked seven times, in one form or another, if we will be eating or if we already have.

The refrigerator, too, shows Mary's handiwork. It is so filled with labeled casseroles it resembles the compacted matter of a collapsing star. I can't even find the coffee, eggs or milk. Looking at those piled, labeled dishes reminds me of the days just after Peter's death, endless casseroles with the weight of grief and the taste of ash. My stomach roils. I am feeling a certain amount of expertise having successfully stripped the bed, started a wash, handled the horror of the bathroom, and dressed and groomed Father. I make an executive decision. We will avoid the forming black hole of the refrigerator. Father and I will go out for breakfast. This is strictly against instructions, but we are grown men, one of us at least. We know how to comport ourselves in public.

EVIDENTLY, WE don't. The trouble starts with my car, which is not his and Mary's, which has obviously been fashioned with the sole, sinister purpose of befuddling an already befuddled mind. He cannot find the door handles, the seatbelt, the window button. He is uncomfortable with the way the seat slants slightly back. He sits forward, hunched and ready for disaster.

"This isn't the car," he tells me. "Where did you get this car? This is somebody else's car."

"It's my car, Father."

"I don't know this car."

We repeat this conversation in varying forms, eleven times, all the way to the beach.

I choose the little café on Hendry's Beach. It will not be overcrowded midweek, and we will be able to sit outside and watch the surf. Typical of summer, the fog is still lingering at the beach. It is gray and somewhat bracing. A second sign of trouble swims into visibility as we pull into the parking lot. Hendry's Beach is no longer Hendry's Beach. It is now Arroyo Burro Beach. When this happened, I have no idea. It is as if a small piece of my past has chipped off and floated into the ether without my knowing. Now, it would seem, entropy is attacking my past. I could graph it, place each incident along a descending line—sleeping in late, cleaning my own father's bottom, emerging from the fog, right beach but wrong name, the familiar face of the stranger beside me. I could calculate where we are heading. Chaos.

It is too cold for Father at the tables outside, even though they cluster beneath glowing heat lamps. He proclaims this enough times that the people sitting around us smile sympathetically and nod. One elderly lady with a deep tan offers him her knitted sweater.

"I know you," he tells her, beaming. There is something in his wide, welcoming eyes that makes her retreat, shaking her head, clutching her offered sweater in protection.

We settle ourselves inside. It is warmer, quiet and nearly empty. The espresso machine makes him jump each time milk is steamed. "What is that?" he asks each time over the insistent screech and gurgle. I look at my watch. He asks if we have ordered, on an average of once every 1.38 minutes, until our food arrives. With his agreement, I have ordered him huevos rancheros, a remembered favorite; for myself, toast, juice and coffee. When the eggs arrive, they are no longer a remembered favorite. They are too hot; they are too spicy. They have too much stuff on them, and are, in fact, the most peculiar and menacing eggs my

147

father has ever met with. He shoves the plate, launching it off the table.

I have excellent reflexes. No one in my family knows this, but once I harbored hopes of becoming an astronaut. I knew astronauts needed to be in peak physical condition. I trained, one hundred and fifty sit-ups every morning, one hundred squats, twenty pushups, and forty-five minutes of self-designed exercises to improve my hand-eye coordination. I was quite successful with my secret regimen until I gave it up. I discovered Einstein and realized I could travel much further into the galaxy with my mind than on rocket fuel.

I catch the sloppy plate of eggs without spilling a drop, but the noise and movement has revealed us. We are a trouble spot in the restaurant. Waiters hover nervously, customers inch their chairs away. I switch plates with Father, and he sets into the toast with quiet, satisfied relish. In a state of edgy reprieve, I eat eggs swimming in salsa. We eat in silence. I cannot think of what to say to this man. In a moment of quiet back at the house, I will jot down a list of topics that might interest him.

We walk on the beach, but not far. The sand is soft and deep, higher on the shore, which pulls him off balance. Closer to the water his footing is firmer, but the movement of the waves makes him dizzy. I have to hold his elbow, which is awkward because he has his arms up and his hands plastered over his ears.

"It's so loud," he shouts. "I didn't know the . . . the . . . that is so loud." He gestures at the surf with his free elbow.

People walking notice us. With sympathetic eyes and over-generous smiles, they give us wide berth. Their dogs, however, greet us. Every one of them, every size and shape and color, they are drawn to Father by some innate notion that they have found the one human without boundaries or rules, who will accept their sandy paws and salty snouts in joy, and of course, he does. It is the only time he will peel his hands from his ears. He pets them and talks to them in language that lacks its usual lapses in vocabulary and sense. He calls them all Jack, and they, in return, accept their christening gracefully. The owners stand to the side and wait for their pets to return to them. It is interesting how information surfaces. Somewhere in Father's past, long before us, there was a dog, Jack. I think, judging by current appearances, perhaps he was more affectionate with that dog than he ever was with any of his children. Man and dog are still connected; like the particles along a string, they still resonate with devotion.

I maneuver him back to the car and tuck him into his seat. He sits quietly with a smile on his face, while I get in and reach across him for his seatbelt. We are close, and he smells of salty wet dog, sea air and old man. I press against his unresisting body and grope for the belt somewhere behind his right shoulder.

"That was a good day," he says.

I feel the gathering movement in his thin body. He leans forward into me and kisses me, on a spot he is just able to reach above my right ear, and then he settles back placidly. There is a surge of electricity inside my chest, almost painful. It is our first kiss.

"That was a good day," he repeats as I snap his seatbelt into its trap. "We should do that again soon, Peter."

Peter. I am at sea. I am displaced, homeless, not myself.

"That was a good day, Dad," I tell him. It is only 11:00. We have a lot of time left to us.

Clare:

I am sorry about the lack of contact. I haven't had a chance to look at emails, let alone type one. My dad takes far more minding than I realized, and it

leaves little time for anything else. As you might guess, I am down in Santa Barbara, covering for the absent Mary as she goes to retrieve the pregnant Ellie. Sarah also threatens to descend upon me, with her refabricated mother in tow. In addition, I have had to bail my brother Luke out of jail for beach transgressions. Have I told you about all this? I seem to be losing some of my acuity. Is Alzheimer's contagious? Anyway, I, too, am starring in my own disaster film here, (By the way, I'm glad yours turned out well. I would hate to lose you now...), a family disaster of epic proportions.

Did you think of me? I am grati
Frnt dor—escaped!
    Lo
    M

* * * * *

Sarah:
Don't come.
    Best,
    Mark

A note left for Mark on the door of the house:

If it's cool with you, Willow and I are going to camp in the carriage barn for a while. The landlord's totally wacko about some prize plants Willow's dog Mutt dug up. Ignore the boxes. We'll be by later to move them. Where's the key to the padlock?
    Luke & Willow

Mary and Ellie:
I realize that you have only just arrived but I have been calculating the amount of time that would

be required to wrap up Ellie's affairs and return home, and I am quite certain that you could be here in Santa Barbara no later than next Tuesday. I have put Sarah off from returning, but I must say, I shall be very happy to see you, Mary.

    Best,
    Mark

* * * * *

Mark,
It sounds as if you could use some help. I'm coming down. Two days tops.

    Much, much love,
    Clare

* * * * *

Quark:
Fuck you. I can come if I want to. It's my home, too.

    Sarah

Sarah

*T*here are all manner of homeless. There are families that have been kicked out of their houses or apartments and live in shelters or squats; there are down and outers that inhabit alleyways and the moist, dank underbellies of bridges; there are gangs of runaways that live like feral cats in abandoned buildings; and there are the lost, wandering, solitary shades that slip beneath our notice until we trip over their bodies in the dark shadows of a highrise. The homeless are legion. I have documented their search for food, their tentative social hierarchy, their rough camaraderie or piercing aloneness. The police rouse them, move them on, and so they shift across the face of this city, and then resettle and wait to be moved on again. I find them again and again and take their pictures. Sometimes they will want a copy, and so when I have finished my developing, I will print an extra one and find them again. They will hold the picture in worn, cracked fingers and stare. "There I am," they will say, and be satisfied. The importance of a picture cannot be underestimated.

Ruth is one of the shades. She is nobody. She has no driver's license or state identification card, no memory of a social security number, no Medicaid card. Her story is sketchy, teased from her like delicate threads from a snarled skein, the knot always remaining, irreducible. Her last name or birth date changes at whim. Sometimes I think I have created her, have taken a picture of a cracked sidewalk or a blank brick wall, have carried the image home and exposed it to paper; and then during the plunge in solution, she appears, soft at first, like smoke, and then the edges hardening, the features sharpening. I have developed her. She is mine.

She cannot take a plane or a train. She is an undocumented human, an elderly potential terrorist. She is barred from travel until she becomes a someone. California recedes before us.

"We'll drive," I tell her. "I'm going to lease a car. I already have someone to sublet through August. Road trip, Ruth, what do you think?"

She doesn't care. She is used to moving on, but just as happy to stay put. I may have to use a trail of Krispy Kremes to lead her to the car. I rustle through drawers for some non-oral incentive. She sits on the couch, filling her mouth with Doritos and then chewing. Points of triangles bulge from her cheeks, then diminish with a struggle. I sit down next to her, feeling the sharp prick of crumbs through the thin cotton of my skirt. I hold out pictures.

"See. Don't you want to see them, Ruth? That's Dad. You called him Frank. This is Ellie, my twin, with me at the back of our house; we're hard to tell apart. She's the one smiling at the camera. I'm looking at her. That's Mark. And here's Mary. Doesn't she look like you? We all think she looks like you."

Ruth wrinkles her nose. She squints and prods around her gums with her tongue searching for hidden remains of chips. She sniffs and leans closer. She points to a picture I haven't named.

"That one looks familiar."

"He can't be." I push the pictures into a neat pile, Mary's smiling, protective face on top. "He's dead. You were gone way before then. I took that picture. I took it with his camera. Peter."

"Well, he's the only one that does a thing for me . . . except you. I saw you before. You brought me Chinese noodles. Remember? I love a good Chinese noodle."

I nod and smile. We sit side by side in the darkening apartment, watching the sun slip up the face of the opposite building, leaving it in unrecognizable shadow, something familiar turned strange. Ruth is still, and as ever, waiting for what comes next, but I sit on sharp chips and am ready to move on.

"How about something to eat?"

"Always," is her answer.

When I return with two plates of pasta, dripping with butter and sprinkled with cheese, the photos have disappeared. I think, I hope, she has squirreled them away, added them to her cache of necessaries, the mini-bags of cookies, the wrapped candies from restaurants, the quarters and dimes. She is collecting security, hoarding a future. Perhaps the photos are the first step to becoming a someone. She is adding a past.

LUKE

Willow says she gets a tattoo every time she puts some-thing in the past. Her first, a tiny raised fist on her left shoulder, is from when she was twelve. It commemorates the day she stuck a steak knife in her stepdad's leg and walked away from her house for good. She had two black eyes, a broken collarbone, and the exact imprints of her stepdad's heavy duty outdoor grill spatula all across her back. Twenty-two of them; she counted them in a gas sta-tion bathroom mirror. She waited for everything to heal before she got her tattoo.

"No more parents. No more pain," she says.

There is a tattoo hidden under the soft, short hairs on the back of her head, an eye inked in red with one black tear. She says she got it on her fifteenth birthday, but she won't say what happened, what she put behind her that time.

"It helps me see what's sneaking up on me," is all she'll tell me. "It's my third eye. Ever heard of a third eye? I read somewhere it's supposed to be in the front of your head, right in the middle of your forehead; but mine's in the back, because I got two perfectly good eyes pointing for-ward, so it's a total waste if you see what I mean. I mean what you really need is someone watching your back, right? Right."

I am not watching her back that night on Leadbetter Beach. My eyes are closed. I am settled into the cool sand, and she is on top of me. Neither of us sees the two cops with flashlights behind her. We are busy.

◇

155

Waiting for Mark to come get us I have circled the cell one hundred and eighty-seven times. She is not with me in the cell. If she was she would walk with me, or sit me down, tether me. Wherever she is, she is not walking. She is still. Only her lips move, her tattoos speak. She says it's okay, she's been to jail before, twice.

She shows me the small ball and chain, the handcuffed daisy as we stand next to Mark.

"Once for pot, once for loitering, whatever loitering is, because I wasn't loitering, and I wasn't tricking either, which they said I probably was, but I wasn't; but I have to admit I thought my jail days were over," she says and laughs. "You have led me astray. I may need another tattoo." She hugs me and holds me to that spot while Mark pays our bail. Dad stands at his shoulder.

"Why are we here?" he asks and looks around. "Peter, tell me again why are we here?"

Mark isn't Peter, just like I can't help where my feet take me. They want to take me away, to lead me astray.

We have to pick up Mutt, who's at the pound. Mutt's face behind the wire makes my calves ache. He doesn't jump up or bark when he sees us; he sits there looking through wire. My legs ache and my feet itch and I have to walk.

"I need to walk," I tell her. "I need cans."

She nods and takes my hand. For once she doesn't say a thing, but her tattoos understand.

When we get back to the cottage in Montecito, we leave Mutt and pick up two garbage bags and head out. We will walk toward Carpenteria where the roads are quiet, and the kids throw pop and beer cans out the windows of their cars as if the hillside is their personal dump. I like beer cans for abstract stuff, shapes that get their meaning from their points and edges. These are tricky mobiles to balance, which is what I want, something off kilter that looks as if the slightest breeze will topple it or send it spinning, flying apart.

156

This is one of the three memories I have of Peter, beer cans. Coors, gold and silver. We were stacking them in his attic bedroom. He was giggling, his hands sloppy in their movements, as if he were underwater.

"See Luke," he said to me. "They work just like building blocks. Get enough of them, they take you where you want to go, buddy."

We were building a gold and silver pyramid. He lay down on his back and finished another, and handed it to me so that I could put it on the very top, the last one. He lay looking up at the pyramid.

"Come down here." He reached out an arm.

I snuggled into his armpit, and we looked together.

"Just like an Egyptian tomb, Luke," he whispered. "We made it. The real thing. Don't tell Mary."

I never did.

WHEN WE get back to the cottage we have two bags full of cans, mostly beer, no Coors. I don't work with them. The lady from the big house is waiting on the porch, Mutt tied to the porch post next to her with a length of wire. Above them, a mobile of Coke can gray whales dip and swing, reflecting light and shedding red color onto the woman's face. She is angry.

"Hey!" Willow shouts and is at Mutt's side untying him before I can drop my bags.

"I caught him digging up my bulbs!" She holds up fat, dirty bulbs. They are gnawed, the green tops torn and shredded. "Do you have any idea how much these bulbs cost? Three hundred dollars apiece! They're lilies from the Ecuadorian rain forest! They're very rare!" Her face flashes, red white red white red, in the wind.

Willow stands up. She is nose to nose with the lady from the big house. She flashes red and white, too, and all her earrings and the stud in her nose spark, too.

"Mutt has had a bad day. He's been in jail and so have we and we shouldn't have left him and you shouldn't have tied him up. He's had a bad day. That is so totally uncool because dogs are sensitive, and besides, if those bulbs come from the rain forest and are so rare and cost so much they're probably contraband. Contraband means stolen, Lady. Look it up. I read an article once about how rich people buy contraband plants and stuff that's protected and now the stuff is disappearing. Maybe Mutt is an agent for the Sierra Club or the Nature Conservancy or, or the World Wildlife Fund or something, maybe he's looking out for his fellow wildlife! Maybe he's thinking of turning you in!"

Mutt is sleeping, he is dreaming, his feet twitch in dreamland clover. I don't think Mutt knows he's been set free and put to work for the Nature Conservancy. I don't think he even noticed he was ever tied up. But the lady from the big house has noticed something. She has noticed Willow, I think for the first time. I want to tell Willow that it is better to be ignored than noticed, better to walk by unseen, but it is too late. The lady from the big house is looking at Willow as if she is a squashed pop can, a piece of trash in her personal space. She looks past Willow and right at me. She is really noticing me for the first time, too. Her eyes flash red.

"I don't think this is working out anymore, Luke. I like to support the arts, but this is too much. Either she and the dog go, or you all go." She steps off the porch and heads for the clean, trashless perfection of the big house. I watch Willow, still red and white in the sunlight and wind. Even when she stands still, there is movement.

"Bitch," Willow mutters, and Mutt gives a soft howl from dreamland.

WILLOW SAYS we can move into Mary and Dad's carriage barn. She says anyone related to me has got to be cool about us.

"Unlike my parents, who were never cool about anything to do with me, but I have put that in the past. It's way back there." She waves an arm behind her.

She is wrapping my mobiles in toilet paper she has stolen from Macy's and Nordstrom bathrooms, and packing them in boxes she has found behind the shops downtown. Her fingers are thin and quick and gentle. Two have Chinese characters tattooed on them that she says probably don't mean anything except to her. She calls the tattoos Ted and Kevin.

She wants another tattoo.

"I'm thinking of a bunch of lilies," she says and laughs. "That'll put an end to this place!" She snaps her fingers, and Mutt trots over to her to see what all the commotion is about. She puts her arms around him and hugs him fiercely. He pants over her shoulder and grins. I know how he feels.

"New home, Mutt," she whispers into his fur. "Again."

Willow is not a squashed can. She is indestructible. Her body is a path, a map of all her scars. I am reading her, following her. I am getting closer. She is leading me home.

Dear Himmel,

You mentioned that I might email in the intervening weeks while I was away from campus. In fact, I have some questions you may be able to answer, not of course about myself, but rather in regards to my father, Frank Bennett. As I have mentioned in our conversations, he is suffering from Alzheimer's. From late night research I have conducted via the internet while here in Santa Barbara, I feel he is in quite an advanced stage. Many of his behaviors are strikingly inappropriate. I am wondering at what point

Alzheimer's patients should be moved into a group home or institution? In addition, perhaps you could shed some light on his delusions. He is very insistent in them, and though I have tried, will not be reasoned with. Perhaps you can suggest methods with which to tackle these delusions.

Thank you for any information you can provide me,
    Best,
    Mark Bennett

* * * * *

Mary, Ellie and Mark:
Hello all!! Well, we are on our way! This is the first installment of my coast to coast travelogue. Who knew it would be so hard to negotiate New Jersey—who even knew New Jersey! It took us most of a day to find our way through that state, which by the way is larger than anyone knows. I am not lying to you when I say I thought the state line was just beyond Newark Airport! I was under the impression we could point the car west-southwest, and all would be well. Needless to say, my navigational skills are lacking, and now I know where I get it from. Mom couldn't find her way out of a cul-de-sac! Now she is driving (sans a license, of course) and I am in charge of the map. It took an hour or two of practice in a deserted parking lot, but it's all coming back to her. And an added bonus: When she drives, she talks. This is what I have found out: She once was a trucker! Imagine! This is going to be a great trip. I'll keep you all posted. We are in Pennsylvania now and on our way as soon as she finishes breakfast. I think we'll stop in Amish country (if we can find it!), look around and buy some food for the road.

The AAA guide says they have great pies... I want us to take our time. Prepare yourself, Mark, here we come!

XXXXXXXOOOOOO, Sarah

* * * * *

Dear Mark,

Experiencing some delays here, calculations that need to be run again and paperwork on the trip to be handed in. It may be a week or so before I can get away. Hold on, Mark. You can do it, and I am coming. Promise.

Can hardly wait! Hoping you can hardly wait, too...
Love,
Your Clare

* * * * *

Dear Mark,

To answer your questions, it is entirely up to the patient's family and their individual needs and circumstances when it is most appropriate to move a patient into a facility. However, having said that, most research has shown that Alzheimer's patients remain viable longer when kept in their own homes. As far as the delusions issue, current theory believes that it is easier on the patient if caregivers are non-confrontational when dealing with delusional issues, unless, of course, they pose a safety risk.

Mark, these are all answers easily found in one of your internet searches. I am more interested in why you have *actually* been in touch. For my proffered information, perhaps you will answer these questions: How are you coping with the care of your father? How do you feel about the fact that your sister, Mary I believe, has been caring for him alone for a number of years now? I look forward to hearing from you.

Regards,

Ernst Himmel, M.D., Ph.D.

* * * * *

Dear Himmel,

I can answer your questions quite easily with this quote from my *The New Quotable Einstein:* "Freud was brilliant, but much of his theory is nonsense, and that's why I'm opposed to your analysis."

As always,

Mark Bennett, Ph.D. (cubed)

* * * * *

Mary (and Ellie):

Thank you for the sticky notes. They have been invaluable. I am sorry; I should have arrived earlier so that we could have talked. Thank you also for the casseroles, your foresight and effort are much appreciated. By my calculations, you and Ellie should be coming home soon. I am glad. I miss you.

Always,

Mark (and Dad)

* * * * *

Dear Mark,

You called him Dad! I wonder what this means? I love you. We love you. Things are complicated here. I don't know how long we will be. Ellie isn't well, unhinged almost. I will call tonight.

Love to you both, Mary

MARY

"Mark, it's very disturbing. The entire place is filled with eggs!" I am whispering. Ellie is finally asleep, and I do not want to wake her.

"Eggs? Mary you must be precise. What kind of eggs? Chicken eggs? Are there chickens there?"

"Of course there are chickens here; it's a Greek island! There are chickens everywhere! But they're not chicken eggs, Mark. They're ceramic eggs. She's made them. Hundreds of them, eggs with things sticking out of them, bits of bone and I don't know what. Faces, some have faces that are trying to push through! It's frightening, Mark, really, really frightening. And she doesn't look well." I can hear the panic in my voice, but I can't help it. The words are tumbling out. "And there's a painting she's painted, a self-portrait. It's scary, Mark, like something from *The Picture of Dorian Gray,* or maybe something out of a postmodernist psycho-thriller. It's a cutaway of her body! . . . by the way, there's a rather funny painting of you here, too. Apparently she ran out of egg clay . . . Mark? Mark, are you there?"

"Of course, I'm here, Mary. I think you must be overreacting. These ceramic eggs sound quite in line with her usual, notably bizarre art. As for the self-portrait, I think you are being too dramatic, too literary. I'm sure it's all very normal . . . well, normal for Ellie."

"Are monks and naked devils dancing in circles in your sister's belly normal, Mark?"

"Mary. Mary, I want to talk to you about Dad. Dad is—"

"Mark, I called you. I get to talk about anything I want! This is my call . . . what's Daddy doing?"

"He's talking to the mirror. He stands in front of the mirror and talks to his own image."

"Is he upset?"

"No. No, in fact, it's quite fascinating. He becomes quite animated and surprisingly articulate. I've been graphing it, listing words and circumstances. The surge in vocabulary usage is almost exponential. That aside, Mary, it's disturbing. When are you coming home?"

"If he's not upset, and he seems to like it, I don't see the problem. Just watch for an argument."

"Watch for an argument between Dad and himself? What should I do with the one who starts it?"

"I don't like your tone, Mark. Daddy is not the problem. Ellie is the problem, Mark. What should I do about Ellie?"

"Bring her home and she can have a conversation with Dad and his new best friend."

I hang up. After I hang up, I start to giggle, and then I can't stop. I giggle until I double over with cramps, and tears stream down my face and drip onto my kneecaps and pool in the cracks of my toes. We are all falling apart. As a family, I am not sure we can become any odder.

"What's the joke?" Ellie asks from the door of the bedroom. She is standing, naked and sleepy, one skinny arm scratching bulging belly.

It is fascinating, almost as large as the wall it's painted on, a fresco of Ellie, alfresco. In it, she is turned slightly to the side, a great swath of her body carved away, showing her inner workings. Everything is extremely precise (Mark would appreciate that), everything is extremely clinical. Brain matter, hair follicles, blood vessels, bones of cheek and jaw, nasal cavities, mammary ducts and layers of skin and fat, all rendered with meticulous accuracy. One arm of bone, sinew and tendon props her heavy body; the other, whole and encased in shockingly natural, sun-tanned skin, holds a clear glass to her lips. Water courses down her esophagus towards the fire-lit cavern of her belly. All semblance of science leaves the portrait here. A conga line of monks dance in a weaving circle around a great, glistening egg. The floor of the dark cavern of her belly is littered with squashed intestines and glistening red globs of detritus. Fire erupts from vents and simmers beneath the egg. Along the conga line, the monks' bodies slowly change from sedate cloaked figures to crooked old women in black babushkas to writhing fiery devils with molten pitchforks and emerald eyes. The egg is blue, cool, impervious.

"I have no idea," she tells me when I ask her what it means. "I must have had a stomach ache at the time."

"Does it mean you hate the baby?" I ask. It is almost a whisper, but Ellie's answer is direct and clear.

"Quite the contrary." She eyes the picture, then grins. "I'm very pleased with it."

I don't know if she means the painting or the baby. The painting of Mark is more understandable, more enjoyable. The top of his head is exploding, and formulas, equations, rulers, question marks and all manner of science is shooting out. When I saw it, I laughed out loud. It is absolutely perfect. I want to take it home with us, if possible. By the time the rest of us are done with Mark, I think he will see the humor, the truth in it, too. I hope some day he will hang it in his office.

When I congratulate Ellie on it, she becomes mournful.

"I ran out of clay. I don't like to go out too much. I was using up my paints."

She runs hot and cold depending on the time of day, like this foreign tap water. I am learning when she is approachable. Mornings are not good, but in the after-noons we can pack, we can go for walks up in the hills where we hardly meet anyone except adventurous tourists, children and goats. She warms with the sun. She smiles and stretches out her arms. In the hot afternoons, in the lonely hills, she loves this island again.

I COULD love it, too. It is beautiful. Tan and white, gray and red and olive green, it thrusts from the blue-green sea and shimmers in the sun. On top of it all, the monastery, huge and monolithic, living rock, everything on the island seems to lean towards it, the narrow Cyprus trees, the squat white houses, the narrow steep streets, the people, even the dogs and cats and chickens. When Daddy and I traveled, we visited places like this, picture postcard settings, but being here, living here like Ellie . . . It makes me ache with the romance of it. It makes me stiff with envy until I see what it has done to her.

There is nothing left of her except eyes and belly, the rest of her thin skin and bird bones. She looks like one of her own sculptures. I have done the math. Whatever is inside her is too large for a first baby of only four months. I am sick with worry. What if her painting is prophetic? What if some horrible, monstrous disease is growing inside her? What if all the jealousy and hate she says these people feel towards her has impregnated her, is gorging itself, growing, feeding on her from the inside out? What will I do? How can I save my Ellie? Then, rising from all the panic comes black anger, and I hate this place. I will do anything I have to. I will kill; I will claw my way off this blasted rock.

Only, she won't go. It's the eggs.

MARK

I am having a hard time understanding why Mary doesn't come home. She is all around me here, her books, her house plants and mementos. Her dusty oboe case and music stand. Her sticky notes. We eat her casseroles and follow her orders as if she were whispering in our ears. Every morning Dad sits at the kitchen table and looks around.

"Where is everybody?" His voice is puzzled and lost. He doesn't know her name anymore. He doesn't know she's his daughter, but he knows she's missing. Someone is missing that should be here.

There is a correlation in physics, Holographic Theory. It is the idea that the quantum states of a system in a region of spacetime may be encoded on the boundary of that region. Mary is encoded in the place; she marks the boundaries of home. Whether or not she wants to be, she is still here. She always will be. She is a holograph. We move past her, through her, as we struggle through our day.

We have established a routine: breakfast and then the daily walk that Mary proscribed, along the creek and through it and up to the Mission, then home. I have made some simple adjustments to maximize comfort and expediency. I have bought water shoes, two pairs. We match. Dad chose the color, chartreuse neoprene with pink webbing. I roll our pant legs up, and we splash across hand in hand. At the Mission we sit on the pink steps, and let the sun dry our feet. We have been asked not to go in. So we sit and look out over Santa Barbara and watch the fog slip back from the shore, and when the spaces between our toes are dry, we shake our trousers down and are on our way. This is Dad's territory; he is better at home.

Mary is right to notice. I have changed. I called him Dad. I think of him as Dad. In all honesty, it is hard to feed him and clothe him, hard to wash his body, then rush to dry his chilled, goose-pimpled flesh, hard to change his diaper and have him remain Father. That distance is not possible anymore. We are two astral bodies from far-flung regions, drawing closer, moving in concert, being sucked into the black hole of his disease. So, after all these years, he is my dad. I would call him that, but the irony is he won't respond to it anymore. He did the first few days, but now, no. He is Frank now. He is Frank, and I am Peter. We are both people who have not existed for a long time. We miss Mary.

SARAH

M, M, E:
Ohio—straight roads and corn. Yawn. Columbus a
dump, believe me, I know a dump when I see one.
Some of my best friends hang out in dumps.
    XXXXXXOO, S

* * * * *

M, M, E:

Indiana—better. We did the zoo and children's
museum in Indianapolis. Fun. Climbed through
a gigantic heart and slid down an artery, both
squealing! She (Ruth...Mom...) said she once
picked tomatoes here.

"Nasty, hard, back-killing. Growers treat ya like
dirt," she said. Another piece to the puzzle.
    XXXXOOOOO, S & M (oops!)

* * * * *

M, M, E:
Fabulous bakery in Springfield. We stayed two
days just to eat breakfast there! Visited Abe
Lincoln sights. No new tidbits, but we are on our
way to all of you!
    XO, S

"I COULD go on like this forever," she tells me. She is smiling.
Her teeth are gray and brown. Two are broken and one
missing. Homeless people often have bad teeth. Some
have even been known to die of the neglected infection

169

caused by an abscessed molar, almost like something from one of Mary's Victorian melodramas, a Dickensian kind of death. Ruth, my mother, is no longer neglected. She is no longer homeless. She has me. I will save my money to fix her teeth. Then when she smiles, I will see the happiness and not the want. It is a picture I want to take.

People know her past. It isn't just the teeth. It is something essential that comes from her pores. She is clean and wears new clothes. Her hair is cut and styled. She even borrows my lipstick some mornings, but still people sniff her out. They stiffen when she walks by. I have been noting this for the past week, each roadside diner we pull into, each cracked small-town sidewalk we amble. People stare or look away. They whisper. I see them wrinkle their noses, and I want to slap their faces. I want to kick their fat American shins. I want to reach out and take Ruth's hand and hold on, but I can't. We are not there yet.

It doesn't matter anyway, because she doesn't notice people. She is entranced by the scenery, by the hot wind pushing through the windows of the car, by the bridges and stretches of endless corn and grain. Each motel thrills her. Her suitcase begins to bulge with stolen washcloths and samples of soap, shampoo, mouthwash and shower caps. She is becoming a traveling advertisement for Hampton Inns. Each menu holds the key to manna from God, and the AAA guide is the bible of travel, filled with awe-inspiring side trips to sights and tastes as yet untried. She is becoming a tourist.

Mary, Ellie and Mark:

Missouri now! Beautiful rolling hills of green and gold, brown gentle rivers that slip beneath shady trees. We sat for three hours last night and watched the fireflies! I tried to photograph them.

Doubtful it worked, though. Ruth said it's better to sit and watch and not waste a minute. She is wise!!

Salina, Kansas, next, I think, unless something else catches our eye. We'll be exactly half way across this continent. So much unknown land! So much sky! I am expanding. I may burst! I think it's joy, or maybe just travel...
XXXXXXXXXOOOOOOOOOOOOO, Sarah & Ruth

THE LAND is flat and toasted. We have counted seventy-two grain silos in the last three hours. The wind combs our hair, and gospel music pounds out of the radio. Why is gospel music the only music that travels coast to coast? We have heard this particular song at least three times in every state. We know the words. We sing along, loud and reckless with the road in our voices.

"Yessiree, I could go on like this forever," she tells me.
"Me, too."
We are smiling.

Mark and Sarah:
Top Secret Email!! Mary is driving me crazy! Make her stop! She treats me like too thin porcelain, as if I might break apart and my pieces scatter forever. I'm stronger stuff than that! She is fattening me up, and we walk. We walk and eat and pack and eat and eat and eat and eat and then we walk and pack and eat some more. I am feeling better. I felt the baby move last night, a little toe or finger that prodded me. Mary prods me, too. Too much prodding! And what about the eggs? What will we do with all the eggs????
XXXXXXXXOOOOOO, Ellie

* * * * *

Mark,

Hello Dear. Ellie is better, but still strange. We are making some progress. I have been thinking about Daddy. Better be careful with the mirror, or rather Daddy. He sometimes is quite explosive. Ellie is still egg obsessed.....it's very strange!

    Love,

    Mary

* * * * *

Mary:

I am well aware of it, re: explosive, and in fact, eggs as well. There no longer is a mirror. Dad and mirror had a grave falling out. It was permanent. We are running out of casseroles, Mary. When are you coming home?

    Yours,

    Mark

SARAH

Dear all:
Southern Kansas, Oklahoma, Texas...nothing but
dirt. Why, God, Why?!?
   XXXOO, S

THE CAR begins to chug as we drive through a wide valley
between wind-carved monuments of red and orange sand-
stone that bake beneath a violent blue sky. They have
the tortured look of Ellie's sculptures. The car bucks and
shudders and stops. Death throes. The Arizona desert
watches us glide silently to a standstill. In front of us,
behind us, the empty road spools away and is lost in
shimmering mirage. Around us, the desert is hot and endless and waiting. There is no cell phone service, no roadside rest stop with email hookup to complain to Mary, no
service station squatting under its one shade tree with icy
cans of Diet Coke and a grubby gas jockey to save us. We
are alone.

   "Shit." There is too much dirt and too much sun and
too much sky. Panic oozes from my pores and trickles
down between by shoulder blades. We are going to die.

   "Vapor lock," Ruth says. She is gazing out at the carved
cliffs. Her eyes droop. She is sleepy and content. She is
completely oblivious to our danger.

   "What?!?" I bark. I am gripping the wheel so hard the
sweat from my palms trickles down my wrists.

   She answers without opening her eyes. "Bad gas. Water
in the gas, engine gets hot. Water vaporizes and the gas

can't get through to the engine. Vapor lock." Her arm waves mildly. "Stuck."

Once again I am amazed by the trivia in her keeping, bits of her life that surface and drift off. They are like the heat waves in the distance, a mirage of substance that dissolves as you approach.

"Well, what can we do about it?"

"Don't know. Just telling you what it is." She settles lower into her seat, and it is that simple act of acceptance that makes me explode.

"Well then, it's a fucking useless piece of information, isn't it?!?" I am screaming, incredibly hot and screaming. "We are going to die out here! Open your eyes!! Look around!! There is nothing! Nothing!! We are going to die, Ruth! We should have never left New York. New York has people, people and cars and restaurants and Diet Coke and gas stations where someone actually knows what they're talking about! That's it! That's it, Ruth! Take a little nap. Have a snooze. Too bad if you wake up dead! Vapor lock! Fuck!! Fuck! Fuck! Fuck! We were so close." Now I am whimpering. I can't think of anything else to say; I am ashamed of what I've already said. It is not her. It is not her vapor lock. It is something else, something looming and horrible, and I can't focus in on it because the picture will be too sharp, too final. I rest my head on the steering wheel between my hands and instantly sweat is released. It runs down my nose and into my eyes. It stings. "I hate machines. If Mark were here, he'd probably know what to do. I hate Mark. I hate myself." Ruth is watching me, impassive in her car seat, eyes still sleepy and calm. I am sobbing, a slippery, wet mess. She will not want me anymore, not want to be my mother, not want to be my traveling companion.

She opens the door and slips out of the car. I think she is walking away, but instead she goes around to the rear of the car and opens the hatch back. I watch her in the

174

rearview mirror as she pulls out a blanket. She opens my door and closes the blanket into the top of it; she drops the other end of the blanket and walks off into the desert. I can't see her now because the blanket blocks my view. I won't have to watch her go. I hear the sound of her feet crunching the dirt and rocks, lessening as she leaves. The soft steps pause and start again, then pause, and here they are, getting louder, returning to me. The relief makes me shiver in the baking car. She is tugging at the blanket, angling it away from the car window, making a lean-to with it and two heavy rocks she has carried from the distance. She leans her head into the car.

"Climb out the other side and come over and sit under here. Cooler. You'll cook in there."

I do as I'm told.

Homeless people are monarchs of the makeshift. They can create a habitat from a box, from a tarp, from a piece of rotted plywood and the side of a dumpster. They know the rain shadow of a building and the lee side of an alleyway almost by instinct, almost as if the knowledge had seeped into their skin along with the filth and the certain danger of the street. They are seldom stingy with their space. I have seen them wave an unknown friend into their box, have photographed them there, two lean and filthy bodies settled into a two-foot square, waiting with the patience of Buddha, for the rain to stop.

I sit down beside Ruth in the plaid patterned shade. It is cooler than the car. A breeze ruffles the blanket and dries my sweat until my skin feels stiff and immovable. To the left and right of us is the verge of the endless road, glimpses of red monuments worried into fantastic shapes by wind and time. They are like the homeless, adaptive, resolute to remain. I am small next to them.

"Ruth," I whisper. "I'm so sorry."

She grunts in response.

175

"I brought you all this way, and now we're stuck here. We were almost there, almost, almost home, and now we're stuck. I'm so stupid. I don't know why I did this . . . I don't know why I always . . . I'm so stupid. You must hate me."

She is looking at me with her eyes that are like this desert, bright and hard and waiting.

"I don't hate you," she says. "You brought me all this way."

When she says it, the words are turned around, and I can glimpse that it has been a gift, this trip, a gift that even my anger and blubbering can't destroy. Here is another bit of her, shimmering and distant. I want it to be real.

She does it then. She reaches out across the heated desert air between us and puts an arm across my back. It isn't a hug, really; there isn't a contraction of muscles, an additional emphasis of affection, a gathering close. This is as far as she is willing to go. It is enough.

"It's not the vapor lock," she tells me. "You're scared 'cause it's almost over. You're worried about getting there."

She is right. There is a click as if the shutter has opened, and I can see, colored truths that harden into black and white. For the last few nights now, when I lie down next to her in cheap motels, and close my eyes, I see flashes of New York, snapshots of the two of us at restaurants or at home, sitting on the couch watching TV, our naked feet side by side on the coffee table amid popcorn crumbs and drying sweat rings from our glasses of milk. I fall asleep and dream of us. In my dream, I go over and over our time together, our trip, and it is a line of photos that almost fills the walls of a gallery. I pace the gallery, back and forth, back and forth, past the pictures, stopping to examine them then moving on, my steps stopping and starting, echoing in the empty space. I am alone with my steps and my photos. It is a sign of a good photographer, a true artist, when you stand and stare and want to get into a photo. More than anything you want to be absorbed into it; you want its cool surfaces, its lines and shadows to be your home.

We sit in silence together for a long time before I tell her, "When we were growing up, I was always the one to come up with the ideas, the plans of what to do, how to terrorize the daily help, the Marias, how to skip out of school . . . I would come up with the plan, and before I could have even a second thought, Ellie would be half a mile ahead, doing it. I was always catching up. This is the very first time I've ever done it all by myself, but it still feels like I'm catching up. I don't know what to do."

She is right. It is that simple. I have ended my travelogue. It has been days since I emailed anyone. I don't want to go home, bringing my little offering, my twin to Ellie's news. Ruth is more than that now. I want more than that. I want this road, this angled piece of shade, this old woman with her mysterious knowledge and waiting eyes to be my home. We could do it; we are adaptive, resolute. We could go on like this forever.

I look over at Ruth. She is smiling.

"Gotta finish whatcha started," she tells me.

Of course. I will do as I am told. She is my mother. I crawl from beneath our tent.

"Where ya going?" she asks.

I look back at her. "To get my camera. I want to remember this. I want to remember this place, this exact moment."

She nods, leans back and closes her eyes. "Get me some chips while you're at it."

Yes, I think. That will make the picture complete.

ELLIE

$\mathcal{M}$ary is my heroine. This is how I will always remember her. If I were to paint a picture of her, to sculpt her, it would be as Athena, my warrior goddess, armed in gold, wisdom shining from her face, ready to go into battle for a just and noble cause. Me! She is like a character in one of her novels, and I am her sidekick. Together we are an amazing story.

We are almost finished here. The gallery owner has come from Athens, selected what pieces she wants and left. She has admired my fresco, lamented its attachment to the wall. It's worth a fortune, she says. She says she will talk to someone, see if it can be removed and sold. But I told her no. It needs to remain. Its colors have seeped deep into the rock of this house; it is the part of me that remains behind, my gift to this place. What she has not taken, Mary and I have hung or set out on every available surface. My little house has become a museum. We will take the painting of Mark. Mary insists. All that remains are the eggs, one hundred and eighty-seven. They line the walls like little soldiers, weary and bereft. They need a home.

"I can't leave them, Mary."

"We'll think of something," she says and hugs me.

It is market day. The farmers have brought their goods and produce down from the hills. At the edge of the harbor, there is a whole square filled with stalls of trinkets and cheap art for the tourists. The crowds are thick and avid, sunburn-hued Brits and Germans, lean, cool Swedes, loud, brightly clad Americans, all scrumming to buy what they'll later discard. The real business of the market is farther back from the harbor in the warren of narrow streets: vegetables and fruit just picked, barrels of olives, home pressed oil, cheeses, mounds of wild greens and herbs, nervous lambs and kids destined for someone's table. There is bickering and laughter. Every price is negotiable, but every buyer, every seller knows the true worth of each item. Only a fool pays what's initially asked, a fool and my own Mary, that is.

We are shopping for a last supper. Tomorrow we take the boat to Kos, then the plane to Athens, then the plane to L.A. It will take a few days. We don't think of that; we think of what we want to eat. I haggle on Mary's behalf for lamb meat for stew. We buy red wine and garlic, onions, potatoes and carrots. At another stall we get fresh herbs and greens for a salad, at yet another, a thick slice of feta and a small bottle of thick, cloudy olive oil, hand pressed by the wrinkled old farmer's wife whose emphatic nod, toothless grin and waving hands pass as a language between Mary and herself. Mary would like to be adopted by her, but I make her move on. At another stall we pick a round, flat loaf of bread. Putting my hand underneath it, I feel its heart is warm still, a small spot of heat like a secret wish. I stick my nose deep into the cracked crust and breathe in. Someone's hands have shaped this, kilned it. It is art. I have to swallow my saliva. The baby kicks. We are hungry!

At the last stall, we buy five fat tomatoes of a red so intense, so passionate, only the sun and clay and the people of this island could have created it. And there's the rub, as Mary's Hamlet once said. With the land and the sun, the clay and the passion, there are the people. That's where all the trouble lies.

"Putana." It is hissed from behind us. "Mayassa, skila."

We are adjusting our purchases. Mary wants to carry it all. She is balancing a basket on her hip and tugging at two

179

plastic bags that I won't let go of. We turn together. Stavros' mother, flanked as usual by a gaggle of local crows, stands with her fists on her aproned hips, scowling. Mary smiles. Her sweet face is uncertain, suddenly worried.

"Did I not pay enough?" she whispers to me through her smile.

"She didn't sell us anything, Mary. She wouldn't," I tell her. "That's Stavi's mom. She just called me a whore, a witch, and . . ." I think a minute. "A bitch. A nicely placed parting shot, I'd say."

"Oh!" Mary's eyes are round and her face is pink. She's blinking rapidly. She still has that silly smile plastered on her face. "Oh!"

"Mary, it's okay. I'm used to it. It's fine." I pull in my side of the plastic bags to start her moving up the hill towards home. A crowd is forming. They have the eager, hungry faces of wannabe bullies at a fight. "Let's go, Mary."

"Oh! Well that's just—" She lets go, but only of her side of the bags. "She shouldn't—" She's shaking. "Well!" She takes two steps toward the women, turns back to me. "She really said that?" Her eyes are dilated; the smile has slipped, and I think, watch out, mom of Stavros, here comes Mary, big sister of Ellie . . .

I've seen Mary stand up to teachers, to principals and vice principals, to irate neighbors, the police and even once an entire fire squad. She has saved Sarah, Luke and me more times than I can count. She is small and slender and light of color and voice; she is generally placid and quiet, but here is a word to the wise: Don't get between Mary and one of her chicks. Stavros' mom is not wise. She spits. A stream of saliva shoots from between her teeth and lands about six inches from Mary's feet.

"Oh!"

The smile is back on Mary's face. She is trembling, but her back is straight and stiff. She walks toward Stavros' mom, the basket of produce still clutched to her side. Her steps are firm, the first one lands right on top of the glob of spit. She obliterates it. It is beneath her notice. She stops in front of Stavros' mom, grinning ear to ear. Stavros' mom answers her with a scowl and a lifted chin. Mary has turned her attention to the contents of the basket. With one hand she is testing the tomatoes, checking them for ripeness, for heft. She takes her time. Stavros' unwise mom continues to scowl. There is a caw or two from her cohorts. They think they have won. What can this puny, pale creature possibly do or say?

Mary takes the biggest, reddest, ripest tomato and holds it right under Stavros' mom's nose. Mary squeezes and the tomato erupts, covering the woman's face with gobs of mashed fruit, spattering the closest of her cronies. Clear red juice and pulp slide down Mary's outstretched arm. She opens her fingers and drops the mangled tomato at Stavros' mom's feet, then slowly and very, very deliberately, she wipes her hand on the woman's dress and returns to me.

The gasps number about the same as the shouts of laughter, but Mary's unplanned reprisal is executed ten paces from the bright blue front door of the police station, most of the occupants of which are watching, along with about fifty other witnesses. An open and shut case, Mary is dragged off. She does not go peacefully. There is only one thing to do: lug all the groceries up the hill, gather every euro we have between us and bribe the local constabulary.

"This is for her bail," I tell them in Greek. I place a handful of euros on the desk. "More than enough."

"She's a danger!" The sergeant nudges the coins with a plumb finger and shrugs hugely.

Mary is not helping her case. In the back of the little building, she is kicking the door of her cell. The walls vibrate. "I have rights!" she hollers. "Call the embassy! I want a lawyer!"

I put another handful of euros on the desk. It is my last.

"She's not a danger," I say smiling. "She's just a little angry, and besides," I add, "we're leaving tomorrow. We won't be back. Ever." It is the truth, I realize, and suddenly it is just fine by me.

The sergeant eyes the bribe and shakes his head. He reaches below the desk and pulls out a soggy paper bag. Pink-tinged juice drips from the bottom.

"Evidence," he tells me.

I rifle in Mary's purse.

"I have traveler's checks."

DINNER IS superb. We scorn table and chairs and sit on the floor in the middle of the room, watched over by one hundred and eighty-seven eggs. Mary allows me one glass of wine; she allows herself many more. We giggle and drink and eat until we are quiet, replete.

"Look at the way their little bits are all reaching out to us," she says quietly, pointing to a line of eggs with her wine glass.

"What are we going to do about them, Mary? They need us."

Mary scrunches up her half-drunk face. She takes another sip, then another. The third sip stops the wheels turning; her face unscrunches.

"What we need here," she tells me, "is a bit of irony."

We work all night. We cut small squares of paper, and I write out the words "thank you" in Greek script for her to copy. I didn't know she could do calligraphy. I paint a small wild flower on each card as she finishes. The notes are beautiful. We gather the eggs up in bags and set out. It will take many trips. We start at the top. The monastery is pale blue in the moonlight, the shadows deepest black. Small gas lamps light the courtyard. We climb the courtyard stairs and set an egg and a note in front of each monk's cell door. A fat white cat is our only witness. From the monastery we work our way down the streets of the village, each front door of each house. At the priest's house, I leave two with my note, one featureless, smooth and cool blue as the night air, the other with just the hint of a face emerging from the red speckled shell. I save Stavros' house for last. There is only one egg left. It is a large egg, yellow as dawn. From just about the top of it, an arm reaches up, its palm open, its fingers outstretched to the sky. In the palm I place the note and the key to my house. When we are finished, the sky is lightening, and there is no time left to sleep. The ferry will be here in two short hours. We climb the hills behind the town, watch the sea and sky. We watch the coming day.

It is the perfect gift, pregnant with meaning: for each of them, a handful of their little island, shaped by me. They are not a wasteful people. They never turn down a gift, no matter how little they want it. They will find a use for my eggs. I envision egg doorstops and egg paper-weights, colorful, mysterious eggs that lurk just inside windows and beckon to passing tourists. It shall become know as the Island of Ellie's Eggs. Each of them shall have a little piece of me, and they will keep it, because they are a thrifty people. They know the true worth of everything, even the things they bargain away. I am a gift. I will be with them always.

MARK

*S*ome days it feels as if I have been here forever. Whole days pass in which Dad sits for hours on end without moving or saying anything. On these days I am the anxious one, unable to focus on anything of import, nervous in the face of his silence, incapable of coming up with one thing to say. What can we talk about? We exist in different galaxies. The distance between is too far. So I sit with my *Quotable Einstein* on my lap. Occasionally I read a quote to him; his eyes move to my lips. No response. Other days he is unable to settle, is constantly on the move, worrying the floorboards with his shuffling. The rest of the time we muddle through. This is the delicate stasis we have reached. We have a schedule and rules, which I follow and Dad ignores, or doesn't even know exist. He is dictated to by his urges and I by him, and what looks to be utter confusion and disorder is actually a system. The mathematics is there. A recent, gleaned quote from Einstein: "One thing I have learned in a long life: that all our science, measured against reality, is primitive and childlike— and yet it is the most precious thing we have." Applicable, I think. I am in charge.

Luke and his girlfriend, Willow, are moving into the carriage barn, if moving in consists of a mattress, a hibachi grill and six marijuana plants. The rest of the numerous, carefully packed boxes are Luke's mobiles, hundreds of them. The girl, Willow, set about settling in immediately. She is, as Mary feared, pierced and tattooed, but she is equally unafraid of dust, spiders and hard work. She is a balance of interesting forces, much like Luke's mobiles, alive with movement, and I see Luke's eyes and feet are constantly drawn to her. She has two traits in total accordance with Dad. One, when she speaks, she is almost wholly incomprehensible, and two, she has a tendency towards disrobing which is inappropriate and disconcerting. Luke doesn't seem to notice, and the three of them get along extremely well.

I offer this example of my first conversation with her which will, I think, convey the extent of my meaning, not to mention my discomfiture:

Clouds of dust are rolling out of the open doors of the carriage barn one morning as Dad and I return from our walk. We decide to investigate. I know Luke plans to move in, but I have hoped it will wait until after Mary's return. Alas, no, it now seems. Luke is nowhere to be found, but the girl, Willow, is there, barely visible in the dirt she is raising from the carriage barn floor.

"Hey!" she hollers when she perceives us standing in the door, and begins waving about the air with her broom. When the dust settles, it becomes quite clear that she is wearing nothing but one of those women's undergarments that seem to have no visible back to them, and nothing on top at all. I will not go into the number, placement and scope of piercings and tattoos she sports. I will only say that Ray Bradbury's Illustrated Man has nothing on Luke's Willow. I am rightfully speechless; I believe Dad makes a low whistle.

She must notice, because she laughs and says, "I'm naked, well, except for dust."

She drops the broom with a clatter that makes both Dad and me jump, and begins scrubbing at herself and shaking her head. When she finishes, she is indeed less dusty, though no less alarming. Dad steps behind me, and we both take half a dozen steps back. She pursues us, thrusting out her hand.

"I'm Willow. Remember me? We met in prison!"

Dad, astounded and charmed, steps out from behind me. "Oh yes! I remember that! That was fun!"

Willow laughs outright and hugs him, lets him hug her back too tightly, and doesn't let go until he is ready. An imprint of her body in dust and wood shavings is sketched on his shirt and trousers when they step apart. She turns to me, and quite frankly I am panicked that she might accord me the same greeting, but instead she grabs my hand and pumps it.

"Willow," she says grinning. "Prison."

"Indeed," was all I can manage in return.

At this point she bends over to retrieve the broom. I am in the process of questioning the utility, indeed the comfort, of backless underwear when she catches me staring and has this to say:

"You're probably wondering why I'm naked cleaning, but I'm naked a lot, so that's the way I am, because I feel that the human body is a naked vessel, kind of like a canvas, and what we put on it means a lot, and like I think we should show the original artwork, man. I mean this is the way I am, man. The air needs to circulate over the skin. The wind needs to touch us. The cosmic wind of truth isn't going to find us if we're hiding in clothes! Clothes can suffocate you, man. Don't get me wrong, 'cause I wear clothes, just not many, thank you sunny California! I mean, why wear clothes, especially when you're cleaning, 'cause it's way easier to hose off a body than scrub a bunch of dirty clothes, and anyway, I'd have to sit around naked and wait for them to dry 'cause I only have a couple things to wear anyway. What do you think, good logic, huh?"

I nod. There is really nothing else to do. Other than a vague reference to the cosmos somewhere toward the middle, the entire speech is completely incomprehensible.

"I bet you always wear clothes," she says with her wide, white-toothed smile.

This I can answer: "Always."

However, what she says has obviously struck a cord with Dad. He collapses to the ground and tugs his shoes and socks off, reaches for his belt. Chaos. Enter Luke, yard right, with a huge, elderly dog, black, tan and white, who is overjoyed to see us all, despite the obvious fact that, other than Luke and the mostly naked Willow, we have never set eyes on each other. He lumbers over and jumps all around me, then discovers Dad. He drops his fat rear end down next to Dad, who is still disrobing, and the two of them stare at each other, both with huge grins. The dog licks Dad's entire facial surface, and Dad, in return, throws his arms around the dog.

"Jack!"

Of course.

"Well, his name is Mutt kind of," Willow says, but she is smiling a loopy, sad smile, and her eyes are shining and wet as she watches Dad and the dog. "Only kind of, though, 'cause that's what I named him when I found him, 'cause that's what he is . . ." Her voice diminishes as she speaks, until at last she says in a throaty whisper, ". . . a mutt. Jack's a better name. It's a real name, like he belongs or something. Let's call him Jack."

And it is settled.

"Hi, guys." Luke stands there, bemused and untethered as Dad. He smiles at Willow in open accomplishment. "I'm back."

It seems they are staying.

Mark and Daddy,
Will be arriving two days from tomorrow late.
Much love to all. Can hardly wait to be home.
  Love and kisses,
  Mary and Ellie
P.S. Have you heard from Sarah?

I AM standing right next to him when he slips and falls. I am running a sudsy sponge over his nether parts, which he considers a form of painful torture. I could not be gentler without actually not touching him, and the fact of the matter is he has to be cleaned, but he complains, whimpers, howls sometimes. Luke and Willow are downstairs making breakfast. There is the smell of French toast drifting to the upper landing that is quite enticing. I am unclear whether this is what distracts me or whether it is the large soap bubbles that slide down his back which have caught my attention. The mathematics involved in the structure of a bubble is enormously complex and fascinating. In fact, it is believed that the distribution of matter in the universe has the characteristic of soap bubbles and filaments, the soap bubbles consisting of large areas of low density gases of cold dark matter. The structures of nature exist on every level from the subatomic to the cosmic. A comforting thought. That is what I am thinking, and then he is no longer there.

It is as if some great interior shift in balance has happened inside of him, and he is suddenly feet in the air, first buttocks, then back and finally head down on the tile of the shower. The crash is enormous, the following silence just as large, overwhelming the tinny sound of the running water, the soft drum of running feet on the stair. Soap bubbles knocked free of their moorings float in the void where he has stood. First the dog, then Luke and Willow are in the shower with me. We kneel in suds, water spattering over our backs. Dad's eyes flutter open, and my lips stop moving. I realize I have been praying.

Einstein has quite a bit to say about God, though none of it conclusive, I must admit. I have always considered myself a disinterested agnostic, assumed Einstein to be the same. God's existence has little relevance to me, to my life, my work. I have always felt that if physics could prove that God existed, then perhaps he (or she, I beg your pardon, ladies!) would hold more interest for me. At times, Einstein seems to be a believer, at others not. However, in my current perusal of his quotes, these three stand out to me: "What really interests me is whether God could have created the world any differently; in other words, whether the requirement of logical simplicity admits a margin of freedom." "To assume the existence of an unperceivable being . . . does not facilitate understanding the orderliness we find in the perceivable world." "Isn't all philosophy like writing in honey? It looks wonderful at first sight, but when you look again, it is all gone. Only the smear is left." Ah yes, Einstein, but now answer me this. Why do we sometimes pray?

Dad seems okay. His eyes can track, his arms and legs move on cue. Strangely, he suddenly knows Luke's face and name; however, as per current and every changing norm, he doesn't know his own. We pull him upright, and Willow rubs him down first with a wet towel to remove the remaining soap, then with a dry towel that she tugs from beneath the newly renamed Jack's haunches.

"Warm," Dad smiles down at the dog, then winces, and we almost lose him again as he reaches up shaky arms to wrap around his, no doubt, throbbing head.

There is a trip to Medcenter, an emergent care facility. There are x-rays, a CAT scan, an alertness test, a general physical, and a medical history. There is tapping with a small rubber hammer, listening with a stethoscope. A diagnosis emerges. Dad has had a fall. He is a sixty-six-year-old white male who is unharmed and remarkably physically healthy. He has all the classic symptoms of advanced, early onset Alzheimer's disease. He will have a terrible headache and will be sore and stiff for at least a few days. There is nothing to be done for the Alzheimer's. No surprises. We go home. We feed him ibuprofen and put him to bed, where he curls up into a fetal position and closes his eyes. Luke and Willow wander downstairs to finish our long overdue breakfast. Jack and I stay. We each take a side of the bed, Dad in the middle. We both watch Dad intently. Occasionally, Jack turns his attention to me. I sense a certain sad disappointment in his gaze. I sigh. Jack sighs.

What we don't know in this world is prodigious, whether it is God's existence, or the fate of the universe, or the simple reason for the structure of a bubble. A sudden shift in balance, a man falls, a bubble pops, and in an instant the world is different. Something is lost. We know a little less.

Luke and Willow return, Willow leading, carrying the butter balanced on a pitcher of syrup, and in the other hand, a carton of orange juice. Luke follows with a serving tray heaped with plates of French toast and empty glasses. Dad rises to the smell. We all sit on the bed, Jack included, and have a midday picnic. Dad smiles, wincing as he chews.

"I have a terrible headache. I don't know why I have such a terrible headache," he tells us and offers Jack another piece of toast from the end of his fork.

Hello all,
Mom and I expect to reach LA in the next day or
two and will see you all soon after. We lingered a
bit in Arizona, but are now once again on our way.
Sarah

Luke and Willow, this added coefficient, settle in and suddenly our days change. Dad spends time with them. He wanders in and out of the carriage barn unhindered by closed doors with the dog padding at his heels. Luke has shown surprising foresight by hanging all of Dad's woodworking tools out of reach in the rafters. Willow talks at Dad in her inexplicable language, and Dad nods and smiles.

He digs up Mary's flowers, and Luke follows behind, carefully replanting. He and Luke sit on the back steps and stare into the yard in a silence of perfect accord. When they sit and are too quiet too long, or when they become restless and wander the precincts of the yard in aimless agitation, Willow reins them in. She sets them to work with a made-up repair project, some small bit of cleaning, a dog walk around the block, an errand to the store and back. She is watchful and gentle and fiercely protective. Mary would approve.

They are hanging the last of the mobiles. The eaves of the carriage barn drip with reflected light. There is a job for everyone. Luke lifts the fragile mobiles from the box, carefully disengaging any tangles and hands them one at a time to Dad. Dad holds them up to Willow, who stands on a ladder, nails between her teeth, hammer in hand, piercing the eaves and hanging each mobile. I sit on the step with my *Quotable Einstein*. It is my job to watch, to offer eyeballed adjustments in distances between mobiles. It is evidently Jack's job to hold me to my post, to sit on my feet and pant at me, to drool on my left knee.

Luke is wearing his coveralls, Dad a pair of boxers and dress socks, and Willow is wearing something comprised of strings and holes, the surface area of which, when added together, might equal a square of toilet paper. The dog and I are clearly overdressed for the occasion. Dad's ensemble allows a stunning view of his bruises, black and a deep bloody purple. They run the length of his spine, tattletale tattoos that scream abuse, but don't seem to bother him.

Luke bends over the box, reflected light from the slivered aluminum spiking up into his face. Dad stands with both his arms raised, a mobile swaying from each hand, and Willow leans back, one slender arm grasping the ladder, the other reaching out and down, tattoos singing its length, to catch the upraised mobile. The wind stirs.

The mobiles come alive; they whisper and stir. Fractals of light scatter and dance off eaves and walls, off arms and faces and dazzled, blinking eyes. Spectrums of color slip across the air. Dad laughs.

He looks over his shoulder to me. "Look, Peter, look! Look at the light!"

Here is another quote of Einstein's: "Even old age has very beautiful moments."

Mark:
I will leave here by 6, so that I can be with you no later than noon. Shall I bring lunch?
  With much love and anticipation,
  Clare

CLARE IS finally coming. She will be here tomorrow, and I am not ready. The stack of books and videos that I had hoped to use as tutorials, or at least as reference, have remained in the shopping bag in which they came. I have gone to bed each night exhausted, then lain awake minutely calculating the next day's activities. I don't know how Mary does it all. Frankly, I'm not even sure how she keeps him in clothes. He has flummoxed me, yet Mary seemed always on top of things here, and with time to spare to micromanage, via telephone or email, all of our lives, too. Were there times when she called in panic or confusion, and I didn't notice? I consider myself an acutely observant person, and yet I begin to wonder. Does the oboe go unplayed? Are the books stacked neatly on their shelves, dusted weekly, but never read? Mary, all this time I have counted you as the one in the center, the one who has looked up into the sky and watched us rocket away. I have always thought of you as being there when we returned. Now I see that though you have been here all along, you are distant, too, an isolated outpost of the universe, traveling a lonely course, waiting to be found.

There is a supposition held by some of my colleagues and aptly named The Big Crunch. It is an extension of the Big Bang theory that contends that the universe will not expand indefinitely, that it will reach some point of maximum distance and then will reverse its course. It will collapse. They conjecture it has happened before, will happen again and again, a continual process of expansion and contraction for eternity. Herein lies another metaphor. I will be more careful with them from here on. I see now I have played with metaphors from the safety of science, but proximity changes the game. Our universe is collapsing. Each wandering star is coming home: Luke, Mary, Ellie and Sarah . . . these other elements, too, this woman Ruth, Luke's Willow, and my lovely Clare. I have come home. For perhaps just this once, I am at the center. It will be a complex configuration, chaotic in fact, but calculable, not beyond my powers. I will gather them in, order and adjust them, and then once again we will all be on our way.

PART THREE

A CONTRACTING UNIVERSE

FRANK

$\mathcal{A}$ whole bunch of us live here. There are seventeen or twenty-three. The boys live way up on the top floor and the girl on the middle floor and there is a whole floor for Peter and me and Jack. When my parents decided to move to the mountains, I had to get rid of Jack, but now he lives here with a whole bunch of us. I don't know what we're going to do about dinner. Did we already have it? Sometimes I forget. That girl will tell me. She's the one. When my parents moved to the mountains she took over. No hugging, that was the rule. No hugging, no hugging the dog, no dog. She said it's not good to get too close to anything. That's why my parents moved to the mountains. They're way up there, but I can visit any time. They grow their own food way up there.

I don't know what we're going to do about dinner.

MARK

I can see that arrivals are very much like the testing of a theory. What one has surmised will happen will either be proved true or not, in which case, it is time for another theory.

Clare is the first to arrive, with lunch as advertised, the smell of Panang Chicken, Pad Thai, Satay and Tom Gai soup preceding her to the door. The doorbell rings, and I am unable to speak or to rise from the couch where I am sitting with Dad. I fear it is as Himmel explained. I am suffering from juvenile longing. In my particular case, the symptoms are acute. The doorbell rings again, and Jack starts barking from the backyard. I am beginning to feel a tightening in my chest, a churning in my stomach, when Dad rises to answer the door. Tiny spots like fermions vibrate across my vision. I might pass out. Dad pulls open the door and stands there saying nothing. The protocol of politeness has escaped him long ago, I am sure. I cannot see Clare from the angle of the couch. There is a rectangle of day and in it Dad's slightly stooped back, his large head and the aurora of his chaotic hair blocking the entering light. From the open doorway, there is the extended silence of sizing up. Then Clare.

"Hello. You must be Mr. Bennett. I'm Clare, Mark's friend. You look just like him."

"I don't think we have any Mark . . ."

"Dad!" It is barely a squeak, but it creates enough of a break in the surface tension that seems to hold my body in place. My legs thrust me upright and propel me to the door. No longer words via email, she is here, beautiful, symmetrical, terrifying. We have grown intimate through electrical impulses via a modem, through simple binary code, but she is here now with all her Thai food and complexity, and I have no words for her. I am a blank. In that instant I forget her name.

"Mark," she says, and the tiny black fermions return, arcing through my vision, dragging bits of the light of her smile behind them.

"It is?"

"What?" She is grinning now.

"Your name?"

"I thought we already ate." Dad is looking between us, an uncertain smile creasing his face. "Didn't we?"

From the back of the house we hear the door bang, followed by Willow's ecstatic war cry, "Food!"

"I hope she's clothed," I say to no one in particular. Classic entropy.

Clare is laughing. She puts the carrier bags of food in my arms, turns to Dad and kisses him on the cheek and whispers conspiratorially, "Let's eat again anyway." Then she turns back to me, holds my face in her hands and kisses me. "Oh good," she tells me. "You're just as I left you." She brushes between my dad and me and leads us into the house. I am reminded again of the elemental force of her. I am glad of it. Dad and I follow, drawn into her wake by kisses and gravity.

Dad stage-whispers to me, "We must know her."

Yes Dad, I think we certainly must.

Clare slips into the configuration of our day quite easily. Willow talks all through lunch, something to do with Thailand, where she has never been but knows she would love if she ever did go, and a Thai masseuse whom she seems to have loved a little too well and never should have. Luke says nothing, because he doesn't, and Dad chews noisily because he does. Clare behaves as if we are all quite normal, which is clearly not the case. I sit and listen, watch Clare and gain mastery over my physiologic responses to her. I calculate slowing heart rate, pulse and breathing; I monitor clearing vision. By the end of the meal I should be able to speak in full sentences. I eat Pad Thai and graph the probability of success of this encounter. As Willow's conversation circumnavigates the globe, and seemingly its men, probability drops; but then Clare takes over and tells us about her recent trip and the new Hadron Accelerator. I am able to contribute. Success indicators rise. Willow waxes poetic, though incomprehensible, on the cosmic consciousness and what nuclear explosions do to it. A sharp dip. Dad declares the meal over by suddenly stating, "I have to go!" He proves the matter by voiding in his pants before he can come to a complete standing position. A near vertical drop in probability and the end of the mental exercise, except for this: as I rise to marshal Dad, Clare reaches across the kitchen table and takes my hand and squeezes it, hard and sure.

"Mark, I'm glad to be here . . ." she says. Her fingers slide from my hand. "Come on, Willow, help me with these dishes and we can argue cosmic consciousness."

"Cool enough," is Willow's response, and suddenly, oddly, I am immensely grateful to her, to her distracting tattoos and magenta hair, to her inconsequential jabber and her alarmingly incorrect openness to all things.

"Thank you very much for a very fine meal, Clare," I say. There it is—a whole sentence.

Clare presents a solemn face to me. "You are very welcome, Dr. Bennett."

"Who's Dr. Bennett?" asks Dad. "How did I get so wet?"

Clare and Willow stand up grinning at each other. Willow bends down and smoothes Luke's hair, kisses him on his forehead. He looks up blinking with sudden awareness and smiles.

"Hi," he says. "I'm here."

I think I will leave probability in these women's quick and capable hands.

After lunch, Willow and Luke take Clare to view the carriage barn, and I take Dad to the toilet, change his clothes and settle him down in front of the TV with Animal Planet playing quietly and Jack installed at his feet. Gravity tugs me out towards Clare. The two women stand under the eaves, heads tilted up gazing at mobiles. Clare reaches up a slender arm and delicately nudges a mobile of gray whales clad in brilliant tones of Fanta soda cans. Her face, her hair, her T-shirt and jeans are suddenly alive with threads of light.

"They're wonderful, Luke," she whispers, and her breath stirs the whales further. "Such incredibly perfect negative space. They're miraculous."

Luke beams, smitten now, too. Behind me, the door creaks open and slides back into place; Jack slips past, rump swinging as if he has not seen these people in a millennium at least, and I feel the presence of Dad beside me.

"Mahogany," he says, and by now I have lived with him long enough to not be surprised, to know that it is a compliment, a word from his past that has suddenly lit upon his thoughts at the sight of Clare, lean and strong with casts of Fanta red light racing over her hair. "Good wood," he adds and steps off the porch to join them.

AFTER CAREFUL consideration, I install Clare in one of the twin beds in Ellie and Sarah's room. Ostensibly, the house has five bedrooms: Dad's, Mary's, Luke's (all the furniture of which has been plundered and reestablished in the carriage barn), Ellie and Sarah's, and mine. This does not include the attic bedroom and bathroom that Peter once occupied. No one has used it since his death. For the one night we are alone together, Clare is stationed far enough away from my bedroom to be only slightly less distracting than the satisfied noises that rise from the carriage barn, and occasionally from the lawn, on the summer night air. The bag of books and materials that are as yet untouched are stashed under my bed, but create an imaginary lump that keeps me awake. I am unclear as to why I am unable to approach them. What would Himmel say? Instead, I spend two hours and thirty-two minutes reading through Einstein quotes until he, too, mocks me: "Falling in love is not at all the most stupid thing that people do—but gravitation cannot be held responsible for it." And add this: "I admit that thoughts influence the body." All aspects tallied, it is an extremely difficult night.

THE NEXT morning, Mary calls once from the tarmac as the plane rolls toward the gate, twice while she and Ellie are waiting for their bags and once again while they drive north. She is not happy with me.

"It's fine about Clare, Mark," she tells me four separate times. "I'm glad for the chance to meet her. But this Willow creature? Really, Mark, I told you to take care of that. I bet you haven't even made the appointment for Ellie to see the doctor tomorrow."

"I did," I reassure her. "But Mary, Willow's been—"

I hear Ellie shouting at Mary's cell phone from the distance of the passenger seat, "Who's Willow? Clare's there?! THE Clare?!! I want to talk to Clare, Mark! Clare and I need to talk!"

"Mary, you can't let Ellie talk to Clare. Tell her—"

"Shush," Mary says, presumably to Ellie, since I am talking in a reasonable voice at moderate volume. "And what have you done with Sarah? Why isn't she there yet?"

"Mary, I haven't heard from Sarah since her last, and to my mind, ominous threat that she would be here in a few days."

"Did you email and tell her not to come?"

"Not that time."

"Mark!"

Circumstances proceed from bad to worse as, of course, could have been predicted, when Mary and Ellie pull into the driveway. Ellie immediately lumbers out of the car, insisting, "Where's that Clare?! Hello, Dad! I'm pregnant. Long story." She gives him a peck on the cheek and rushes off before he can react, yelling, "Clare! Where are you hiding?!"

"Hello." Dad smiles into the space where Ellie just stood. He reacts quite differently to Mary; he has no idea who she is, as indeed he probably has no idea who Ellie is, but for Mary, it matters.

"It's your rule, Auntie," he tells her as she tries to hug him, and he backs up.

"Daddy, I'm not her. It's me, Mary." Mary's arms are still stretched towards him.

"Ha!" Dad turns on his heel and stomps toward the backyard.

I watch her face turn an alarming red, and she begins to tremble. She watches his back, then turns to me for an explanation. I am torn between following Ellie and saving my secret and my dignity, or helping Mary. Mary wins this round.

"He calls me Peter, Mary, but he doesn't even know who Peter is anymore. You know he . . . I mean, it's quite normal for Alzheim—" It is the wrong explanation, because now she is angry.

"Shut up, Mark. I don't need your pseudo-expertise and grand theories right now. Just get the bags."

When Mary walks off after Dad, it is with the steps of someone who has lost the feeling of the ground underneath her. I gather Mary's two suitcases, Ellie's six duffle bags and a bulky, flat crate that must house some sort of painting, and muscle everything to the base of the stairs. There is laughter erupting from the kitchen. I have chosen incorrectly. I should have followed Ellie.

WE TAKE a walk on the beach after supper that evening. Clare produces a pair of small, spongy ear plugs for Dad. Mary is impressed. I am pleased. We proceed slowly up Hendry's Beach, a disorganized group. Luke, Willow and Ellie chase the waves and stop to examine any artifact that has washed up. Clare holds my hand and Dad's elbow, and Mary is on the other side of Dad, quietly trying to establish a connection. I am not sure which of them is the more lost. Jack lumbers between the two groups. Our progress is continually impeded by Dad insistently greeting every dog out for an evening stroll. They are all "Jack" to him. A modicum of consistency is always comforting.

"If I'd known he loves dogs, I would have bought a dog," Mary continues with the slightly martyred air since being snubbed by Dad. "I like dogs. I like dogs, and I consider myself a very huggy person!"

"We have a dog now, Mary," I soothe. "We have Jack."

"He's not ours. He's hers." Mary is squinting rather malevolently at Willow, who is standing knee deep in ocean and draping seaweed over Luke and Ellie's shoulders. She has crowned them each with a half clam shell.

"Yes, Mary," I tell her gently. "Jack is Willow's, but it would seem that Willow is ours."

"Look at her, Mark. She's not something anyone would want."

"Perhaps that's her appeal to Luke," I counter.

"Mark—"

"How can we be walking up the beach, and the sun's setting right in front of us instead of off the coast in what ought to be the west?" It is a deliberate attempt on Clare's part to steer the subject in a safer direction, north in fact, which is the direction we should be walking, but

203

we are not. Really, Clare continues to exhibit her exemplary value. The question allows me to explain to her the physical situation of Santa Barbara in relationship to the ordinal directions. Unfortunately, it allows Mary a further opportunity to pout. She is ominously silent, and if one could stomp in the soft sand of Hendry's Beach, she would be stomping every step.

"Look at all those colors," Dad says. "I can't remember what that's called. Sometimes I can't remember things," he confides to Clare.

"Me, too," she tells him, nodding. "Isn't it annoying?"

"What is?" he asks, and the two of them stop to greet a contingent of three Welsh corgis that suddenly puddle and writhe around their shins. Clare and Dad kneel down to accept adulation.

I turn to Mary. She is still scowling at Willow, who, in turn, has found a nest in Luke's arms. The two cling together and walk awkwardly up the beach. Ellie mimics them from a short distance behind, her arms out and around ocean air, stumbling drunkenly, perfectly happy to amuse herself alone.

"I've never known you to be unkind, Mary."

"I have to protect him, Mark."

"That's Willow's job now."

Mary stops and sighs. She stares back the way we have come. Stars are appearing, light from suns that may no longer even exist. Our tracks weave down the beach, disappearing into the coming darkness.

"I'm tired," Mary states. "I want to go home."

Dad has heard her. He rises from a squirming mass of fur and looks around. "Uh oh," he says. "I knew we were lost."

We arrive back at the house to find that Sarah and her counterfeit mother have materialized and installed themselves on the couch, in matching Disney T-shirts and mouse ears no less, and are watching a pay per view movie and eating our leftovers. Honestly, could my family become any stranger? It becomes more obvious to me every day that entropy affects the mental processes as well as the physical world. The entire situation is made more bizarre by the following: Dad steps through the door, sees this Ruth woman and begins to beam.

"There you are!" he laughs. "I've been looking for you!"

"Hi back at you," the Ruth woman replies with what I consider a very cagey answer.

"You're here," Dad says and wraps his arms around the woman. To her credit I must admit she lets him, and in fact, pats him, though gingerly, on his back. He holds onto her for a long time. There is a great deal of hugging and patting while everyone else in the room watches, their faces registering either astonishment, shock, triumph or puzzlement, depending upon their particular mental capabilities and relation to the situation. My face, I believe, must be a mask of incredulity. Dad breaks the spell by trying to kiss the imposter on the lips.

"Whoa there, old boy," she says, stepping back.

"Frank," Sarah prompts her.

"Hah!" I announce my well-placed skepticism.

"Shut up, Quark," Sarah counters.

"Jeanie," Dad croons and effectively shuts us all up.

SARAH AND Ruth disappear upstairs to unpack. I convene an emergency meeting in the kitchen, participation mandatory.

"Now that you're all here," I tell them. "I just want to say—"

"Isn't it amazing?!" Ellie enthuses.

"It's more than amazing," I say. "It's absolutely ridiculous!" One doesn't need to be a Himmel to know what's going on here—evidently I am not the only one who suffers from juvenile longings. I could clear this matter up if they would only listen. They don't.

"Do you think it's possible?" Mary's voice is small and uncertain. Jet lag has quite obviously unhinged her.

"Who is she?" Luke asks. He is either taking over Dad's role, or hasn't been paying attention, both possible and not mutually exclusive.

"Jeanie," Willow helps him, though she has no idea who Jeanie might be.

"Their mom," Clare tells Willow. I have personally kept Clare abreast of each of my family's little dramas, except, of course, my own.

"Our long lost mother!" Ellie cannot be contained. "Of course, it's possible. It's more than possible! It's necessary, it's stupendous, it's perfect! I'm pregnant and Sarah finds Mom!"

"You're pregnant?" Luke says, flabbergasted.

"It's very cool. It's synchronicity, man!" Willow, of course.

"It's almost Dickensian." Only Mary could say this and be pleased by the implication; and indeed, in her low voice I hear it clearly now, the hope, more than a whisper now, a veritable roar. She wears a tremulous smile. Tears threaten.

"Mary, surely you—"

"Mark," Clare places her hand on my arm. "He did seem to recognize her."

Traitor. I give her what I hope she will recognize as a very stern look. Hysteria in the room is on the rise. Everyone is talking at once; the meeting is a shambles.

"It is quite clear to me," I raise my voice above the din, "that no one here is familiar with, or perhaps has forgotten (this for the wavering Clare), the premise behind Ockham's razor." Everyone is staring at me. At last, I have the floor. "Ockham's razor is a credibility test. It's also known as the Law of Economy and the Law of Parsimony. In physics, we

206

use it to eliminate extraneous hypotheses, particularly metaphysical conceits. 'The simpler the explanation, the better,' sums it up, I believe. For example, we have a man, our father, who has Alzheimer's disease, who calls me Peter without remembering exactly who Peter was, and doesn't recognize his daughter—you, Mary—who has lived with him her whole life, and yet recognizes a complete stranger as his wife, Jean, who left nearly thirty years ago. Explanation one: The laws of universal synchronicity (I admit, here, perhaps, I was a little cruel to Willow) place the elderly, runaway, and now derelict mother in the path of her daughter, who just happens to live on the same, and opposite side of the continent as her, and also happens to photograph the homeless as her own personal attempt at expression. The daughter recognizes her and brings her home where the cosmic circle is completed with smiles and hugs for all. Did I mention that the mother, gone all these years, has been held captive by aliens and just replaced on that particular spot on Earth?" I wait for an argument. There is none. They all continue to stare at me. I continue. "Explanation two: she is a stranger, an opportunistic, elderly, homeless person. Dad doesn't know her; he speaks purely from the delusions of a damaged mind." I know I'm on dangerous ground, but I feel I must make them see. "It's just as likely that woman is our mother as it is that Ellie received that child through Immaculate Conception." Now, we are all quiet.

At last, Luke speaks. "I don't get the whole razor thing."

Willow hugs him. "I liked the first explanation."

"Me, too." This from Ellie.

"It's late. I have to figure out where everybody's sleeping," Mary says. Her voice sounds deflated as she leaves the room. I know it is hard, but I feel I have done what I must on behalf of truth, justice, our family and . . . and science.

207

Ellie follows in Mary's wake, mutters as she passes me, "I wouldn't be talking about virgins if I were you."

Luke and Willow, attached as usual, head toward the carriage barn. Luke's voice, muffled against Willow's magenta hair, can be heard, "That was confusing."

"Yah," Willow answers, tugging him through the door. "But kinda cool. Mark's way smart. I think I might have read about that Ockham guy. It all sounded kinda familiar." The back door closes behind them.

Clare turns to me and looks into my eyes. She reaches up and strokes my cheek.

"I'll prove it to them, Clare."

"You're way smart, Mark, but sometimes you're way stupid, too, and a bit mean." She smiles at me, a little sadly it seems. "I'm going to go help Mary."

Meeting adjourned. I am left alone in the kitchen with Friar Ockham and his very bloody razor.

SARAH

"*I* think that went really well!"

I am so excited I am bouncing on my old bed. I feel as if I am eight years old again, and one of my harebrained schemes has gone even better than expected.

"We're in, Ruth! I've brought home the biggest fish. Ellie's baby is nothing to a real life mom! Of course Quark's going to be a jerk. What's new? That Clare seems cool, and way too normal for Quark. How she can stand him, I don't even want to know!" I cannot contain my triumph. "Don't worry about him. I can handle him. Hey! Did you see Luke's girlfriend's tattoos? Stunning! What was her name? Doesn't matter. I wonder how those tattoos would photograph? Oooh, now there's a cool idea! God, I sound like Ellie!" I flop back on the bed and take a big breath and let it out slow and easy. I look over at Ruth. She is perched on the end of Ellie's bed as if she will be asked to get up and leave at any moment. She scratches aimlessly under her Mickey Mouse ears and stares at her shoes and waits for dismissal.

"You're home, Ruth . . . Mom. How does it feel?"

"Humph," Ruth replies, and lifts her head to eye the closed bedroom door. "Where'd you say that bathroom was?"

I'm sure that it's not that she doesn't know. She just doesn't remember. Yet.

MARK

I am relegated to Peter's room. Sarah has claimed the twins' room for her and that woman. Mary will remain in hers; Ellie will take mine. It is unsettling to stand here after so many years. An army of cleaning women, the "Marias," we used to call them, have tidied, dusted and straightened untouched items every Thursday since the date of Peter's death. His school desk, uncluttered and polished, his book cases still filled with the youthful readings, his double bed with its Grateful Dead spread only slightly faded by the sun from the attic windows, on the walls his posters for The Doors, the album *The Wall*, Goldie Hawn go-go dancing on the set of *Laugh-In,* all are signs of a life truncated in the midst of an unfortunate early 70's fetish. Gone, but not a single clue as to why. The grateful dead do not speak. We are left to interpret the leavings and go on from there, an echo of the big bang in our ears. When I look around I see there is nothing to interpret here. It is as I have always suspected. We are the only leavings.

There are strangers with us now, people who have not lived in our skins. They walk through our rooms, see the detritus of our lives, but they do not have our history. I suspect that Willow, tattooed and pierced, replete with her own ether-filled theories, has had her own cataclysmic past; and certainly this homeless woman of Sarah's, this Ruth who now sleeps among us, harbors some terrible loss. Surely, no one chooses the street. What do they think of us as they look at us now, packed together in this place of memory, all of our idiosyncrasies rubbing up against each other, causing friction. We are odd, even I have been considered somewhat odd on occasion. Hence, Himmel. Do they understand why we are . . . we? What does Clare think of us? What does she think of me?

MARY

"*I* know he's kind of odd, but he means well . . ." I am holding one side of a clean sheet and snap the rest out over Mark's bed. Clare catches it as it floats toward her. The two of us force it down over the trapped air above the double bed.

Clare smiles as she tucks in her corner.

"I just didn't want you to think he was always so bossy and . . . well, kind of lecturing all of the time." Mark is ours and we love him, but I am not sure how the rest of the world takes him. I concentrate on my side of the bed, but even with my head ducked behind the bed, I can hear Clare chuckling.

"But, Mary," Clare's head suddenly pops up from her side of the bed. She is smiling. "He is! He's Mark."

I am so tired, so raw, this relief feels like cool water running over my skin. Here is an opening, a chance to explain. I grin. "Oh Clare, he has always been so difficult. It's just terrible how awkward he is all the time. I want him to be less . . . Mark, but then that would be such a sad thing, and, anyway, he can be so . . . so very sweet. . . ."

Clare is stuffing a pillow into its case while I do the same with its mate. Clare shakes her head. "I know that, too. I just don't get it . . . he's so infuriating . . . but then I . . ." Clare shrugs. "He's . . . so endearing . . . and somehow . . . I . . ." She smiles helplessly.

"He tries very hard." I can't help it, my voice sounds encouraging. "And, then he's so very brilliant. Brilliant people can sometimes be so . . ."

"Infuriatingly right?" Clare poses it as a question.

"He means well," I try to sum up.

W stare at each other for what Mark would calculate as approximately three quarters of a minute. That is all it takes. We are laughing. My laugh is near hysteria; Clare's is rich and deep and full of this new, shared understanding of all the disparate, glorious parts that make up my brother. Listening feels good. Among all the sharp, unspoken subjects in this family, this one has been blunted, smoothed. It is workable. We run our capable hands over the sheets until every wrinkle is gone, then tuck edges firmly under the mattress. We pound and mold the pillows, then replace them, plump and inviting at the head of the bed. Finally, the duvet is shook out and stretched and folded at the bed's foot. We stand back to admire our work, smile and link arms. The perfectly made bed. We are up to any task.

"Ellie should be very comfortable," I say.

"Where do you want me tonight?" Clare asks.

I know about the carrier bag of books beneath the bed. I noticed them when I brought Ellie's duffles upstairs. I looked through them and put them back. Research. My poor Mark. How does Ellie know these things? Honestly, this family. I am always catching up. I will let this one go, will let it loose in the world. Mark will be okay. He is in safe hands.

"Look under the bed," I tell Clare. "Then decide."

I can hear the crinkle of unfolding plastic as I leave the room, then minutes later, even over the sound of water from my faucet, Clare's warm laughter.

MARK

Clare arrives at the top of the attic stairs carrying her suitcase in one hand and my bag of instructional materials in the other. I am reduced to instant confusion, extreme embarrassment. I am speechless, sweating, trembling, miserable. I fear for my health, my sanity. This is not as I have planned. Oh entropy, can't you just give me a break? Can't you just leave me out of the equation this once? Clare places her suitcase on Peter's desk. She brushes past me and goes to the window with the bag of books. She sets the bag on the floor and bends over, carefully opening the bag, slowly pulling out the top item. She is so graceful, so beautiful; the moon through the window reflects in her hair. She is a source of light, a distant star, unreachable, speeding away. She straightens, her eyes on the book in her hands. From below I hear Willow's laughter, Luke's, "Give me some covers." They are nesting under the stars. Clare smiles.

"*The Art of Masturdating: A Guidebook for Single Heterosexuals.* Who writes this stuff? I don't think so, Mark." She tosses the book out the window.

I hear the book hit the roof slates. There is clatter, sliding, then the silence of the drop.

From below: "Ow! Hey!" Luke's voice.

Clare raises an eyebrow. She has two more books in her hands, and reads aloud the titles, "*The Feminine Mystique, The Kinsey Report . . .*" She reaches back into the bag. "On video, too, no less."

Out the window they go. Clatter, slide, silence.

"Hey! Hey! What the fuck?" The outdoors protests.

I think I might throw up. Where is a black hole when you need one?

"*What Women Want Men to Know* . . . I'll look through it and let you know." She drops the book back into the bag, grabs another, a video. "*What Women Want.* Oh Mel, you're all that women want," Clare croons. "You're better looking than him, Mark, taller, maybe smarter, though now I'm questioning that." She drops the video into the bag, collects the last two offerings. "*The Girls' Guide to Hunting and Fishing.* I actually read that. I think you need to be kept in the dark, there." She launches the book.

From below, "Come on you guys! Give us a break!" Luke.

The fermions have returned to my vision. They weave and dart, vibrate like the strings of my grand theory. The rest is darkness. Clare is relentless.

"*A Very Lonely Planet: Love, Sex and the Single Guy.* Definitely not." The book sails through the night air.

"Ow! Shit! What the hell?"

"Get a flashlight, Luke." Willow speaks.

Clare laughs. She has one last book. She opens it, runs her fingers over the illustrations, ancient, intricate, richly colored. She flips a few gold-leafed pages, walks towards me carrying the open book. "Now this," she whispers as she passes. "This we can use."

There is light and movement in the yard below.

"Holy cripes, Luke!" Willow hollers. "Cha-ching! Jackpot! Manna from heaven! Eureka!"

Clare smiles and sits down on the bed, pats the spot beside her. Remarkably, some shreds of motor function remain to me. I do as I'm bidden.

From below, Luke's comment is decidedly muffled. "Must be Ellie."

"Bless her, baby! Oh man, are we gonna have some fun!"

"Now that," Clare says as she leans toward me, "is what I'm talking about."

W‍HEN A‍RCHIMEDES discovered the means by which to determine the proportions of base metal in Hiero's golden crown by using specific gravity, he uttered this triumphant exclamation: Eureka! "I have found it." *The Oxford English Dictionary* states the correct spelling is actually heureka, though admits to its rarity. With my apologies to the *OED*, I choose the popular rendition.

Eureka! I must echo the ancient and eminent scientist as well as the delightfully ignorant but prophetic Willow. Eureka!! I have found it. Gravity—specific, general, special. Clare's gravity is no longer an unknown. I must dig up my *Quotable Einstein* from the couch downstairs. Clare and I will peruse its pages together. What has he to say of this phenomenon? I think he would be proud of me. I know I am. I am renewed, invigorated. My theories are intact. I look forward to the challenges of tomorrow, and the successes they will bring. Oh, Willow, you are so right, my girl. Cha-ching!

This note left taped to the refrigerator:

Wake up sleepyheads! Mom and I are
dropping Ellie off at the doctor's then going
grocery shopping. This fridge is totally empty!
Sarah

Below it, this message also taped:

Everybody still asleep so Luke and me got
Frank up and took him for a picknick at the rose
gardens at the mission. He likes roses. Back soon.
Willow

This message left on the answering machine that same morning:

Holy shit!!! Twins!!!! TWINS!!! Holy shit!!

216

MARK

*I*t seems as if we have returned to a time before the Big Bang. We are remarkably compacted here. Too compacted. Drama simmers. The inestimable Himmel would have a field day. I observe and wait for the explosion, my participation minimal. Mary watches Willow with a cold, hawk-like eye, despite the fact that Willow remains as always, oblivious, virtually naked and vociferously cheerful. Willow has taken to selling Luke's mobiles at the biweekly farmers' market downtown. In the past two weeks she has made a surprising amount of money. She dutifully hands it over for groceries and rent to Mary, who scowls and gives it to Luke who gives it to Willow. Clare came up with the idea and helped Willow with the business license. My Clare! Ellie teaches Clare the twins' Double Talk. Clare's quite amused with the language and as adept as one would assume her to be. I hide my annoyance and listen. What will I hear?

Sarah feeds her erroneously assumed mother as if the old woman and not Ellie was the one about to give birth. Sarah is in an artistic frenzy. She has taken to photographing all aspects of Willow, a definite step up from her homeless oeuvre. She has commandeered one of the upstairs bathrooms (mine, in point of fact, as one would guess knowing Sarah) and is in the process of extensive preliminary developing. The Ruth woman assists. Her residence here continues to irk, but I have taken steps, this letter sent yesterday:

July 14, 2006

Paternity and Genetic Solutions, Inc.
2104 Wilshire Blvd., Suite 707
Los Angeles, Ca 90314

Attn: Lab Consultants

Dear Sirs:

    Enclosed you will find in separate Ziploc
bags, hair from myself (whose paternity,
of course, is unquestioned) and a Snickers
wrapper from the woman currently living among
us and claiming to be our missing mother. I am
certain of both samples. Indeed, I am the one
who offered the woman the candy bar, having
first warmed it in my hands so that much of the
chocolate coating would adhere to the wrapper.
She is remarkably and continually ravenous.
I knew she would lick the wrapper and supply
an adequate DNA sampling. I am quite pleased
with my ingenuity, to be quite honest. I look
forward to a test result that will confirm
what can be the only statistical certainty.
The imposter will be unmasked! I add only that
this is a matter of some urgency. I await your
speedy response.

Sincerely,

Mark Bennet, Ph.D.

Enc.

ELLIE GROWS; she is her own expanding universe, evidently
expecting the birth of twin galaxies. Her moods have
swung from chaotic and occasionally ecstatic, to moody,

morose and an exceedingly unattractive bitter. When Sarah is busy, Ellie feels neglected. She paces and mutters. She puts her hands to her belly and stares at us with tragic eyes. She drags Dad on frenetic walks from which he comes home tired and confused. Mary warns us we must be gentle and do as she says. Mary tut-tuts, juggles the mood swings, soothes the feelings, puts words in all of our mouths that we would never be willing to say to each other. She begins to fray, like the pages of an over-used reference book. She's coming apart.

Dad, Luke and I are relegated to the periphery, our orbits far-flung and inconsequential. We bump against the walls and each other, and feel the discomfort of traveling too close to the gravitational mass of women. They set us to work or set us spinning off, feeling unwanted. It is a remarkably big house, but there is too much contact. Our molecules collide. Yes, I expect an explosion soon. I would decamp to the north and get back to much neglected work if it were not for Clare. She is here, inexplicably enjoying herself among the strange and volatile assemblage. So, I am here. Hers is the heavenly body that draws me.

Sarah

Ann,
How is everything at the gallery? I am working on
something truly incredible here, a single subject:
Willow, my brother's girlfriend. She's young and
absolutely beautiful and covered in tattoos! Each
tattoo has history! Now don't make faces at this
email—don't judge. I've enclosed a file with some
of the photos. I know you'll agree, but let me
know anyway.
    Best,
    Sarah

She has a tiny, delicate strand of barbed wire that rings her left areole, her nipple is pierced. When I use a macro lens I can see the exact edge of each tattoo, the precise line where ink gives way to pale skin, each tiny hair, each pore, the way the skin has healed around each piercing, yielding to the wound, making it art. Willow up close and personal. I shoot her sitting nearly naked in the lawn chair eating a lime Popsicle, snuggled with Luke sharing a joint (better not show Mary that one), at the kitchen sink, illustrated arms sunk to the elbows in soapy water. I get in close and photograph every inch of her. Sometimes I think if I zoom in enough I'll see just how deep the staining goes. I tried black and white, and I'll probably keep some of those photos for contrast, but Willow is a full color subject. It isn't just the tattoos, their vibrant, carefully rendered hues; it isn't the flamboyant crop of wild hair or the sparkling array of studs and rings. It's the tender pink young-girl skin, flawless, lineless; it's the sparse constellation of tiny tan freckles across her nose and shoulders, and the unblinking, open clarity of her light blue eyes. Every inch of Willow is a snapshot of her life. She points and laughs and fearlessly matches stories to the art of her body. Ruth hands me lenses and nods and even sometimes grins in understanding. When I look at them together, I see the ways that they are the same. It is as if the aperture has been held open too long. They are over exposed; life has singed them. I will show it. We are creating something, the three of us. I envision a gallery exhibition, a book. The photos will be textural, almost painful, tender as newly pierced skin. People will want to reach out, to touch, to protect each inch of revealed skin and ink. When I hold the camera in my hand, I can feel how each picture will be. My fingers tingle. It's that immediate. The collection will be extraordinary, truthful. Even Mary will see Willow's beauty.

ELLIE SULKS. She doesn't have a reason. She is the one who trumped me. Twins always trump a missing mom that no one seems to have missed anyway. Except me. Isn't that the great game of our childhood—twins conquer all? We didn't need anyone but each other. We shared a skin, a face, bones. We used to switch places, and no one could tell. Except me. She always wanted, had, first choice; she rushed ahead, was the first to do, the first to be. She wants to go back, wants to speak our old secret language. She would like to switch places like we used to, but things are different now. She envies the camera in my hands; she envies my art, my freedom. Sometimes I catch her watching me, watching us. If I took a picture of her at that exact moment, would I catch the sharp spike of jealousy in those eyes that mirror my own? She doesn't have a reason, but I am her twin. I know just how she feels.

Sarah,
I was skeptical until I saw them, but you are right. The photos are wonderful—a touch of Mapplethorpe maybe, yet something else there too—vulnerability is the word that comes to me unbidden. It's a new direction for you. I sense something big here, Sarah, for both you and the gallery. Good luck to you in this and hurry home. We need to talk timeframe and space. I want to see more!
Best,
Ann Hulse, Naked Eye Gallery New York

MARY

I don't need pictures of that naked girl plastered all over the walls. One thing's for certain—we are now all quite aware of what Luke sees in her . . . of her. I need those pictures gone. No, that's not the only thing I need. I need Sarah to step back from the "major talent" role and help out a bit. I need Ellie to drop the "tragic queen" pose. I need Mark to alternately stop mooning over Clare and telling me what to do. I don't need hired help with Daddy, Mark, and it doesn't matter who the hell Ruth is! Mind your own business. I need the excellent Clare to take him away. I need Ruth to stop eating. It's astounding, and honestly the only reason I truly doubt her connection to this family. None of us has ever eaten like that. Scratch that last thought. I like Ruth. She is an ancient Oliver Twist. "More, please." It's strangely endearing, really. Ruth can stay the same. In fact, Ruth, go ahead, turn cannibal, eat the others! I feel like Daddy. I'm groping around in my memories for something and coming up empty-handed. Did we ever all get along?

Of course, I don't say any of this. I'm their Mary. We each have a role. I smooth ruffled feathers; I ooh and aah; I cajole and encourage; I cook and clean. I listen. Secretly, I plan. I know what I'll do. I'll run away. I'll join the circus. I'll juggle cats. I have experience.

ELLIE

I have always been the one who sees, who hears, who knows secrets. I see Luke and Willow roll like puppies in the grass under my window at night. Vapor rises from their dew-wet backs. I hear the rustle and thump of bodies colliding above my head, Mark's deep murmur, Clare's throaty laugh. Happy couples. Happy? They're like freaking rabbits. Sex is all around me. Rapture. But not in this narrow room. Perhaps these twins weren't the Immaculate Conception, but it looks like I'll be pretty damn immaculate from now on. I hate it here.

There is movement inside me, the beginnings of life and the end of it, too. The rhythm of restless fetuses, two little eggs, one little egg split in two, they change everything. I know.

Art is all around me. Luke's mobiles glitter in the sun; they go out into the world and bring home a living, bring home fame, for him and Willow. Clare and Mark, heads bent together over a laptop are unaware how the equations reflect and light their faces. Symbol and meaning scroll down live flesh. Flesh as art. Sarah explores every inch of Willow's, discovering its exquisite beauty. Sarah spends hours in the bathroom next to my room, and I hike all the way to the other end of the hall to pee ten times a night and thirty times a day. The photos begin to fill the walls of Luke's old room. The sun gilds every photo on the walls and each grain of the wood floor. It would be a good place to paint, to sculpt. Mary says it will make a wonderful nursery. Another narrow prison.

I wander the house and run my fingers over the furniture, along the bookshelves, the cabinets; I gaze up at the tiny paintings on the wall, bees in the bookcase, vines that cling to the arch of a doorway, a cascade of blush roses that seem to almost creep in from the window and lay across the sill. Sarah always said they were Mary's, but I think she's wrong. I think they were our mother's, not that Ruth, Sarah's Igor. She could never have produced something so delicate, so achingly sad. We humor Sarah, but we all know. I think my mother painted them, and then something happened. We happened, and that was the end of it. My parents were artists, their memorials surround me, sticks of furniture and daubs of fading frescos. I take Dad for walks on the beach, both of us unbalanced and awkward in deep sand. I point out the light on the water, the shapes and colors of the cliffs. "Uh huh," he says, but his eyes are unfocused. He no longer sees. We walk until we are tired, and then we sit and watch the waves slide like hands and sculpt the planes of the beach. I am not the ocean. Sand slips through my fingers.

Mygy hygands eyegare eyegemtygy. Mygy fygingygers eyegare rygestlygess.

My hands, my fingers want clay. They want work. They want the smooth muscled skin of a man's chest. They want friction, control. They want passion. I press them to my belly to still them. I say to them, "Feel that. Babies. A little Sarah, a little me. A new beginning." My fingers are not fooled; they feel more than that. They feel the urgent push and poke of necessity, of history, of desertion and madness. My fingers feel the babies grow and my art recedes; the babies want and my time slips like retreating waves into a dark and formless sea. I was an artist, but then Mary made me give all my eggs away. Except these two. My hands feel empty.

I have always been the one who sees, who hears, who knows secrets. Here is a secret of my own: I don't want the babies. I never did, not really, even when it was only going to be one. I remember that. This is not the future I wanted. It was just a joke, dancing under that stupid saint's canopy. It was a dare, like one of Sarah's clever little ideas when we were young, a little lark that would leave us rolling with laughter, and someone else standing among the wreckage. Little ideas, big consequences. I don't want them.

Thigere igare tigoo miganigy igof igus higere. There are too many of us here, in this body, in this house. Their happiness crowds me.

I hate it here.

FRANK

There's a bunch of us that live here. At least twenty of us—boys and girls all mixed up together. New ones keep coming. It's noisy. They keep changing the bathrooms around. I'm thinking about moving out. My parents have a place in the mountains. They grow their own food. They have a mine, and they work deep in the ground, bringing stuff up. They said I could come any time. I have a dog, Jack, and he could come, too. They said I could help with the . . . the . . . you know, the wood that they put up in the mines. They said there's plenty of food. They grow their own food up in the mountains.

I don't like arguing. She came to the house to live. She said we don't argue in this house. Just keep it to yourself. Keep everything inside. That was a long time ago. So I did.

I don't like arguing, and I don't like how they keep changing the bathrooms.

LUKE

I like Dad. It's something new for me. He doesn't know I'm his son, but we sit together in the sun, and Jack pants at our feet. We're quiet together. It's okay that he doesn't know me. We're even now.

All I ever had were my feet to tell me what to do. "Feet don't fail me now." Willow told me that line. I like it. Mary's not too nice to Willow. She doesn't say anything, it's her body, the way her face and feet turn away as quick as they can if Willow's in front of her. Willow's like the wind. She's constant. She doesn't notice, just flows around it. But I notice. It makes me want to take Willow's hand and walk away.

There are holes in the rafters where the mobiles hang. The gray whales are gone and two constellations and two fish and one rainforest animals and seven of the abstracts. The abstracts are Dad's favorites. He stands under them every day, smiling up, reaching to set them in motion. He's always gentle as if they were glass or young children. "Who ever did these things did something really great," he tells me. It feels good when he says that, even if he doesn't know it's me that did it, and I'm his. Then we settle down in the sun, and Jack drops at our feet with a huge sigh, and soon he's panting, making my ankles moist with his breath and thumping Dad's bare feet with his tail. Willow will come out soon with something for us to drink, and then she'll flop down next to Jack and rest her head on his neck. Mary's not too nice to her. I can feel it in my legs. It makes me want to walk. It reminds me that there are cans waiting, waiting to be collected, to be snipped and bent, to be made into something. Something beautiful. I have been neglecting cans.

MARK

I predicted correctly. Oh, entropy, you rule the known universe.

Boom.

RUTH

*T*hat girl, Sarah, she says I'm part of the family now. They're okay, kind of goofy is all. They want, but they don't know what. They feed me and I have my own bed. Then I saw the envelope sitting on top of the pile of mail that comes through the slot. They don't even have to walk to the street to pick up their mail here. It comes sliding right through a fancy little brass hole in the door. I heard it and I said I'd go get it. They were playing that game, and I didn't want to sit around and listen to them tearing each other up, so I went for the mail. I picked it up and saw it and knew right away. I put it down on the little table by the door with the rest of the mail, and I went upstairs to get some things. I won't take much, just these clothes and some little snacky things I've been saving.

She said I was part of the family, but I saw the letter. That Mark. He's the sneaky one, thinks he's smarter than anybody else. There's smart and there's smart, and I'm no idiot, either. I watched that Sally Jessy and that handsome Maury Povich. I saw a show on it. That envelope was from some paternity testing place, stamped right on it, "Confidential Results." Oh well, it's been nice. Food's been decent. I liked that road trip. We had a ball.

This town is not such a bad place. That Sarah, she took me all around. There's lots of bums. They hang out down by the beach. They sit on nice clean grass under skinny palm trees. Imagine that! The sun just sparkles on that sea. All the bums are just warm and squinty-eyed and relaxed. Once, we even passed these two sitting on a wall down toward the bottom of that main street, two bums, one of them holding open a little white box. Eating sushi. Where else in the whole damn world will you see two bums sharing secondhand sushi? It won't be such a bad place. Nothing like having your own bed and sitting next to a friend with a bowl of Fritos between you, and that handsome Maury on the boob tube. Nothing like that.

MARY

*I*t's my fault. I said we would play the game, such a simple childhood game. I thought it would bring us back to what we were back then, six kids together in a big house. I used to make them play it when the bickering started, Sarah and Ellie torturing their little brother, Luke, Peter and Mark flinging snide remarks and couch pillows at each other. Ordinary kid stuff. "We're playing the 'Say Something Nice' game. Everybody come sit down." They would all moan and grouse, but Peter would back me up. I could give him that look, and he would back me up. He was the little father of the family. "Okay, you start," I'd say to one of them. Then whoever I had picked would think a minute and have to say something nice about someone else. It couldn't be something simple like, "I like your hair." It had to be true, heartfelt. At some point I would say, "Mark, say something nice about . . ." whoever. The minutes would spin out. Mark would think; we would wait. We would wait and wait and wait. Eventually, the single gleaned item from years of coexistence would surface. "Ellie, I believe you are the alpha twin," or "Peter, I think you are capable of doing better in math." Remarks unknowingly calculated to cause discontent. If we were lucky, which we usually were, Ellie would lose patience. "Mark, it's so easy! Like this . . ." and compliments would drop like pearls from a broken necklace and scatter glossy rewards around the room, small things, easily offered, soon forgotten. Ah, but that moment of glow. The point is, though, the game worked, even with Mark's occasional fruitless ruminations. It made us think about what was best in us; it kept us together.

Sometimes I think that we're characters in a book; I think that some idiot author is toying with us, has set us in motion with a double tragedy, has something in mind for our ends, and now only has to fill in the parts between. We are stuck in ourselves and cannot respond to each other out of character. There's our third tragedy. Will we ever change? Will we ever learn?

Daddy is sitting watching the Animal Planet channel in the living room and we are seated around the dining room table. Mark starts by saying something really lovely to Clare, and I am thinking that it is a good beginning, if not actually following the rules, because let's face it, there's nothing wrong with that relationship, when Ellie suddenly calls foul.

"That's cheating, Mark. Clare's not part of the family, and besides, you're just saying that because you just want to fu—"

"Ellie!" I stop her. "Say something nice, if not to Mark yet, then someone else. To Sarah."

Clare looks like she's been slapped.

Ellie stares at me for a second, says, "All right then." She turns to Luke. "Your mobiles are wonderful," she says. "They're the only real art that's happening in this house." Ellie gives Sarah a sideways glance and then beams at Luke. It is at this point that Ruth leaves the room.

"Mail's here," she announces as she gets up.

Besides the sound of the mail sliding through the slot and the television from the living room, there is the hollow sound of Luke's feet, tapping a nervous staccato beat beneath the dining room table. He looks confused and frightened. He turns to Willow. She is grinning ear to ear.

"You see! I told you how totally cool your stuff was. This is a great game! Can I go?"

233

"No," I say, and just like that, I too have broken the rules.

"I don't remember this game," Sarah says quietly. "I don't remember ever playing it."

"Sure you do, Sarah." There is something in Ellie's voice that is sharp and bright and brittle as glass. "We used to all play it before Peter shot himself. That must have been right after you stole his camera."

"Ellie!" I am shouting. "Stop it! Stop it now! What has gotten into you?"

Now it is my turn. Ellie turns to me.

"Stop what, Mary?" Her voice is low, intense, mean. "Stop saying that Peter blew a hole in his body and made sure we could all share in it? Stop saying that Sarah took his camera and then slept on it for years like she was trying to hatch it? Stop saying what? The truth? That's your problem, Mary. You never want the truth. You just want some made up idea of happy families. Here's another truth. You want to know what's got into me? Two babies, that's what. They're like hard, tight little fists. They're like rocks. They're my happy family. I don't want them. I hate them. I don't want any of this!"

Sarah pushes herself back from the table. "I'm going to find Ruth," she says. Her voice is so small and so young. It is raw and new-formed. Ellie has done this; she has ripped something between them. This time she has gone ahead and made sure that Sarah will never follow. Sarah leaves the room, and Ellie watches. They look so different.

"Ellie," I beg. "Please." I turn to Mark. I want him to take on the role. I want him to be the little father. "Mark, say something."

"Hormone surges," he says. "Ellie is experiencing hormone surges, quite clearly. You shouldn't let it bother you. Sarah shouldn't let it bother her, and I might add, the camera is irrelevant. That all happened a long time ago. I know you don't like my theories, Mary. But I stand by them. It's mathematically provable. Peter's, uuuh, event, clearly marks the boundary for this family. We, our paths, begin after that sad occurrence. I repeat, nothing before has relevance."

We are all looking at him, expecting more. It is Ellie who breaks the silence.

"That's very convenient for you, Mark, considering you have your own guilty little secret concerning Peter." Her hands are shaking, and I know that very soon she will shatter and fall apart. I know because I raised her.

"I don't know what you are referring to," Mark says. His face is a blank.

"I heard you, Mark. The day before he shot himself, I heard you ask him his class ranking, and poor, stupid Peter, he just had to open his dumb mouth and tell you. He was your big brother and those were the kind of things he did, things that always turned out badly, like sharing a favorite thing, or pretending he could do something when of course he couldn't, just to impress us all. It always turned out badly, but mostly for him. So he told you, and you said, 'Wow, that's like idiot level. That's only the fifty-second percentile. I didn't think I knew anyone in that part of the class. You should have asked me to tutor you in calculus and physics. You should have asked me for help.' You just had to rub his nose in it, Mark. Perfect Mark. Mark the Quark. Five years younger and a million times better. You said, 'I have the highest average in our class. I'll be giving the valedictorian speech at our graduation.'"

"No," I tell Ellie. "He didn't. He wouldn't." I turn to Mark. "You wouldn't." I will him to reassure me, but he sits absolutely still with all of us, even Clare, staring at him. I think, yes, he might have said this terrible, this unforgivable, this last thing, because even though he has always been light years ahead of us, I still know him. I raised him, too.

Mark sits absolutely still. Luke's feet beat a call to retreat even though he's the only one who's been left unscathed, the only one who's culled a compliment in our little game, but then here's another truth, the truth of Luke: He's never been unscathed. Since birth, he's carried the damage of proximity. The TV in the other room provides an unnaturally loud, whiny jingle about cat food, and then Luke's continued tattoo is answered by another set of feet. Sarah is running down the stairs.

"She's gone!" she screams. "She's nowhere. She said she went for the mail, and she found this, and now she's gone."

Sarah flings an unopened envelope she has mangled in her clenched fist at Mark. It bounces off his head and drops to the table. He slowly raises his hand to his forehead, and Clare takes the letter and smoothes it. Clare's lips move as she reads the face of the envelope. She looks up to Mark. Sarah is crying.

"It's my turn," Sarah sobs. "It's my turn to play. Quark, you think you're so much cleverer than all of us. You are. You are, but you're a monster! You're not human."

She stands in front of us, her hands pressed to her face; her whole body convulses with sobs. I jump to my feet to go to her, but Ellie is there first, putting thin arms around her shaking sister. Sarah shoves her away and runs from the room.

"Sarah!" Ellie screams, reaches out. Her voice chases her sister's retreating back, then splinters into tiny, terrible shards.

It is quiet except for the TV, inanely cheerful in the next room, and then Willow reaches out and takes Luke's hand.

"Let's go for a walk," she says.

She gathers him up into her painted arms and leads him out. Clare rises, too, slowly, carefully. Still holding the unopened letter she slips from the room. Mark jumps up to pursue.

"Clare!" he calls. "Clare!" Sarah is wrong. His voice sounds terribly human.

Across the table from me, Ellie is looking at her out-stretched hands. She turns and holds them out for me to see.

"What have I done, Mary?" In her voice is the little girl of thirty years ago. "What did I do?"

Something has happened here, a cataclysm. Our world has flown apart, and here I am again, at the center, reaching out for the pieces.

DAD USED to say he liked wood because it whispered stories to him. It told of lean years and years of plenty, of obsta-cles that obstructed or that were avoided; it told of the chance of a new beginning with each branch. Dad loved wood because it required him to interpret. Each piece he touched, he fashioned into something either beautiful or useful, exposing the heart of that unique tree. People bought his works of art, his consoles, or tables, or chairs. They ran their fingers over the surface and felt the beat of the wood's heart; they sat down and settled back and felt embraced by story. I want stories of my own; I always have. That's why I read. I read and I read and I read and I have learned everything he said the wood ever told him, except I have learned it about people. That's what books do, they interpret the heart of us all.

Once a major celebrity bought a piece of Dad's fur-niture from a local artisans' gallery downtown and then commissioned a dining room set. It was the point of branching out for him, his new beginning. It was three years after Peter's death, my first year at the University of Santa Barbara. I stayed at home until Luke graduated. In that time I completed high school, a bachelor's and a master's and began a doctorate in English Literature, all right here in Santa Barbara. I raised four children and lost one. In that same time, Dad went from carving statues of a woman that he burned one by one, to making cabinets and shelving, to building Peter's coffin, to creating furniture for stars' homes and art galleries and museums. Slowly, I became caught up in his wood's story and all the stories that my siblings carried home to me. I let go of my own. I don't mind, really. I use my skills. I look into the heart of each of my family. I read them.

ELLIE

*I*t's my fault. I don't play the game right. I never do. I don't know why. I say terrible, unforgivable things. How can something be true and still a terrible lie? I've always been the one who sees, who hears, who knows. I keep secrets. They are like babies, sharp little fingers and toes, insistent fists and elbows and knees. They want out. They want to wreak havoc and change the world. I haven't been careful enough. I haven't been careful at all. They are out now. They are what I have created. It is my fault.

MARK

Clare is leaving. Her suitcase is open on the bed. She bends over it, carefully folding brightly hued T-shirts and soft, faded jeans, a sweater the color of chocolate, an emerald skirt. The sun from the skylight encases her, enhancing the brilliance of these tokens of her life. She lifts a hand and tucks a stray strand of hair behind a perfect ear. The sun gilds her hair, brings out the jeweled red tones, the spectrum of a retreating galaxy. Her fingers are quick and sure, long and graceful. Her body forms an elegant lambda as it bends there by the bed, as she prepares to leave.

In the early 50's, physicists discovered a particle they dubbed the lambda, based on its telltale shape, the upside-down V of that Greek letter. Three quarks travel along the tracks of the lambda. Occasionally, one of the quarks behaves badly, gets too close to one of his fellows and obliterates himself. The lambda flies apart. Even so, the lambda is considered essentially stable. Though its existence lasts only a fraction of a billionth of a second, it is ancient in terms of subatomic time. If put on a par with the cosmologic time scale, the lambda would far, far outlast the sun's existence. Propelled by some interior mystery, the quark orbits the lambda a trillion times, before it trips up and ends in disaster. A trillion times sounds like it would take forever, but it doesn't. It has passed before the thought is even formed. Clare is leaving. It's too soon. It seems like she was hardly with me at all.

"Clare." I don't seem to be able to move beyond the top of the stairs. She has claimed this room. She has taken

240

over Peter's space, filled it with her own disappointment, her own anger. "Clare," I beg admittance.

She shakes her head, sticks out a hand to repel me.

"Clare."

She unfolds and turns to me. "Just tell me. How could you do it, Mark? How could you say that to your brother?"

"Clare, I don't even remember saying it. I was thirteen, Clare."

She shakes her head again. "How could you *ever* say it? How could you do this?" She points at the envelope that sits on the bed next to her open suitcase.

"What's in there is science, Clare. It's important. It's the truth."

"No, Mark! There's science and there's truth, but they are not always the same thing. Can't you see that?" She throws up her hands. "Aaargh! You're so . . . you're not . . . what is wrong with you? Sometimes I wonder just what planet you are from!"

Oh boy. Here we are again, the eternal echo of my sisters. "Clare, if I came with you—if you could—if I . . ." My voice trails to silence. Could what? If . . . then: It is a hypothesis I can't begin to form.

We are quiet in the overcharged air of the room. Ions dissipate, settle. From below there is the sound of further entropy, calling voices, running feet. For me, the center of the universe is here, though, in this room. Clare is the essential particle I orbit. She is my lambda. I am her quark.

Clare shakes her head again and waves her hand toward the stairs, aiming vaguely where my family has scattered. "You have to fix this, Mark."

"How?"

She won't answer. She has turned back to her packing.

In high school, Mary once dragged me to a play at a small theater on Anacapa Street. *The Importance of Being Earnest.*

There is a line from it that has become quite famous, I think. I have heard renditions of it now and again, applied to any number of articles. It has even proven occasionally apt in my own field, though I must admit, I haven't the clarity of mind at present to come up with an example. It's quite an amusing line. Unfortunately, in our current situation, its application sheds its charm and becomes simply accurate.

"To lose one parent may be regarded as a misfortune; to lose both looks like carelessness."

Dad is gone.

I MUST hand it to Mary. She waits until Willow and Luke return from their walk before she panics, searching every place in the house he might have tucked himself away first, then asking the neighbors if they have noticed him wandering off. Evidently, they have let down their guard because we are here to watch him, clearly a mistake on their part. When Luke and Willow return, sans Dad, and Willow is in tears because Jack is missing, Mary continues to have the presence of mind to call Sarah on the slim chance that she has taken Dad with her to search for Ruth.

"I can't find her, Mary." Sarah's wails are audible over the cell phone. "I've looked up and down State and East Beach, even Milpas, Mary. I can't find her! Oh, Mary, what am I going to do? I have to find her!"

"Sarah, honey, is Daddy with you?" Mary's gentle voice travels along a dead wire. Sarah had hung up. "Sarah hung up," Mary says and sets the phone in its receiver. "I don't think Daddy's with her." She turns to me.

"We seem to be experiencing a mass migration." My attempt to raise the situation from despair with a modicum of levity is not appreciated.

"Mark, you are not above this. You are not five hours up the coast offering useless advice and stupid theories. You're right here in the thick of it. Please, please, *for once* just help me."

She is my sister, Mary, the one who always listens, who agrees and accepts. She raised us, and though I have always felt I needed it less than the others, I think now, perhaps, she raises us still.

"We need a map of the city," I tell her, and when she has run off to her car to collect it, I call the police.

Ellie floats downstairs to join us, looking red-eyed, rumpled and tragic. When she hears that Dad has disappeared, she throws her arms up into the air and wails, "My fault! This is all my—"

"Shut up, Ellie." Mary's voice is sharp and final.

Ellie's mouth snaps shut.

"You can do Lady Macbeth on your own time. We need you to stay here in case the police call or Daddy manages to find his way home."

Ellie manages a nod.

When the police arrive to file a report, it is Willow who can provide a description of what Dad is wearing, down to his brown socks and the orange polka dot boxers she has put over the diaper we have been putting him in lately. She tells the police what he has had for breakfast and on which side of his head his hair is parted. She says he wears a bracelet she made of blue, lettered beads that carries his name, Frank Bennett, and that every piece of clothing, except the boxers which have been borrowed from Luke, has his name and address in it. She did it herself, weeks ago, with a Sharpie. She tells them that Dad has been talking lately about his parents in the hills, but warns them that that doesn't mean that's where he's headed. I watch Willow talk; I watch the two policemen as they take the information from this tattooed, much-pierced girl, clearly impressed with what she says, what

243

she has done. I watch Mary watch Willow. Emotions buffet her face: worry, failure, reassessment, gratitude.

"I think he's with my dog, Jack," Willow tells the policeman. "Jack's like Lassie or Rin Tin Tin. Not that he looks like them, because I don't even know what Lassie and Rin Tin Tin look like because we weren't allowed to watch TV, but I've heard what people say and stuff, and anyway Jack doesn't really look like anything, because he's a mutt and he's just black and brown and white and tan with a big tail that wags, and he can grin but he's missing a couple of teeth so it's kind of scary, but he's a really good dog and he'll watch out for Frank just like Lassie or Rin Tin Tin, but Frank might be frightened or worried and Jack's just a dog . . ." Willow is suddenly again in tears. It is to Mary that she runs, our Mary, who will always open her arms. Luke hovers in their orbit, miserable and shuffling.

"Maybe I should go look, Willow," he offers. "I could walk."

Once the police have left, I am able to establish a grid of the city and distribute quadrants to everyone. Sarah is called and told to watch for Dad wherever she is. Willow, revived, convinces Luke that we will cover more ground in the VW bus than on foot, and he is so relieved that she is no longer in tears that he will agree to anything. They take off for the hills. As Mary and I are about to separate into our cars, I turn to her. There is something I must know.

"Mary . . . Mary, was it really useless? All the information and advice these past years? I tried very hard to make it relevant . . . helpful."

Mary looks into my face; she reaches out and runs her fingers down my cheek. It is a light touch, soft and lingering, a touch like the gentle, remembered fingers of a long departed mother.

"No, Mark, not useless. I was always glad of it."

Mary is lying. She has been lying all along.

244

Clare is right. Up in Peter's bedroom packing her bag and waiting for us to clear out so she can slip away, Clare is right. It is part of her perfection. There is a difference between science and truth. I think she means between the head and the heart. In all the time I have known her, Clare has always been right. I haven't listened. I could turn from the car and go up to Peter's room and tell her, tell her she is right, but Dad is somewhere out in Santa Barbara with the toothless, grinning Jack as his only protection, a frantic Mary, a distraught Sarah, a marginally operational Luke looking for him, and Willow seemingly our only hope. Clare is right. I need to fix this.

ELLIE

I hear them leaving, the cars starting up and heading down the driveway. The VW sounds like castanets. I don't think it has too many more miles left in it. Above me, I hear Clare, the clunk of her suitcase on the floor, the awkward, weighty steps on the attic stairs. This is my fault, too. How can I fix this?

It is a struggle getting it out of the narrow door of the closet. It is heavy and awkward, still in its original crating from the flight. I don't know how Mary managed by herself, but if she did, I can. I have to stop twice on the stairs and readjust my hold, and I'm completely panicked that I'll miss her; but I catch her as she's closing the boot of her car. Her face looks scrubbed as if she has tried to wash the sadness off of herself. Her eyes are red and look sore. I know the feeling.

"You love him." I don't mean it to be an accusation, but I'm a little out of breath and it comes out huffy sounding.

She doesn't say anything. She stands there with her arms at her side and her keys beating a slight jingle against her thigh.

"I didn't mean any of those things I said back there. I didn't mean them."

"They're accurate, though."

"No, Clare. They're all lies."

She shakes her head and looks away.

"You have to have this," I tell her, and thrust the crate into her arms. "It's for you."

"Jesus, Ellie, it's huge. What is it?"

I grin at her. "It's for you. I do things big."

She smiles back for the first time, but her voice still sounds sad. "I noticed that about you. What is it?"

"You'll see when you open it," I tell her. "Only, don't open it until you're not quite so mad at all of us. Please," I say.

We stand looking at each other for a time with the crate between us, and then she finally says, "Okay. It's a deal." She smiles again.

I open the back door of the car and help her slide the crate in. We hug. I hold on hard.

"You're one of us," I tell her. I tell her in Double Talk so she'll know it's true.

"Thank you," she says, and then she goes.

I'VE GIVEN her my art, my last piece, the painting of Mark, brought here all the way from Patmos. It was to be a joke, a tease. I wanted Mark to hang it in his office or on the wall of his lab, to have his co-workers say, "That's so him!" This is better; this is what it was truly made for. She will see that the painting is accurate, too. It is truth. Art has that power, paint or clay, any medium, even photography. It brings truth to the surface. Clare will love the painting. It will make her laugh; it will make her understand. It is so him, and she loves my brother, Mark. The art will make her call him back to her. It is the one thing I am sure of. Art.

MARK

*O*f course I am the one who stumbles across her. I am beginning to notice that fate has a rather wicked taste for irony. I am driving slowly along West Beach, the southern boundary of my quadrant when I notice a solitary figure sitting in the sand, a head of gray hair, a familiar set to the shoulders. The distance from the road is enough to engender the hope that this is Dad, but after I have parked and tripped across the endless stretch of soft beach I see that it can't be. It is Ruth. She is sitting with perhaps a half dozen bags of chips arranged around her. Her knees are drawn up to her chest, and she stares out at the ocean and the fog bank that skulks just off the coast. When I reach her side, she looks up.

"Ruth, Sarah's looking for you."

"I'm here," she answers.

"I'll call her." I pull out my cell phone.

"They asked me for change." She is staring out to sea again.

"Who?"

"The bums way down the other side of the beach. I was planning to settle in there amongst them, and they asked me for change." She fights a tremor in her voice, "Like I wasn't even one of them or something." Sarah has done this.

"May I sit," I ask.

"Not my beach."

I sit beside her, but she will not look at me. I put my cell phone back in my pocket. We sit together in the uncomfortable sand and look out at the ocean.

"It was a day just like today that we buried my brother, Peter, the same fog bank heading in, the same breeze and heat," I tell her. "Mary played the oboe."

"I never said I was your mother." Her voice is belligerent. "I never said that."

"I know, Ruth. Listen, I . . . I . . ." I have done this.

We are silent again. I remember that the music hung in the air, clear and steady, and then seemed to drift out over the cemetery cliffs to be lost above blue waves and white caps where the fog gathered and waited.

"The thing about quarks," I tell Ruth. "The thing about quarks is that in many ways, in many ways . . ." I am stumbling over my own words with this old homeless woman. "In many ways, quarks are the basis of everything. Well, in fact, strings are, strings of energy, but that hasn't been proven really. I mean the math is there, but it can't be tested yet. But quarks now, quarks are real. Did you know that quarks make up approximately ninety-nine percent of the mass of the universe? They travel around the proton at almost the speed of light. Think of it. It travels the lambda a trillion times before it self destructs and takes the lambda with it. All in less than the blink of an eye. Really, I mean, if you want to put it poetically, the quark sets the universe in motion. But, but, but here's the thing, Ruth." I glance over at her. I have her attention now. She is staring. It is a response I seem to engender.

"The thing is, well, it's that the quark doesn't know what it's doing. Well, I mean obviously, but I mean metaphorically, too, if you know what I'm saying."

Ruth doesn't respond. She continues to stare. I must take it as encouragement.

"The quark might set things in motion . . . it might be the heartbeat of the universe . . . it might cause all kinds of destruction and decay. I'm sure it does. Look at the lambda—but I'm straying from my point here. The point is that it doesn't know it's doing it. It doesn't mean to,

Ruth." I am not sure I have been entirely clear, and of course, I assume Ruth is less than a novice when it comes to physics, but I truly hope she understands.

However, there is very little indication from Ruth. She continues to stare, then shakes her head with some bemusement.

"Isn't that all something?"

"Yes," I answer. "I suppose it is."

I remember the smell of the newly cut grass at the cemetery. I remember the smell of the sea and the cry of the gulls that mixed with Mary's lonely music. I remember the fog came in before we finished. There was moisture on every blade of grass and each wild strand of my sisters' hair. I remember it beaded on Dad's beautiful handiwork deep in the hole, until they pushed the dirt in and covered it up. I remember before, weeks, months, years, a different lifetime. I remember Peter's laughter and the dull percussions of the pillows he loved to aim at my head. I remember the weight of his hand on my shoulder, the sudden weight of his loss. These are my memories. I have devalued them.

"Did you hear what my sister Ellie said to me at the table?"

Ruth shook her head. "Gone by then."

"She said I said something terrible, something unforgivable to my brother before he died. She said . . . she implied it was my fault he killed himself." Saying it is like ripping something open in my body; it is like taking a gun to myself and pulling the trigger.

"No," Ruth says simply. She is shaking her head. "Not so."

"I think she could be right," I say.

She shakes her head still. "Not so," she confirms. "I had six kids and two husbands, one of them a shit who beat me and my children and ran them off. I've been a drunk and a bum. Though that sweet Sarah calls it homeless, I know homeless and I know bums, and I was a bum. I was things I don't even want to think of anymore. I've been all over. I've seen people kill themselves. Seen them do it lots of different ways. Well, maybe not lots, but some. It's not ever just one thing, not just one thing that some idiot said or done to them. It's a buildup of matters. Lots of little things, and it's not even that, because nobody makes you kill yourself but you. Fate happens in small things, like little messages, but it's what you do with them that makes the difference."

This is the most I have heard her say at one time. She is eloquent with experience.

"Thank you, Ruth." I have been wrong.

She is fighting with a snack-sized bag of Doritos, her face fierce and ardent as she tries to open it. The upper edges finally separate. She grins with delight.

"Chip?" she offers.

Frankly, I have avoided watching Ruth and food. It is not an attractive combination. She is somewhat toothless (not unlike Jack the dog) and wholly careless and immoderate in her habits. She eats with her mouth open, and I am in constant fear that something unappetizing will fall out then, and perhaps worse, will be scooped back up and put back in. Her fingers worry me. Even by her own account, they have probed unimaginable places. I envision stinking dumpsters, slop-filled gutters, reeking corners of derelict factories that even rats avoid, but those same fingers are offering me something more than chips.

"Please," I say. If I am to eat crow, accept absolution on my tongue, it might as well taste of nacho cheese.

We finish the bag. Ruth eats three-quarters of them, then licks her index finger and collects the crumbs from the dark recesses of the bag.

"That was fine," she enthuses. "Should we have another?"

I push myself to standing, reach down and offer her a hand up.

"I need to be looking for my Dad."

251

"Gone? Better find him before he gets himself into some trouble."

"Yes." We are in agreement. "Will you help me?"

She grins and hoists herself up without my help. "Sure. If you buy me a milk shake."

"It would be my pleasure," I tell her.

On the way back to the car, I call Sarah. She is out of range so I leave a message on her cell.

"Sarah? Sarah, it's . . . it's Mark. Your brother Mark. I have Ruth with me. She's okay. I'll bring her home." I swallow. "Sarah. Listen. I opened the envelope." The lie is sharp and hard, a foreign substance in my mouth. "The results are inconclusive, Sarah. It could go either way." I hang up quickly. I can feel sweat where my collar meets my neck, and my arm pits are swampy. I am very glad I could leave my message on her phone. I could not have done it face to face.

"You lied." Ruth is looking up into my face as I hold the car door open for her. She slides into the passenger seat, and I walk around the car and join her.

"How's that feel?"

"Strange," I tell her. "Better, perhaps."

"A trillion orbits?" she muses as we head for In-N-Out Burger. "I wish I had a nickel for every one of them."

"Fifty billion dollars. You'd be buying the milkshakes."

"Imagine that!" she chuckles, then sighs. "I would have, too."

WILLOW

We find him, well mostly it is me because Luke keeps getting distracted by beer cans and pop cans on the side of the road. He wants me to stop so he can hop out and get them, and after a while I let him, but at first I am trying to keep him focused because I have to do that a lot with Luke, because he's an artist and artists live on a whole different astral plane. That's why his mobiles are so amazing, because he brings special knowledge and a different understanding of time and space when he comes back to our realm to get some work done. You should try making love with someone from a different astral plane; it's like so amazing. Fireworks, man, and images and heat and it's so, so, so, so WOW. It's totally cool. That's just Luke. He's not dumb or anything, because I know that's how some people see him, even his family sometimes acts like that, but he's not, he's just *out there, man.* I can be out there, too, because I have a touch of the astral. That's how come I know how to find Frank, I mean, I know I told the police that he might be heading for the hills up behind Mission Canyon and all, and we were even going to look, I mean, he had been talking about his parents that live up there. Can you believe how old they must be? I mean, he's, like ancient, so they must be totally dusty. Luke says he thinks his dad's parents have been dead for a long time, but he's not sure, and I think you can't just discount what people say and think. You can't just discount people because they have Alzheimer's or are old or all different looking because, hey, there are things going on in their heads, man. They have thoughts and feelings. They have validity, man. Validity. Frank says his parents grow their own food which is very cool when you think how old they are. Right on, old folks! Anyway, I get these feelings, like the day I met Luke I knew all day something really cool and totally shaking was going down sometime, so I was just looking out for it and there was Luke in his bright yellow prison coveralls ambling down the road. Is that so cool? I am telling you, man, I know things. Someday when I got the fifty bucks to waste, which we will get because we are making a total mint off of Luke's mobiles and we are going to be so famous, anyway, at that exact moment I'm taking myself down to that psychic lady on lower State and checking it out. I bet you anything I know more about my future than she does. My future's sitting right next to me. Lukey, baby boy, you are my man! Woohoo! Back to my feeling. I get these feelings, and anyway we are driving along and I'm getting one, really strong, I mean we are all set to go do the dirt roads up in the canyons and then work our way down and I think hey, maybe he got stuck on Alameda Padre Serra because there's no real streets that go up from that road until you hit the roundabout, so we start heading along APS and we keep stopping for cans. It is a total goldmine. Man, some people have like no respect for the environment. Uncool, but then we pick them up and it's cool again! Anyway, I am getting kind of worried, because we're not seeing Frank, and I am beginning to wonder if my feeling is wrong because I have had wrong feelings once or twice. Once, I had a really good feeling about this guy who liked to be called Rocko, I mean his real name was Sean which is a perfectly nice name, but he's like always, "Call me Rocko! Call me Rocko!" Okay, Rocko, whatever you say, I mean, I should have known, but I was going with this feeling and then he ups and steals my decrepit Mazda that was still running and everything.

I mean, man, I only paid fifty bucks for it, but still that is just so low, and it had all my stuff in it, because I was kind of living out of the back seat, and so I had to steal a bunch of stuff to get started again, and that's just bad Karma, but I figure it's really not my bad Karma anyway, because good old Rocko's the one who totally led me astray. He can eat my Karma, man. In your face, Rocko! So anyway I'm getting really worried again because what if this feeling is a Rocko feeling, and what if Frank is somewhere and he's really frightened or hurt and Jack can't help him because it's like a really big hurt that a dog can't handle alone. We hit the roundabout and start wandering up the roads that lead up off of it, first one way then the other. We go up Barker Pass and Nicholas and turn on Chase and there he is! It's a total miracle! He is standing at a mailbox and some old lady is talking to him and there is Jack sitting all patient and concerned right at his feet. It's a long way for two old dogs to walk. I bet they're tired. As we roll up to them to collect him, I can tell by the look on the lady's face that she's kind of nervous of Frank, I mean he looks pretty normal only a little vacant, but by now I bet he's filled that diaper of his, and besides when you start talking to him he kind of pulls you into his confusion, and I'm cool with that but for some people I think it's scary. I think they talk to Frank or look at him and worry they'll be like him some day. They shun him or act all jolly and fake. It's uncool, but people can't help themselves, because they go around being scared or sorry all the time; that's the way people are. It's just sad. That is just no way to live your life, man. You have to face your future, man, you have to embrace it. You have to do something about it! So, this lady looks kind of startled and concerned and we pull up and that totally doesn't help. First of all, Frank doesn't want to come home, and he acts like he doesn't know us which he might not because sometimes he doesn't, but only for a while then he's fine. Well, this totally freaks the old lady out and you can't blame her because here's some confused old guy all lost and everything clinging to her mailbox with both arms, and here's a guy in bright yellow prison coveralls holding a couple of squashed cans, and here's this girl with all these tattoos and piercings which for old people is just completely wrong, and the old lady starts getting all excited, and that's when the police show up, I mean boom, there they are. I figure some neighbor saw all the commotion and called them. It's Montecito there. It's a pretty stuffy neighborhood. I mean Oprah lives there and everything. They're careful. Luke lived in Montecito on that freakazoid's property who bought all those stolen rainforest lilies. Like I say, some people have absolutely no respect for this planet. Bitch. Well, this old lady doesn't turn out to be a freakazoid lily-snatching bitch at all, because she totally saves us. It doesn't seem like it at first, though, because she just stands back and watches the whole melee. That's a great word. I read that someplace; you'd be amazed at all the magazines and even books that get dumped out instead of put in the recycling; it completely sickens me, but on the other hand it's like a private library if you don't mind doing a little digging, so that's kind of cool. Melee is like a kind of funky fight, which it is, believe me. I am trying to explain, and the police already have Luke in handcuffs. Assholes, I mean, he isn't doing anything, he never does, just standing there, and you can't count a couple of cans as a dangerous weapon or anything. Can you? Such assholes, and Jack is not being any help at all because I am explaining all about the day and the game and my feelings I get, and I admit it's taking a long time, because these things take time, and then I am trying to prove that Jack is my dog by calling his name, but Jack will not budge. He is one exhausted pooch which is sad but totally unhelpful, and the cops are trying to put Frank in the cop car. Assholes. And he totally doesn't want to go and he is getting totally overwrought and agitated and feisty and swinging at everyone.

"Look! Look!" I just scream it, because it is total chaos and they already have one handcuff on me, and I'm afraid they're going to hit Frank with a billy club or something, and so I kind of wrench free and grab Frank by the shirt. "He's got his name and address on his collar! And on his pants!" I show them that, too. "And on his shoes! Pick up your foot, Frank and show them!"

Frank does and everybody even the old lady can see his name and address except the shoes are a little worn down because of all the walking and they can even see that by his name is a little daisy drawn with a smiley face in the center so whoever finds Frank will know that there is someone out there who loves him and is missing him.

"I did that," I tell the police.

And the old lady speaks up and says, "I can vouch for them. I know them." And we all just stare at her, I mean, even Jack stares, and then I run and give her a great big hug and the dangly part of the handcuffs kind of clonks her on the side of the head and she doesn't even mind. She is one very cool old lady.

"You are a very good daughter," she says, which just totally blows me away because it is the first time in the history of this planet Earth that anybody has said that to me, and I get all kind of misty, and I think, wow, now there's a total turnaround, and I think maybe I did something so very, very cool for once, but I can't really think what it is because I'm just all of a sudden overwhelmed because she thinks I'm Frank's daughter, and I think that's pretty amazing because when you think of it, I am. I mean, I found him, just like Jack and Luke. I found him and now he's mine. We are making a family and it's getting bigger and bigger. There's room for the old lady if she wants to come in!

So the police are uncuffing Luke and telling him that he ought to think about wearing something else, and really, when you think about it, it's pretty honest advice, and Luke just nods and asks for his cans back and gets his dad and Jack into the back of the VW, and Frank is totally cool with that because he might be a little confused at times but even he knows that ending up in a police car is not good. We all might look a little strange but we're not total fools.

I don't blame the police though, because they're just doing their job, I mean, they might be complete ass-holes sometimes, but it can't be easy being suspicious of everyone all the time and always looking for the bad side. That has got to be a bummer, man. It must totally wear you down. So I have some sympathy and anyway, if I was a policeman and I took a look at us, I might think we were kind of sketchy, too; let's be honest, like, I know when people see me they just see my skin and they kind of freak. Mary does, I know. She won't really look at me, and she's kind of mean. Sarah and Ellie are artists and that's how they see me, as art, and I bet that old Ruth has seen lots of things worse than me. Mark just got used to me, and besides I don't think he really looks at people anyway. He's ubersmart, and I think when he looks at people he just sees molecules zipping around or some-thing. Mary's different because she sees everything, and when she's looking at me she doesn't like what she sees. I'm glad Luke hasn't noticed. That would make me totally sad. He'd want to walk away, and I just got him settled.

I'm not going anywhere, though, because I know my future. I don't need a crystal ball, though that would be pretty cool. I've got a family to look after. I'm going to work on Mary, and she's going to come around to me; it's going to take time but I have one of my feelings about it, and it's a good feeling, not a fake Rocko kind of feeling. The astral plane is speaking to me. She hugged me. I was so worried and sad and Mary hugged me and it felt so, so, so, so, so good. I tell you, it's a sign. There's going to be way more hugs in my future because I just know it, and that is just the most totally cool thing on Earth.

SARAH

*W*hen I see her I want to hug her, but I don't. Not yet. I say, "You didn't leave a note or anything. You didn't call. You just left me."

It is the strangest thing. The words seem so familiar. I can hear my voice say them, and it sounds as if they are rehearsed, with the perfect ring of truth, the perfect combination of sadness and reprimand. It is as if I have been saying them over and over, every day of my life.

"Well, I'm back now, so I don't need a note," she tells me. "I guess you're stuck with me."

I guess I am. Now we hug.

I THINK we'll go north this time. We'll pack the car with our few things, pack our photos and recordings of Willow, pack our mutual love of the road, pack our anticipation of coming meals in out-of-the-way diners and overnight stays in motels we'll plunder for loot. We'll head up the coast all the way to Vancouver, B.C., and then east. I can show Mom the redwoods at Muir Woods, and she'll love the little towns along the coast. I'll show her the place where Hitchcock filmed *The Birds*, and then when we are back home again, we'll rent the DVD and sit on the couch with the lights out and a big bowl of popcorn, extra butter the way she likes it. Between here and my apartment, my couch, my bowl of popcorn, there is a lot of road to travel, Portland and the Olympic peninsula, Seattle, the Canadian Rockies, Calgary, a thousand miles of open land and fields of grain, lakes and forests. We've consulted a map. We know where we're heading.

I can't forgive Mark for what he did. I can't forgive Ellie. I always thought we were the same, but I'm beginning to see that the surface of things doesn't always tell the whole story. I know Mark found Mom and brought her back, and I heard what he said on the cell phone. It was nice of him to tell me. It must have been hard to be so wrong. He doesn't really believe, though, none of them do, but it doesn't matter, because *I know*. The truth is seared on my heart like a negative. They are unbelievers, and I can't forgive them, but I have a theory. It is the theory of focus, of perspective, and aperture. When I hold the camera up to my eye, I am in charge. I can adjust the aperture to set the subject in harsh light or gentle shadow; I can zoom in on the hard lines or pull back, widen my view, give my photo perspective, distance. Here is the key: zoom back and the hard lines blur, the shadows soften. Distance heals.

Mom and I are going home. Every mile will present a picture, an adventure, a moment in time when we are together. We will keep in touch along the way, mail snapshots and emails. They can follow our progress. Their inboxes will be filled with snippets of us. Gathered together, pasted onto the pages of an album, they will look like a life.

MARY

Ellie is in the swing, and Daddy and I are on lawn chairs, Jack underneath his feet. Sarah and Ruth have left; Mark is upstairs packing, and Luke and Willow are in the carriage barn producing noises I don't even want to classify. Luckily, the sparrows in the hedge are in the midst of a vociferous quarrel, and Daddy is humming something tuneless but distracting. Daddy is very happy today, and that makes me glad—sad too, but mostly glad. We have been granted a reprieve, something I am finally willing to pray for and be thankful for.

WHEN THEY brought him through the door, he looked so tired; but he stopped at the door and took in his surroundings, and his face lit up in a smile.

"Here it is!" he said. He saw me, then. "Mary!" he said.

"Daddy!" It felt so good to say that. I didn't want him to come home and be called Frank as if he were just visiting, as if everything that had come before he stepped out that door didn't mean anything at all. At that moment, I decided. I will never stop calling him Daddy, and if he doesn't respond, I will simply reach out and touch him and gather his focus to me.

"MARY," ELLIE murmurs and the swing creaks below her.

Here is someone else who needs attention.

"Hum?"

"Mary, she barely said goodbye. I said I was sorry, and I hugged her, but it was . . . I don't know, like reaching for a piece of clay and finding out it had hardened before you could work it." Her mind wanders. "The same thing happens to paints if you're not careful; they get all hard and useless in their tubes. It is so annoying really . . ."

"What do you do about it?"

She muses. "Well, you can't do anything about the paint. It's a total waste, but with the clay, you can soak it, soften it, turn it back to slip."

"Maybe that's what you need to do with Sarah."

Ellie is quiet.

"She just needs a little time, Ellie, a little distance."

"Wigee igare thige sigame cligay."

I have never been able to understand the twins' language, have let it be noise, have let it be secret. The distance between noise and word is so slight and so vast. Meaning is everything.

We sit listening to Daddy's tuneless hum, the birds in the hedges, Luke and Willow's lust turn slowly to laughter, then thumping and coughing. They are up to something else.

"What I said about her taking the camera really happened, and about Mark, too. I shouldn't have said it, I know that; but what's really bothering me is that I did something, too. I said something to Peter that was really rotten. I'm just as much to blame, and I didn't say anything. I made them think that it's all their fault."

"It's nobody's fault. He didn't tell us, Ellie. We don't know why he did it. It's nobody's fault."

"Mary, that's easy for you to say. You didn't do anything."

"Ellie, the night before he shot himself, Peter and I were sitting on the floor in the dark in his room. We were talking about all kinds of things . . . you know the way kids do. I don't remember a word of it. I've tried all these years to remember one single word, but I can't . . . I stopped him; I said I wanted a glass of milk, and I'd be right back. I went downstairs, but I never came back up. I went outside and sat on that very swing. I thought someone was coming, and just once, just once I didn't want to be upstairs looking down. I wanted to be here, right here with him."

"Your personal Peeping Tom," Ellie says and smiles.

I nod. "You knew? He never showed up that night. I waited and waited. He never came. There were probably other nights he came back, but by then Peter had killed himself, and what was important had changed. Peter might have been trying to tell me something, Ellie. I can't remember a single word."

"I didn't know you went out that night, Mary."

"You can't know everything, Ellie."

"I thought I could."

It is evidently getting hot. Daddy is struggling with his shirt. He has one sleeve off and is pulling at his buttons as if they are foreign objects that have landed on his chest to do him harm.

"Let me help, Daddy." I get up and kneel at his side.

"What are these things?" he asks with irritation.

"What if I'm like him, Mary?" Ellie's voice is barely a whisper. "What if I'm like her? Our mom. What if I can't do this?"

Daddy is trying to pull the half-unbuttoned shirt over his head while my fingers still work on the front of him. We are in a hopeless tangle for a brief second, until I give in and let him yank the shirt from his body. Buttons fly.

"There," I tell him and laugh. "That worked."

He grins and settles back, and I turn to Ellie. This is the real problem, I know, the problem that is weighing on her. She holds too much inside; history haunts her. I take her hands. She has beautiful hands. They remind me of Daddy's, long and slender, strong and skilled. They are

264

hands capable of creating great beauty, of losing every-thing in their art, of causing pain and neglect.

"You're not them, Ellie," I tell her simply. "That doesn't have to be your story. I'm here. I'll always be here. Luke and Willow are here, at least for now. I think Mark is right, though God knows I'll be the last to tell him; I think when Mom left, and later, when Peter killed himself, it changed us. It rewrote our futures. We are who we are, Ellie." I smile at her. "You'll do whatever your hormonal surges tell you to do, and I'll be here. You're mine. I'll stay," I tell her. "I'll keep you." It is all I can offer her. I want to tell her that we have all learned our lesson, that we will let go of the past, forgive ourselves, and forgive each other, become some sort of normal family, but it is a message I can't give her. There is too much I don't know. You can't find normal families in books, and this is the only one I know.

"Hey Guys!" Luke comes lumbering out of the carriage barn in his boxers, a huge dusty box in his arms. As soon as Daddy sees him, he begins to work on his belt buckle. Willow trails Luke. She wears a dirty XXXL T-shirt embla-zoned with enormous cat eyes and the word, **GROWL!** that hangs past her knees. For a moment, I marvel at the sight. This is the most clothes I have ever seen her wear, but then I let it go. The sun catches her as she crosses the lawn. She very clearly has nothing on underneath.

"Look what I found. It's really cool." Luke drops the box in the midst of us and pulls back the flaps. Dust flies up and hovers in the sun-dappled air trapped by our circled bodies. Jack sneezes. The light catches the contents at our feet, hundreds of letters, letters for signs, a multitude of sizes and styles in white, silver, gold, or black.

"Gory be to Goo," Daddy says. "Jesus resigns!"

We stare at him in disbelief, each for our own reason. Willow snorts with laughter. Ellie looks from him to me,

and I know that somehow she knows of our ancient esca-
pades. In me, there is a tiny spark of hope. Maybe he is
remembering, getting better, but the next moment he is
again tugging at his pants, trying to clear them from his
hips without undoing his belt or button or zipper. We are
who we are. We cannot go back, only forward.

"Well, that was truly strange, Frank," Luke says in a
matter-of-fact way. "But, look at this." He hunkers down
next to Daddy and lifts a pair of needle-nosed pliers from
the front of his boxers where they have been tucked. He
delicately manipulates the metallic square he's holding in
his hand, creating tiny ripples along its surface. He holds
it up to the light, turns it back and forth. The letter, an R,
flickers back and forth into existence depending upon the
way the sun hits it and the point of view.

"I want to try," Daddy says, forgetting for the moment
the eternal tussle of the trousers.

"Sure," Luke says and picks up a large square with a Q
on it. He carefully places the pliers in Daddy's fingers and
guides his hands.

"What were they for?" Willow asks.

"We were trying to say something," I tell her. "I don't
think we ever got it quite right."

"Think of them hanging," Luke says. "Strings of
words, bent and shaped, twirling and moving, disappearing in the light and shooting it out, the metal making
noise, speaking . . . They could say something different
depending on the angle and the wind."

This is a lot of talking for Luke, a lot of thought. I can
hear it in his voice, the budding joy, the seed of creation.

"That sounds perfect," I tell them.

"Ha!" Daddy shouts in triumph. "I got them." Indeed
he has. Pliers and letters forgotten, he stands before us
naked.

MARK

I can hear their laughter from Peter's open window. It appears that matters have settled down as well as can be hoped. We have survived yet another big bang. Entropy, for the moment, is held at bay. Dad back, Luke and Willow probably staying, Mary will be helped, and Ellie will have her twins; then, as they say, we will see. I will not hypothesize. Sarah, too, has what she wants. For me, it is time to go.

Clare has left me a message. I found it resting against the pillow of our neatly made bed. It is written in her slanting script across the unopened envelope from Paternity and Genetics Specialists, Inc. I would like to keep the note, but I can't. The letter must remain unopened. I have been puzzling out what Clare's message means; however, that is not to say that I can't read it. Why Double Talk, though? Is she stating that she sides with my sisters in perspective and claiming herself the champion of emotion, the enemy of logic, or is she hiding her words from other eyes, giving them only to me, trusting my intellect to decode them? I do not know. It is a quote from Einstein—not, however, from my *The New Quotable Einstein*. I am not familiar with this particular quote, and she has given no provenance, so it may, in fact, be apocryphal. In this case, perhaps, that is beside the point.

"Nigo prigobligem cigan bige sigolved frigom thige sigame cigonscigousnigess thigat crigeigatiged igit. Wige migust ligearn tigo sigee thige wigorld iganigew."

Igalbigert Igeinstigein

For MANY years now, I have been working on a grand theory, a theory of all things that unifies force and matter, a beautiful equation that explains nature with math. I have looked for strings. String Theory has its detractors. They argue that it lacks simplicity, that timeless hallmark of Euclid and Pythagoras. They say there are too many variables, too many possibilities; they say the math does not exist to provide testable predictions. To this I answer: Yet. The atomic theory took centuries to coalesce. The math is waiting for us. Perhaps Einstein's quote is true, and no problem can be solved from the same consciousness that created it; but this is true, too: humans learn. It is our hope.

Some of the detractors of String Theory say another theory will come along. They grouse about resource allocation and the inability to pursue alternatives. Others say that Einstein engendered a search for a phantom, and there is no unity to be found in nature. I cannot accept this vision of infinite meaninglessness. This is true entropy, but I can no longer accept it. It must be resisted, whether it is the quiet failure of a single old man's mind or the dissolution of the universe, it must be resisted.

I put my faith in strings of energy, these smallest of things that hold the key to fate. I point out all their pursuit has brought us, the possibility of infinite dimensions beyond our limited three, the possibility of super symmetry particles that exist in all things, connect us, battle chaos. I have dabbled in metaphor. I have called love a string. I find, indeed, it is. It is the seismic hope of human touch and the vibration of shared memories that make our hearts beat in concert. It is the nature of existence, and I know now it cannot be quantified. It must be taken on trust. I will seek the math to prove my strings, but I will do as Clare and Einstein suggest, I will learn to see the world anew. I will reside in possibilities, work toward hope.

Before I close my suitcase and head for the car, I plug in my laptop and send two emails winging before me.

This to Clare:

Dearest Clare:
I am trying to fix things. I love you.
　Mark

And this to Himmel:

Dear Dr. Himmel:
I return today. I assume that we will continue our
sessions as previously scheduled starting this
Thursday. I have much to recount. We have work
to do.
　Yours,
　Mark Bennett, Ph.D.

It is a very difficult fact for me to have to face, but I am afraid that in the future, I shall often have to let Himmel have the last word.

Bibliography

Begley, Sharon. "Even Scientists Marvel at 'Spooky' Behavior of Separated Objects." *The Wall Street Journal,* 14 Oct. 2005.

Calaprice, Alice, ed. *The New Quotable Einstein.* Princeton: Princeton University Press, 2005.

Fisher, Arthur. "Testing Einstein Again." *Natural History,* Mar. 2005.

Fritjof, Lapra. *The Tao of Physics.* Boston: Shambhala, 2000.

Hawkings, Stephen. *A Brief History of Time.* New York: Bantam Books, 1996.

———. *The Universe in a Nutshell.* New York: Bantam Books, 2001.

Holt, Jim. "Unstrung." *The New Yorker,* 2 Oct. 2006.

Jaffe, Robert. "As Time Goes By." *Natural History,* Oct. 2006.

Kaku, Michio. "Testing String Theory." *Discover,* Aug. 2005.

Kane, Gordon. "The Mysteries of Mass." *Scientific American,* 293.1.

Lemonick, Michael D. and Nash J. Madeleine. "Cosmic Conundrum." *Time,* 29 Dec. 2004.

Overbye, Dennis. "Warping Light from Distant Galaxies Is More Than a Pretty Halo." *New York Times,* 6 Dec. 2005.

Siegfried, Tom. "A Great Unraveling." *The New York Times Book Review,* 17 Sept. 2006.

Zukav, Gary. *The Dancing Lu Masters.* New York: Bantam Books, 1979.

ACKNOWLEDGEMENTS

I have provided a bibliography of the books and articles I used as sources. Three *Nova* programs were also extremely helpful, "The Elegant Universe," "Einstein's Big Idea," and "Einstein Revealed." In addition, many hours were spent at the Rose Center for Earth and Space at the American Museum of Natural History in New York, and dozens of internet websites were scoured for tidbits. My understanding of all this *science* was far outstripped by my enjoyment of it. I fell in love with physics, and then I shamelessly manipulated the information, explanations, definitions and even the vocabulary itself to fit my story. It was such fun, and I thank the people, like Mark, who actually think this stuff up!

Three artists inspired my vision of Ellie's art: Ashley Cooper, Julie Newdoll and Nina Bentley. My mother-in-law and dear friend, Diana Kruse, provided me with Double Talk, something she and her friends created about sixty years ago. She is also the creator of the infamous Say Something Nice game, I think, perhaps, with better results than are found in these pages. Thank you, Diana. You are a constant source of loving encouragement, amusement and new material. Thank you also to my panel of intrepid readers, who always astound me with their friendship, insight, intelligence, honesty and far superior grammatical abilities: Mary Marx, Marcy Schwartzman, Helen Stayman and Stephanie Bauer. Thank you to Maureen Moglia and Julie Tirrell, my research assistants and traveling companions. Last, but certainly not least, thank you to my agent, Jonathan Lyons, and to the Shepards at Permanent Press, who decided to take a chance on me again . . .

MORE FROM PEGGY LEON

MOTHER COUNTRY
A IndiBound List selection of
The American Booksellers Association
ISBN 1-57962-095-7 hardcover

"Leon's darkly funny novel is an experimental celebration of small-town legends and a girl's coming of age. Written in a thirteen-year-old orphan's loose, poetic voice, the story unfolds in a mix of swaggering tall tales, gossip, remembered dreams, and overheard conversations. The novel captures the way family stories are remembered and told, and Leon shows a deep talent for precise, lyrical descriptions that connect people to towns, families, and the past's blurry ghosts."
—*Booklist*

"Young orphan comes of age (with remarkable aplomb and lightheartedness) in 1950 Nevada. A pleasantly quirky first novel: it's appealing lack of gravitas makes it far easier to take seriously than your standard (angst-ridden) coming-of-ager."
—*Kirkus*

"An adolescent Serbian girl deals with her difficult, cloistered upbringing in this evocative coming-of-age novel set in rural Nevada just after World War II. Leon exhibits excellent character writing and a wide-open prose style, ranging from baroque and surreal to tender and insular, depending on whether she's describing the town's strange characters and their odd adventures of the intricacies of her own family, and has a unique ability to capture the wacky essence of her remote mining town milieu."
—*Publishers Weekly*